THE BLUE PILLOW CASE IN THE KINGDOM

Roger Lawrence Quay

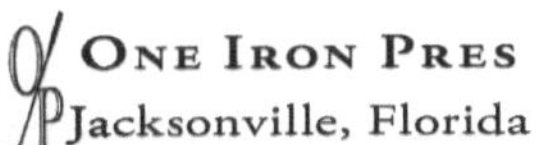
ONE IRON PRES
Jacksonville, Florida

Book and cover design by Sagaponack Books & Design

Illustrations by Hannah Amidon

ISBNs
978-1-7355640-3-6 (softcover)
978-1-7355640-4-3 (hardcover)
978-1-7355640-5-0 (e-book)

Library of Congress Catalog Number: 2022919148

Summary: Dylan returns to the Kingdom of Bonita, a parallel universe, where he finds missing members of his family and learns of a twin brother he didn't know existed.

YAF019010 YA Fiction / Fantasy / Contemporary
YAF001020 YA Fiction / Action & Adventure / Survival Stories
YAF038000 YA Fiction / Magical Realism
YAF027000 YA Fiction / Humorous

One Iron Press
Jacksonville, FL

Printed and bound in USA
First Edition

Acknowledgments

First, I owe a debt of gratitude to Clifford Martin. Although he is no longer with us, I can still hear him saying, "Keep writing!"

I cannot express enough thanks to my dedicated copy-editor Beth Mansbridge. I was lucky to have found Hannah Amidon, a talented and accomplished artist, for her whimsically appropriate illustrations. I would also like to thank Ann Pace Sutton, for her persistent and creative copywriting flair, and to Frances Keiser for her excellent publishing guidance. My sincere appreciation to numerous friends and family for their enthusiastic support.

Most of all, my deepest appreciation goes to my wife, Carol, whose boundless encouragement and patience made my vision a reality.

Contents

Humankind cannot bear very much reality.

—T. S. Eliot

PROLOGUE

"Oh, Chloe, what are you doing here?" Isabella says in a sad voice.

"Sorry, Mom. I heard voices and I thought it was Alex. Where are we?"

"No questions right now. Just stay still for a minute." Isabella throws a match into the fireplace.

"Aaaah," someone utters. "That feels *soooooo* good. Thank you. Well, who might you be?"

"It's me, Isabella, my daughter Chloe, and my buddy, Hari." She gives the German shepherd a quick stroke.

"Aaaah, thank goodness you have returned. It has been written that one day you would return to help us take back this land, so the legend is accurate. This is wonderful news, Princess Xandra," the excited voice responds. "You have been sorely missed, and you are needed now, more than ever. The Rockland rebels have been devastated—completely wiped out. The king is searching for Prince Mako. Everything is in chaos. But now that you are here, all will be well."

A curious Chloe asks, "Mom, who's that talking about a princess? I don't see anyone."

"That's Grock, honey. I'll explain in a minute."

"Okay, Mom."

"Thank you, Grock. I do have a few questions, if you don't mind. I would like to stay and chat with you. I don't have much time. I do love our discussions, and it has been a long time, but I need answers." Isabella prompts Grock.

"Aaaah, I so do miss our discussions."

"Have you seen my son, Dylan, or my daughter, Alessandra, recently?" Isabella asks.

"Indeed I have."

"And when was that?"

"Let me think. Yes, your son Dylan came through first, about eight days ago. He was a nice fellow and seemed very confused. I didn't realize he was the son of the great Princess Xandra. That indeed would have caused a stir."

Chloe screams, "You saw Dylan!"

"Please be quite, dear, Grock is talking."

"I saw Alessandra two days ago. She was looking for her brother, and he was looking for his grandmother. Is everyone lost in your family?" Grock inquires.

"To tell you the truth, yes. I have come to take them all back home, without a battle."

"Be careful out there, Princess. Things have changed since you have been here. The once peaceful kingdom has turned into gloom and doom. Death and destruction are everywhere! The king and queen have destroyed our land. Now that you are here, we can reclaim our land. This is so exciting. I have already alerted the few rebels that remain nearby."

"Do you happen to know where my children might be at this exact moment in time? And possibly, my mother?"

"Yes, Dylan is with the Trefars, and Alessandra is in the palace with your mother, who goes by the name of Socreen."

"Thank you so much. You are very wise, and tremendously helpful. When I have more time, we will sit and chat, but for now I have to depart at once. Soon I plan to return with everyone, so we can continue our conversation."

"That would be nice, Princess Xandra. I have all your gear," Grock replies. "Please be careful."

"Thank you."

Grock, a rock hut in the Kingdom of Bonita, is recalling how Princess Xandra became known. She was named by T, the most famous of all the Trefars and their current leader. Many years ago the Calypsos attacked the Trefars village. The Calypsos were an outgoing group that changed positions daily: one day loyal to the king, the next day loyal to no one. Their warrior skills were highly regarded, and one day the Calypsos leader, Fang, decided to attack the Trefars by surprise. The attack was unwarranted and aggressive. Many died on both sides.

The attack happened while Isabella was visiting with Tara, T's mother. When the fighting finally subsided, T ran back to his mother, who was sitting there, knitting, with three dead bodies next to her, and Lil Magik in her hand. T turned around and saw a wounded Isabella, along with twenty-seven dead Calypsos. Isabella had a small gash on her leg. Otherwise, she and Tara were unscathed. T never asked and Isabella never offered: How in the world could she defeat so many single-handedly?

Lil Magik is a knife. When held correctly, the blade disappears. It's as if you're not holding a knife at all. Big Magik is a sword that has the same features as Lil Magik. Isabella was holding Big Magik.

T pronounced Isabella to be Princess Xandra, for defeating these daunting attackers all by herself. Five days later, T attacked every Calypso village and wiped out every Calypso off the face of the kingdom. All were killed, young and old. The Calypso race was terminated that very day.

Isabella starts to change into her Princess Xandra clothes, and Chloe's eyes are as big as a house. "Mommy, what is that outfit? You look like a warrior queen out of some movie."

Grock laughs out loud. "Small one, she is the greatest warrior queen in this land. Princess Xandra is feared by all in this kingdom. The king and queen will not be pleased that she has returned to fulfill the legend's promise."

"Chloe, put on these shoes and take this jacket," Isabella says, handing them to Chloe.

"Why, Mom, I must be dreaming. I can't see who's talking. Where is this Grock?"

To complete her outfit Isabella grabs Big Magik, and says her goodbyes to Grock. "You are the greatest of all the rock huts throughout the kingdom!"

"Thank you, Princess. That is a great honor, coming from you," Grock replies.

Chloe is certain she must be dreaming. Grock is so excited, it sounds as if he has started to cry. A slot in the rock hut opens and they all depart. The first thing Isabella notices is the smell of smoke and the stench of death. Destruction is all around.

"Okay, Hari, let's head straight for the Rockland village. There I hope to find my good friend Gaylok. Once I get some information, we can head for the Trefars," Isabella commands. "Gaylok is the Rockland rebel leader," she tells her daughter.

"Mom, am I dreaming?"

"Yes, dear, you are."

Within two minutes four giant zebras appear out of nowhere and bow in front of Princess Xandra. Jacob introduces himself as the master zebra, and presents his second mate, Hayley. They also travel with a giant eagle, Razor.

"We are here to help you, Princess Xandra. What do you need?" Jacob inquires.

"We could use a ride to see Gaylok. That would help immensely."

"Yes, of course." He bends down so both Princess Xandra (Isabella) and Chloe can ride together on Jacob.

Chloe says, "Mom, that zebra can talk. This is one wild dream. I love animals that can talk."

"Well, then, you're going to love it here, because all the animals can speak. Keep a tight hold of me."

"Okay, Mom. I'm ready. Let's go get Dylan and Alex."

"Don't forget Grandma."

"Oh, right. And Grandma."

Jacob and Hayley take off like bolts of lightning. Hari follows. The huge male German shepherd can also speak and be understood, and is one of Isabella's protectors. Hari has a mate, Teri, a Rottweiler. She stayed behind in Key West to heal after sustaining a gunshot wound.

To learn much more about each character and the past events, read Book 1, "The Blue Pillow Case."

Chapter 1
YESTERDAY

My name is Dylan Michael Cabrella, and my story continues to perplex anyone willing to listen. I am your typical love-stricken and confused teenager, living in beautiful Key West, Florida. And by the way, my young life is soon to be over. I have probably ruined the relationship with the most stunning girl in the world, my self-proclaimed girlfriend, Violet. I want her to be my girlfriend and I'm fairly certain I screwed that up. Acting like a buffoon in front of Violet at a high school party didn't help my case. Even though I was unknowingly drugged, it didn't matter. I was so despondent I needed to get away, and away I went. I am now in this place called the Kingdom of Bonita. It is not upon the earth, but deep under the earth's surface, where another world thrives. Plus, all the inhabitants, human and nonhuman, can communicate with each other. Before arriving in this kingdom, I was despondent and having vivid dreams. Nightmares, really. I never imagined this new world was real; nevertheless, it is.

My mother, Isabella (nicknames, Bell, Bella) is an animal and marine biologist veterinarian. She is very accomplished and well respected in her field. She is also a martial arts expert. She basically raised us three kids on her own. My parents got divorced when I was very young, and Mom changed her name from Cabrella-Bland to Cabrella. I have two sisters, one older and one younger. My older sister, Alessandra, nicknamed Alex, is twenty-one. She goes to college in Missouri and is studying criminology. She is a wicked black, blue, or red belt martial arts expert. I can't keep up. All I know is she can kick everyone's butt, which includes me. My other sister, Chloe, is ten years old, and is a clone of my mother. I call her "CC," Cloned Chloe. She is a Miss Goody Two-Shoes. Extremely obnoxious. She is following in my mother's footsteps and will most likely become a veterinarian. I wanted a brother, not sisters. Of course that wasn't up to me.

It's been over fifteen years since anyone in my family has seen my grandmother. My grandpa, Vincenzo Cabrella, was just released from prison for the murder of my grandmother, Elizabeth Cabrella. When, in reality, she is stuck in this same place I transported to, the Kingdom of Bonita. I was recently made aware of her situation. Grandpa kept telling me that he was going to get Grandmother and return home.

I recall when I asked, "Where is she?"

His response was "In the kingdom."

"How do you get there?"

"You transport via the blue pillowcase."

"Why didn't you get her earlier? She's been gone for fifteen years."

He responded, "The blue pillowcase, recognized as a transporter, has been malfunctioning."

Apparently, he thinks it has been restored. I thought at the time it sounded like a case for the FBI; they could call it "The Blue Pillow Case."

Grandpa was ready to get Grandmother, so I tricked him and went in his place. Not sure if that was a good idea on my part, because now I'm also stuck in this place. My objective was to find Grandmother and get us back home before my mother discovered my plan. That turned out to be a complete flop. My idea hasn't worked out so well, and since my life in Key West was so dull and dreary, I thought why not go on this adventure. Grandpa was talking crazy, so I assumed everything he was saying was nonsense. How wrong I was.

After listening to Grandpa, it was easier than I ever imagined to get transported. All I did was put my head down on this blue pillowcase and, in a blink, I arrived in this other world. I was found, wandering around, by a girl named Tabitha. She's the new love of my life. She doesn't know it yet. I'll get around to telling her. I actually thought there would never be another true love other than my Violet. Now I may have found one.

Tabitha eventually brought me to the Trefars village, where I train. My life has changed dramatically. I am now sitting within a Trefars camp. The Trefars have been busy teaching me the skills of this Prince Mako guy. It seems the prince has disappeared and cannot be located, so the leader of the Trefars, T, wants to transform me into this prince. I am being trained by the Trefars to impersonate the prince. Supposedly, one day this prince will reign over the kingdom. Now that the real prince is missing, I am being groomed to replace him. No one—other than the Trefars—knows about this plan or hoax. The actual prince is somewhere in San Francisco, California. I guess we look so similar that no one would know the difference, almost like we are identical twins. Since twins are outlawed in the kingdom, this may be an easy task. All I have to do is convince the king and queen that I am their son.

Trefars are elf-like warriors. They ride elephants and are unmatched in their fighting skills. They live in their own compound in the kingdom and maintain everything on their own. They have no attachment to the king or his way of controlling every aspect of your life. I have no idea how many Trefars exist. My guess is it's in the thousands. They have been very kind to me. I almost forgot—they have no sense of humor. All they do is work, strategize, and practice their warrior skills.

I am in the continuous care of a Trefars named Igagbee. He is in charge of my transformation into this prince dude. Seeing that the Trefars are the greatest warriors in the land, I wanted Igagbee to train me in some fighting skills, but that is going unheeded. Even worse than the Trefars not training me was that Tabitha went back to her village in Rockland after its devastation. The king's men wiped out the entire village of Rockland, hoping to find Prince Mako. What they found was a young girl caged with one of the king's trainees, Grando. Grando is a twenty-foot saber-toothed tiger and was left to die, along with Gaylok.

Tabitha and Pup quickly departed for her homeland of Rockland. Pup is a giant female dragon and Tabitha's most faithful and devoted friend. They have never been apart, even before Pup's birth. Tabitha raised Pup.

Pup is not the only dragon flying around the kingdom. Tragoon, and his little sister, Trigon, are also dragons. Tragoon is the largest of the two. Male dragons are usually much larger than the females. Tragoon is loyal to the king, and Trigon's loyalty lies with the queen. Tragoon was last seen off the east coast of the USA.

Rumors are that the prince has not surfaced, and my training will speed up. I need to get to the palace and impersonate this prince guy. The prince and I are also the same age. The Trefars have groomed me to be proficient in every skill the prince excels in. Most of my skills needed lots of training—except for one, swimming. I was told the prince is an excellent swimmer, and I too am a great swimmer, with trophies to prove it. It took lots of convincing, since my other skills were less than stellar. I know deep down if I ever needed to prove my swimming skills, it would be an easy task. The waterways are all dried up because it hasn't rained in over five hundred days, so they had to take me at my word.

"Igagbee, am I ready to do this?" I ask.

"Yes, my prince. You are ready," Igagbee replies.

Igagbee only addresses me as the prince. I guess it's supposed to give me more confidence.

"Prince, it's time for a short break. T has summoned me," Igagbee explains.

"Sounds good," I reply.

I found out that my mom and both my sisters, Alex and Chloe, are also in this kingdom. I hope they haven't come looking for me. If so, I could be in *big trouble.*

Chapter 2

FANCY

Jacob slows down as they arrive at the Rockland border. The devastation is dotted with multiple fires. Screaming is heard. Bodies are scattered all around. Isabella and Chloe jump off Jacob, and start attending to the injured.

"Chloe, this one needs a stitch. Could you finish up with her?" Isabella steps over an injured animal.

"Sure, Mom."

Word spreads fast that Princess Xandra has returned, and everyone starts to have some hope once again.

Isabella, at the side of a small red fox, asks, "Where does it hurt?"

"It feels like my left leg," the fox replies.

The vet assesses the leg. "It is broken, possibly in multiple places, and you have lost a lot of blood." Isabella elevates the leg to take some pressure off the wound.

"Will I live?"

"Yes, of course you will."

"I have never seen a princess before, and now I am being cared for by one, and a pretty one at that. I am fortunate indeed," the fox says.

"Please, try to relax, you need to rest. What is your name, if I may ask?"

"My mom was a jokester, and named me Fancy."

"Well, she was very wise to name such a beautiful fox with a nice name."

At that comment, Fancy grins, showing sparkling teeth.

Hari comes back to tell Isabella that he found Gaylok and he is barely alive.

"I need to depart. Chloe, when you are done with that stitch work, come over here and stitch up Fancy, and put a brace on her back left leg, would you?"

"Okay, Mom, I'll be there in a minute."

Xandra explains to Fancy that her daughter Chloe will finish up.

"My greatest thanks, Princess." Fancy smiles. "I feel better already."

Gaylok's eyes widen when he sees Princess Xandra enter. She can hardly hear him say her name. He tries to get up.

"Please stay still, do not move," Xandra remarks.

After a few gulping sounds, Gaylok says, "I knew you would come. Two of your children came through here and, well, I was hoping you would follow." Gaylok is coughing up blood and looking like death. "I have cheated death many times. Alas, this time I may lose."

"Do not speak like that. You will pull through."

"Your daughter Alex was here and the king's men took her. She was caged with Grando, a large saber-toothed tiger, and he is badly wounded. Your son Dylan is safe for now, with the Trefars. Go see Grando. He saved your daughter's life … but may soon lose his own. He may be able to give you … additional … information. If he is still … with us."

These are Gaylok's last words. Xandra bows down and kisses Gaylok on the forehead. Princess Xandra is approached by a young woman who has been watching and listening to their conversation.

"I am Tabitha, a friend, and the niece of the great Gaylok." She wipes her tears.

"I am so sorry. He was a great man," Xandra responds.

Tabitha is still in shock over Gaylok's death—plus, trying to understand that Dylan is the son of Princess Xandra might be too much for one day.

Many gather around Gaylok's body and a chant begins.

Xandra has to show strength. She knows tears would do no good, and she needs to speak with Grando at once. Xandra is taken to him. Grando is the son of the great Grande. Grande is a thirty-foot saber-toothed tiger, and is one of the king's main guardians. Grando is alive and still caged, and looks like he was left at death's door. Breathing alone is a chore. He snarls at Xandra as much as he can muster, and tries to strike. He can't move, with all his wounds. The survivors are confused as to why the king's men attacked Grando.

"Grando, I can help you if you let me. I am a doctor."

Grando mumbles, crying out, "I am too young to die like this, in a cage. Why not do me in and get it over with?"

"I can help you if you let me."

"What do I have to lose? Go ahead. My own people, the king's guards, did this to me. I don't know who to trust."

"You can trust me. I want to make you well again so you may live a long life, which you so deserve. Let's get him out of this cage," Xandra commands. "Be careful, he is in great pain."

Grando whispers weakly, "Thank you. I would not have liked to die in a cage like a common criminal."

"You are a great, great, grand tiger and the kingdom needs heroes," Xandra responds.

Xandra starts to work on this huge tiger. Many arrows and spears are sticking out from his body. She cannot believe he is still alive.

"Tell me which one hurts the most."

"Not sure," Grando replies slowly. "Maybe the one in my back."

"Okay, let's tend to that one last."

The stitching and cleaning are intense; she is trying her best to save this magnificent beast. She has never seen or dealt with so many wounds at once.

Xandra finally decides to ask, "Was there a young lady with you?"

Grando, almost unconscious, says, "Yes, there was, and they took her. They placed a hood over her head and yanked her out of here. It was as if they were looking for her. She told me she was looking for her little brother, so I am not sure why the palace guards would want her."

"Was her name Alessandra, by any chance?"

"Yes. Alex is what she preferred. We became friends since we were locked up and caged together."

Soon, people and animals approach slowly, bowing to Xandra as she works on Grando.

"Who are you? I have never seen everyone so infatuated with one of non-royal blood," Grando says, amazed. "Why is everyone bowing?"

"I am no one. Just a friend."

Then someone yells, "That is Princess Xandra. She is here to save us all."

"Princess Xandra," Grando says. "My teacher Kaptuk often spoke about a Princess Xandra. He said you were only a legend, a folklore. Your speed and accuracy are unmatched. Is this true?"

"Please be still and quiet. Save whatever strength you have left."

Chloe walks up, her eyes wide open as she sees her mother working on this huge beast.

"Mom, you need help?"

"Is this your daughter?" Grando asks. "She looks like Alex. Don't tell me you're their mother!"

"If you must ask, yes indeed. I am here to take them all home."

He passes out. Xandra works on Grando for hours and hours. After the doctor's last stitch, Grando is sound asleep, along with Chloe, who is sleeping on his front paw.

The next morning, Xandra makes her decision. Grando needs continuous care until he is healed, so she decides to leave Chloe with Grando. Chloe will be safer here since it would be most unusual for the king's guards to return. Xandra believes the sooner she gets to the Trefars, the better.

Grando awakens and is feeling very sore and weak—nonetheless, alive.

"How are we feeling today?" Xandra asks.

"I am not sure. Either way, I must thank you. If there is anything I can ever do for you, let me know. You have saved my worthless life." Grando slouches.

"There is one thing I will ask of you, Grando. My daughter Chloe will be much safer here, with you protecting her. Plus, she has great skills with healing the sick and injured. You will need many bandage changes, and she can do it. Would you watch over her while I am gone?"

Grando again realizes he is out of that cursed cage. "Am I free to go?" Grando asks.

"Yes, you are free to come and go as you wish. If I were you, I would stay still and heal for a few days. You have over a thousand stitches and many deep wounds. I would not move. Food will be brought to you. I hope to be back within a few days."

"Why are you being so nice to me?" Grando asks.

"You are a great warrior, and I have heard you saved my daughter's life. I will always be in your debt." She turns to her daughter. "Chloe, will you be okay here with Grando?"

"I'm not sure. It's kind of scary around here. I do like Grando. He is so sweet."

Isabella thinks, Only my daughter would think an injured and distressed twenty-foot saber-toothed tiger is sweet. "I won't be long. I think it's best if you stay here.

These folks need your care. They would be very upset if you left them. I will leave you all my supplies, so do the best you can. Grando will need his bandages changed daily. Erica will look after you."

Standing next to Xandra is Erica, a giant hippopotamus. She is extremely kind and gentle.

"I do like hippos. You think I could call Erica my friend?" Chloe asks.

"Ask her. I'm sure she won't mind." Isabella smiles.

"Yes, I'll be your best friend," Erica responds, and starts jumping up and down. The ground shakes. When she finally stops jumping, Chloe tries to hug her.

Grando gingerly wobbles over to Chloe, and says very loudly, "No harm shall come to her, or you will have to deal with me."

"Okay, Mom, I'll stay here. Could be fun. What a summer story to tell my friends."

"You're so right, dear. It will be a story for the ages. I'll be back in three days, and if I'll be any longer, I will send word."

Tabitha again decides to approach Xandra, to ask if she is heading to the Trefars. They agree to journey to the Trefars together. Tabitha decides to ride Hayley so they may talk. Pup takes flight to make sure their path is clear, and Hari takes off running. Xandra hops onto Jacob as everyone is cheering and yelling, "Xandra, Xandra, Princess Xandra!"

In the blink of an eye, they are gone.

**

"So, I hear you have met my son Dylan?" Xandra asks Tabitha.

"Yes, I have. I did not know he was a prince."

"He is not a prince, by any means, and I am not a princess—at least, not at home."

"I believe the first part." Tabitha smiles, and they both burst into laughter.

Tabitha has heard Gaylok speak of the legend of Princess Xandra and, until now, thought she was folklore, not a real person.

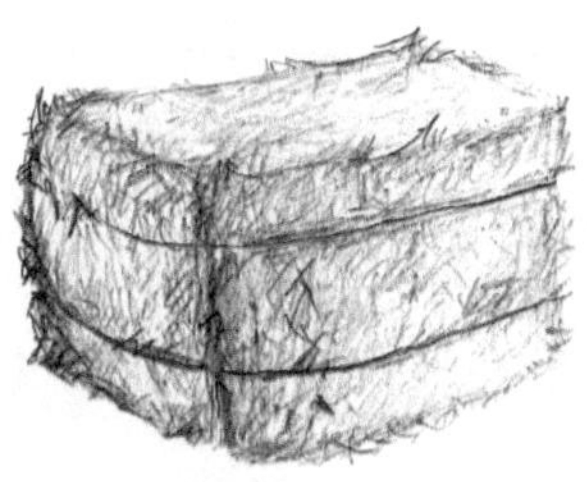

Chapter 3

TRAGOON

Dr. Anthony Rome (Tony) is Isabella's brother. Tony changed his name from Cabrella to Rome. He is an avid world traveler, an Indiana Jones type, and very wealthy. He and his trusted mate, Matt, are trying to find an alternative to the blue pillowcase to transport into the kingdom, but they seem to be having some problems. Matt has never been to the kingdom; Tony has in the past.

Matt is an ex-Navy SEAL, US Marine all the way. Tough as nails at six-foot-four, two hundred and twenty pounds. Matt was arrested in the San Francisco airport parking garage. He was caught with a trunk full of dynamite. Tony sent an attorney to get him released. While Matt is still locked up, Tony arrives in San Francisco to discuss the final release with Brad, his attorney.

"Hey, Brad, how's our boy Matt doing?' Tony asks.

"Not bad, Tony. He's ready to get out of here, that's for sure."

"I bet he is. Are we ready to go?"

"Yep, all set, papers signed, and he's free for now. What a mess he got himself into. Only guy in the world I know who could get into this circumstance. How in the world he got so much dynamite is beyond me!" Brad exclaims.

"It was planted on him, and it's a long story. Hopefully we are going to unravel it soon. At least that's our plan."

"This one was hard to explain, so please keep him out of further trouble."

"Thanks. We will make it right."

"Let's go get the big baby."

They both laugh.

**

"Well, that was fun." Matt gives Tony a bear hug. "What is going on? The last thing I remember is following someone who looked like Dylan, and wham, I wake up in an airport parking lot with a trunk full of explosives."

Brad shakes his head. "Nice company you keep. Okay, guys, stay out of trouble. Matt, please behave."

Matt grabs Brad and gives him a hug.

As soon as Brad departs, Tony asks, "So, do you think you can find the place you last saw Dylan?"

Matt smiles and jumps into the rental car. They head south on Highway 280, towards San Andreas Lake.

Tony wonders why in the world Dylan would be driving to San Andreas Lake.

Matt turns off onto Route 35 and follows Skyline Boulevard to a dirt road. He drives down the road until he runs into a giant gate. A sign reads:

WELCOME TO TRIPOLEE (EEE)
EMERALD ENVIRONMENTAL ENTERPRISE.
WE ARE GREENER THAN GREEN. WE ARE EMERALD.

DO NOT ENTER
PRIVATE PROPERTY
NO TRESPASSING
WE PROSECUTE TRESPASSERS

A small sign reads:

Welcome to the Greenest of Green.
Environmental, Ecological and Conservation Is All We Do.
We Care for All and All We Care for Is Your Future.

"This looks familiar," Matt recalls.

"Okay, now what?" Tony asks.

Matt grins. "I'm going in."

"Great. You just got out of jail, and now you want to break in to a private area. Can you not see the signs that they don't want us to enter?"

"I feel differently. They started this. Sounds like they are asking me to enter," Matt answers.

"Quite an elaborate security entrance for an environmentally safe company," Tony comments.

"Yes, sir, we both are going in, and it's not breaking and entering. I dropped my wallet here. I came back to retrieve it."

Matt gets out of the car and starts messing around with the digital code entry. It's an electric fence, which makes it a little trickier. Within five minutes the gate is swinging open, and Matt jumps back into the car with a smirk on his face. They pull inside and drive the winding road for what seems like another two miles, before they see another giant electric gate. This one is padlocked.

"A lot of security for a company fixing our environment," Tony notes.

"For real. This is unusual. Did you bring my gun?"

"Yes, and next time they will throw you under the jail."

"That's okay. I've got you and Brad to protect me," Matt says with a smile, as he blows the padlock to pieces.

Tony says, "That should wake up everyone. So much for sneaking in."

"They knew we were here when we opened the first gate. These people started it. I'm here to finish it. Gee, what a surprise. Another locked door," Matt proclaims.

They enter a huge warehouse, approximately two hundred thousand square feet. It is dark. No office equipment in sight.

"Furnishings are so overrated," Matt says, scanning his cell phone light over the area.

The warehouse is indeed empty. Not a chair, desk, or paperclip can be seen. Only some type of straw is strewn on the floor.

"I've got to tell you—I wasn't expecting this!" Tony exclaims.

"Me either. Now what? This looks like a dead end."

Side by side, they pace the entire building, trying to figure out their next move.

Matt asks, "Why put straw over concrete floors?"

"Not sure why anyone would do that. The only reason to put down straw would be for an animal of some sort. Let's come back later tonight and see what creatures are lurking," Tony answers.

"Works for me. I'm sure it's much less creepy at night." Matt sighs.

"I'll make a few phone calls while you drive us back to the hotel. We need to get into the upcoming environmental Fourth of July bash. Can't wait to meet the executives of the Tripolee company!"

Back at the hotel, Tony finally hits pay dirt and snags two tickets to the big event.

"All I need is two, Doug, thanks. I owe you one."

"Okay, Matt, we're in. This greener than green environmental ball gala event has been sold out for six months. Hottest ticket in town. Senators, governors, ex-presidents, and mayors will all be there."

"Sounds like a dull event to me," Matt replies.

"Harder tickets than the Masters golf tournament. And, by the way, you're going to have to wear a tuxedo. It's a formal event."

"Of course it is. That's my favorite attire. What man doesn't want to look like a penguin?" Matt smiles.

Neither one of them wants to leave the comfortable hotel room. Both know they have to give the warehouse another inspection. This time Matt packs some of his accessories: a handgun, a diving knife, a crowbar, and two flashlights.

"Diving knife and a crowbar. Really. What in the world do you need that for? Never mind, bring whatever you want." Tony shakes his head.

"My diving knife has many uses. Should I review them with you?"

The gates are as they left them, and it still looks quiet, with no one in sight. Tony suggests to Matt that he start at the other end of the warehouse, and they can meet in the middle.

What are you up to, Tripolee? Tony thinks. He is looking up and down, and soon he is walking on what feels like a hollow spot. He stops and shines his flashlight around his feet. He can barely make out a small tab or hook on the concrete floor even though the straw is everywhere. He pulls on the tab. Nothing happens.

"Hey, Matt," Tony yells, "get over here. I need your muscles."

"I'll be right there. …… What's up?"

"Check this out."

"Looks like a hidden panel in the floor." Matt leans down and pulls at the tab.

Again, nothing.

Tony grins. "What's the matter, you getting soft?"

"If you're going to be that way …." Matt pulls again with all his strength. The floor panel pops open, and Matt falls on his backside.

"That was easy. So much for no one's home. We were knocking on the wrong door," Matt laments.

Tony shines his light down the shaft and sees a ladder heading straight down.

"What, no elevator?" Matt says.

"Doesn't look like it."

They climb down the ladder to the next floor. Tony turns on a light switch and sees computer equipment everywhere. "Must have cost a fortune. It all looks new."

Tony sits and starts typing away on one of the computer keyboards, hoping to find any information. Getting past the firewall is easy. It is a certainty that everyone down here had authorization and passwords were not needed. A topography map of the coast of California pops up.

"Hey, Matt, what do you make of this?"

"Looks like they're trying to review environmental issues."

"This map wouldn't give you that information. This will give you peak, ridgeline, cliffs, valley, slope, and map scale," Tony says.

"Then why did you ask me, Professor Know-it-all?"

"Wanted your opinion. Why are they looking at this?"

"Not sure, but I see an elevator. Let's check out where it goes," Matt yells over his shoulder. He takes out his Beretta Cougar, saying, "Never leave home without one."

"I'm sure that's also part of your probation release program," Tony replies.

"Yep, let's go. What floor do you want? We have plenty of choices. Never seen an elevator with hieroglyphics instead of numbers."

"My goodness, how long did it take for someone to build this monstrosity?" Tony starts to imagine.

"Floor, please."

"Pick one, surprise me."

"Okay. Lingerie, next floor," Matt replies.

As before, there is no one in sight. Each floor is more elaborate than the next. Extravagant chairs, tables, private rooms, all with whiteboards and computers. Some floors are ten-foot high, others sixty-plus feet. Each floor is equipped with high-end furnishings, and not very deep.

"What kind of money do these environmental wackos make?" Matt asks.

"I am now beginning to rethink my business ventures."

"This should be fun. Thirteenth floor, by my calculations. Watch your step," Matt quips.

This floor is completely different. No computers or tables. Only beeping sounds. And then they both see a clock or timer. It reads 24:03 … 24:02 … 24:01 … and is ticking down.

"By my calculations," Tony comments, "whatever is planned happens in twenty-four hours, which happens to be July Fourth."

"Maybe it's for fireworks, the big environmental gala."

"Probably not. Matt, can you stop it?"

"I've never seen anything like this. It looks like it's rigged to blow up something. Not sure what type of explosives are attached. It does look as if someone knew what they were doing. And that's just what I can see. I'm afraid to touch any of this."

Tony says, "The entire ridge that we drove on happens to be on the San Andreas fault line. Any explosion would cause havoc. Why would they want to blow that up? Let me explain to you the worst-case scenario. Repercussions of an explosion would be catastrophic. I'm not sure where to start. I would alert your folks and tell them, and any friends to head east, not north, not south, not west. Straight due east, since we have no idea how far or what this is rigged for."

"Shouldn't we tell the authorities?" Matt says.

"Okay, sure. Let's tell the authorities that the guy they recently arrested with a trunkload of dynamite happened to come across a rigged explosive on private property that someone other than you placed. Oh, and by the way, the bomb happens to be located in a warehouse of the most popular environmental company on the planet. In which we are trespassing."

"Okay, okay, you've made your point."

"No, if this thing can be dismantled, it will have to be done by us, meaning you. Let's see what the next floor has to offer," Tony suggests. "Then we should get out of here."

"Does this mean we're staying for the party?"

"Yes, we need answers. Let's be safe. I will have my pilot, Torch, standing by with *Lucy*. That way we can depart a little before midnight. I'm setting my stopwatch for twenty-three hundred. We need to find Dylan's twin. He may be able to explain what's going on."

"No," Matt replies. "What we need to do is stop this ticking time bomb first."

"I agree. Let's see what a few of the other floors have in place."

The next floor looks like a laboratory. And in the corner of the room is Tony's crate from Africa. It's open … and empty.

Tony's thoughts flash to the neon fish they found in Africa and shipped to the States. It was a wild African adventure that he and Matt were lucky to survive. Tony was hoping the neon fish had special enzymes, and when properly extracted, would provide another way in and out of the kingdom. This fish could be an alternative to using the blue pillowcase for transporting. Tony decided to have the crate shipped to Massachusetts, and when Captain Rogers (Isabella's boyfriend) went to pick up the crate, it had already been signed out by an unknown person. That unknown person was Grull.

Tony barely escaped alive when he had a prior run-in with the hairless albino. Grull is an evil, deformed individual who rides Tragoon, since they are companions. Both are from the kingdom and very dangerous. Grull and Tragoon, a huge dragon, were last seen flying around Tony and Matt's campsite in Africa. Later that evening, their African campsite was completely destroyed. Grull and Tragoon departed Africa and are now in the USA.

"That confirms it," Tony says. "The kingdom has come to us. And they need to be stopped. We need to find Dylan's twin or Grull." Tony lets out a long sigh. "Look at this stuff. It's the same straw that's on the main floor."

Matt attempts to light it. "It won't light. It's flame retardant."

"This may confirm my theory, and you're not going to like it," Tony comments.

Suddenly all the red lights on the wall start blinking and a loud siren is blaring. Both men duck under lab benches to hide, expecting that someone is approaching. After a few minutes, the siren stops and the red lights keep blinking.

"Matt, I think we have company."

"Well, no one is coming down the elevator. It hasn't moved," Matt says.

"You're going to think I'm nuts. I have a feeling we have company upstairs, in the warehouse. All that noise and red lights are a signal that Tragoon has returned, so everyone below is aware and cautious. I think the top floor is Tragoon's lair."

"You must be kidding." Matt sighs.

"I wish I was. I didn't want to alarm you since it was just a theory. I had an unusual feeling that this place was a perfect spot to hide a dragon. Why else all the hay, and if Grull is nearby, so is Tragoon, right?"

"Now, that would be something. Let's go see." Matt hurries over to the elevator.

"Okay, please be very careful. I'm not in the mood to be eaten by a dragon today."

Matt gives Tony two thumbs up. They take the elevator up, and then climb the ladder to the warehouse.

"Open it very carefully and be as quiet as possible," Tony reminds Matt.

Matt pushes on the hatch door. It doesn't move. He tries again. It doesn't budge.

Matt whispers, "Do you think he's up there sitting on the door?"

"Perhaps. Let's go back down and see if we can find another exit."

Chapter 4

FLOBAK

The prince is alive and well. Prince Mako (Michael) is extremely excited about going out in this new world (the USA), without any adult supervision. Every minute he was in the palace, it was as if he had a bright spotlight following his every move. He could do nothing without lots of people in tow. No freedom whatsoever. Being in America is a different story. He is in charge and has complete free rein. His father, the king, and his mother, the queen, are not around to criticize him.

"How do I look?" Michael asks Grull.

"You look perfect, Your Majesty. The king would be very proud of his son."

"Thank you, Grull. I was informed that this is what the concrete-dwellers wear."

Concrete-dwellers are what the king calls people in the Americas. And when the king is referring to the USA, he calls it concrete country.

Prince Mako likes his new look while he stares in a mirror, wearing a pair of black silk-cotton-blend slacks, a blue paisley silk and cashmere blend T-shirt, with an unconstructed black-and-blue sport coat in wool-cotton blend. Flashy socks and Ferragamo oxford shoes. Huge pure-green emerald pinky ring, Omega watch, gold bracelets, and necklace.

The prince thinks to himself that he could get used to this style.

"Wow, you look marvelous, Prince," Flobak comments as he walks into the prince's suite. "Are you ready?"

"Yes, I am prepared. Don't wait up, Grull," the prince commands.

Going out in public with Grull would be a problem. Grull's deformity scares most people and the prince doesn't need any unwanted stares. Flobak will be attending the big gala event with the prince. No Grull tonight.

The prince is finally free of any guardians and out on his own for the first time, ever. He wants to feel emancipated. As Flobak put it, "Let loose tonight"—whatever that means. The prince is staying in the presidential penthouse suite at The St. Regis in downtown San Francisco. Flobak is showing the prince around town. He has been to America and knows his way around. The king nicknamed Flobak "the wanderer."

"We should check out the lounge at this hotel," Flobak announces.

"Sure, why not," the prince replies.

"Do not forget to stay by my side. We cannot afford to lose you again."

When the prince first arrived to the Americas, he was accidentally transported to Isabella's home in Key West, Florida. While there, he saw plenty of photos of someone who looked similar to him. Plus a photo of a young Socreen, whom he knows from the palace. Dylan's missing grandmother, Elizabeth, is known as Socreen in the kingdom. She is also one of the queen's handmaidens.

All those pictures were very confusing for the prince. Why were there so many familiar faces in the photos, in this particular dwelling? He did not understand. And he had to figure out how to get to San Francisco all by himself. He did succeed in getting to San Francisco, still with many unanswered questions.

"You may be asked to consume some unusual drinks and take some potions—drugs. Please resist. Your body is not accustomed to the foreign objects these concrete-dwellers use to abuse their bodies. I will order your food. The foods here in concrete country are much different than what you are accustomed to," Flobak explains to the prince.

"Don't worry, I'll be fine. Let's go."

"How should I address you?" Flobak asks.

"Call me Michael. If you can remember that."

"I shall try to remember, my prince—sorry—Michael it is."

The St. Regis hotel lounge is bustling. Flobak orders two club sodas with lime. Other than a planned party, the prince cannot believe how many people are talking out in the open, and is unnerved.

"I'm getting hungry. Let's get something to eat."

"Yes, Your High—I mean, Michael. I have reservations at the best vegan lounge in town."

"Take me to this vegan lounge."

"Yes, Michael, Your Highness. Oops, that came out wrong."

They walk into the vegan lounge for some food.

After dinner, Michael says, "That was delicious. Now it's time for you to show me what this concrete country is all about."

"Yes, indeed. I have it all mapped out. Next stop, a high-energy dance club," Flobak excitedly remarks.

"What is a high-energy dance club?"

"You asked what the concrete-dwellers do? Well, that's what they do. You can determine for yourself if you like it or not. I see you have your dance shoes on, so let's give it a whirl."

"Okay. Lead the way. It's strange, I don't feel like anyone is following me here."

"I should say not, Your Highness."

The line to get into the dance club wraps around the building. By the length of the line, this must be the place to be—or not to be. Flobak walks up to the front of the line and speaks with some guy standing by the front door.

"Yes, sir, go right in. Venus will show you to your table. Have a great night. The place is rocking."

When they enter, the music is blasting so loud Michael can't believe anyone can stand this vulgar noise. Michael is yelling at Flobak from behind. He doesn't hear a word. They finally arrive at their table and it's a little quieter.

Michael leans over to ask Flobak, "Do people listen to this noise all night long?"

"Yes, sir, they do indeed."

"I thought you said this was going to be fun."

"Relax, it will be. Give it a minute."

With a pitiful look on his face, the prince puts his hands over his ears. A young dark-haired girl who looks like a goddess, skimpily-dressed, walks up and sits beside him. He hasn't encountered anyone dressed like that in the kingdom.

Flobak leans over and whispers in his ear, "She is an Asian beauty."

She says, "Hello, I haven't seen you here before. My name is Kayda. Buy me a drink."

"Certainly. Whatever you like."

Before Michael knows it, there are four girls, each one prettier than the next, sitting at their table. He is usually the one ordering people around, but these girls are aggressive. Michael looks down the table and sees Flobak having a good time. He is surrounded by women, and champagne fills every ice bucket.

"What's your name? Where are you from? Do you work? Do you like girls? How old are you? Can you dance? Do you think I'm pretty?" Kayda has started the inquisition.

"Hold on. One question at a time, please."

Michael is usually asking the questions, so being bombarded with questions is not something he is comfortable with.

"Are you famous or something? This table is reserved for high-end VIPs only." Kayda looks at him curiously.

"First, my name is Michael."

"That's strange. Why does he keep calling you Prince? Which is it, Michael or Prince?"

"That's just between us. My name is Michael."

"You look like a Prince."

"Thank you. I'll be Michael tonight."

"Okay, if that's what you prefer. I like the sound of Prince better. Can I call you Prince?"

"Certainly, you may call me Prince."

The champagne is flowing and everyone is feeling no pain. Flobak is no longer chaperoning anyone. Michael isn't sure who is watching who, and he doesn't care.

"Kayda is a pretty name," he says.

"It means 'little dragon' in the Japanese culture. See my dragon tattoo!" She turns around to show Michael the large colorful tattoo running down her back. "I love dragons. I wish I was born during the dragon days."

"I have a dragon." Michael grins.

"I bet you do. Maybe you will show me later."

"Possibly."

"Oh, I just love this song. Let's dance." Kayda grabs Michael's arm.

The music is so loud Michael can hardly think. *How do these people do this all night long?* All he hears is noise banging loudly.

Kayda leans over to tell him something and he can't understand a word, so he shrugs and smiles. They dance a few songs, and then she grabs Michael and pulls him into the back room.

"Wow, this is so much fun," Kayda says. "Do you want a hit, Prince?"

"A hit of what?"

"What, are you from Mars or something? It's good stuff," Kayda comments.

"No, thank you, I'm fine."

"Okay, more for me, then. You need to loosen up. You're so stiff."

"It's been a while since I have been out." Michael smiles.

"Wait here. I'll be right back." Kayda kisses Michael on the cheek and departs.

Feeling no pain, Michael waves over a waiter. "I like the looks of that. Bring me one of those." He points to a green concoction in a martini glass.

The drink arrives, and he gulps it down. That gets him stumbling even more.

"Hey, handsome, you waiting for someone?" Kayda whispers in his ear from behind.

That last martini drink may have done Michael in; he can't focus or walk too well.

Flobak asks, "Where have you been, Michael?"

"Dancing, Flobak, dancing. I need a break."

Hearing this, the other three girls grab Flobak and take him onto the dance floor.

Michael is a bit intoxicated, and he starts to tell Kayda about the kingdom and dragons.

Kayda beams and says, "*Coooool!* Can you take me there? I just love Komodo dragons. I've never met anyone that owned one. See my emerald golden Komodo dragon bracelet? It's my favorite."

"It is stunning. I need to alert Flobak that I'm leaving."

"He won't care. If you go get him, all those girls are going to want to come with us, and I don't have enough stuff. I am all you can handle. I assure you—I'll take good care of you. Where are you staying?" Kayda asks.

"St. Regis, penthouse suite."

"Nice. Let's go there and keep this party humming."

"Definitely."

The cab ride is quick, and Kayda does all the talking.

They enter the prince's suite, and Grull is there to greet them.

Kayda jumps back and screams out, *"Who's he!"*

"Hello, my dear. I am Grull, the prince's secretary."

"I knew you were a prince. He talks like one."

"Where is Flobak?" Grull asks, grinning.

"I may have departed without telling him. It is not his fault. All mine."

"We shall see. Welcome. Is there anything I can get you two?" Grull asks.

"Wow, look at this view! I'd like a glass of champagne, please. So, where is this dragon and kingdom of yours? Remember, I *love* dragons," Kayda tells the prince loudly.

After hearing Kayda, Michael cringes, knowing that Grull will not be too happy that he has mentioned the kingdom. Michael is not used to drinking that much alcohol. It's not readily available in the kingdom, though the palace does serve it on special occasions. Too much alcohol is like a potent truth serum.

"I see you have been telling stories tonight. Well, if it's a dragon she wants to see, then maybe we should oblige her." Grull smiles.

Grull gets up to answer the knocking on the penthouse door, and Flobak stumbles inside.

"I am so very, very sorry. Somehow we got separated," Flobak blares.

"I will deal with you later. Here you go, my dear." Grull hands her a glass of champagne with a frozen strawberry.

A few minutes later, Kayda has passed out on the couch.

Michael says, "I think that last drink got to her. All this drinking stuff makes you lightheaded, and I do like Kayda. She gave me her contact information. I shall like to see her again."

"Of course. I will take care of her, Prince. You need some rest. It's been a long night, and we have a busy schedule tomorrow." Grull looks directly at Flobak.

Neither Kayda nor the prince is aware that Grull put something in her drink to knock her out.

"Yes, you are right. It has been fun. And Grull, do not take it out on Flobak. I departed without informing him."

"Yes, Your Highness. Good night."

Grull grabs Flobak and says, "Take her to Tragoon. She likes dragons, doesn't she? Well, she'll fall in love with this one."

"The prince wants to see her again," Flobak replies.

"Listen, slow one, all these people will be gone soon, so we may be doing her a favor. Now get her out of here. You're lucky I'm not feeding you as well."

Flobak knows better than to argue with Grull, and alerts his henchmen to take Kayda up to the warehouse where Tragoon sleeps.

When Kayda comes to, she sees a row of giant teeth, and before she can scream, Tragoon has a delicious snack.

**

Tony and Matt are still trapped in the Tripolee warehouse. They continue to search for another exit, and an alarm sounds off again. The alarm stops. Now, only a green light is blinking instead of the red one.

"Hey, Tony," Matt says, "I think your boyfriend just left the premises."

"We better get out while we can." Tony presses against the door.

Matt grabs the trap door and it easily opens. Standing in the large open space, the men sniff a different smell.

"Seeing that a huge dragon has probably been here, there would be an odor," Tony comments.

"No, I mean it smells like burnt flesh."

Tony looks down and sees something shiny on the floor. "Hey, Matt, come take a look at what I found. Not sure how we missed this before. Looks like an expensive woman's bracelet. Do you think he …?"

"You don't think Tragoon just had dinner. Do you?"

"Hope not. Let's get out of here while we can." Tony starts to find his way to the exit.

"Works for me."

They both jump into the car.

"Matt, it's very late. We may have to wait until morning to contact someone about all the explosives. Waking someone up in the middle of the night to explain the predicament may not be our best course of action."

"It's so dark out here, I can barely see the road. What happened to streetlights?" Matt quips.

"Matt, what was that?"

"Not sure, since I'm no longer driving. We're flying—and not on pavement."

Tony hangs his head out the window and he can't make out what it is. Soon they both see a giant talon or claw holding on either side of the car.

"I think your boyfriend found us." Matt sits back, trying to relax.

"I'm afraid you may be correct."

"Any ideas, Doc?"

"Not yet, I don't. This is a new one for me."

"Gee, no kidding. I'm thinking this is my second time this month." Matt laughs.

"We're now over water. I can see that much," Tony responds.

"Hello, boys, having a nice flight?"

"Did your dragon say something?" Matt asks.

"Yes, a grand time," Tony replies. "Thank you for asking. May I ask where you're taking us?"

"Let's keep it a surprise," Tragoon answers.

Matt shows Tony his gun, and Tony shakes his head in the negative.

"Hope you boys are enjoying the scenery. It's a beautiful evening. And, by the way, don't waste your time shooting at me. I may lose my grip."

"What are you and Grull up to, back at that warehouse?"

"Are you familiar with Liquid Megontrolite?"

"No, can't say that I am. How about you, Matt?"

"No, sir, never heard of it."

"It's about ten times more powerful than dynamite, and doesn't leave a trace."

"Why would anyone need such an explosive?" Tony asks.

"That is a good question. You are a smart man, Doctor. I'll let you figure it out for yourself. By the time you comprehend it, our deed will have been done."

"At least that is some refreshing news, that we may live another day."

"What do you take me for, some type of ruthless beast? I have feelings. Grull and I both detest violence."

"What about the woman back at the warehouse?"

"*Ohhh*, she was a lovely morsel. One has to eat. I get very grumpy when I'm hungry. It's your lucky day that I'm not still hungry. Otherwise I can't account for my actions. I am aware that you two may have missed your bath this evening, so let me make it up to you." Tragoon laughs out loud, shaking the car.

Suddenly Matt and Tony are going straight down. Tragoon drags them into the Pacific Ocean, and the water is bitter cold.

"Sorry again for not supplying you with any soap."

"That could wake the dead," Matt says, shivering.

"No kidding. I guess it's better than death, and now I'm freezing." Tony is shaking.

And again they head straight down.

"I want to make sure all your little talking devices are no longer working. Try them now."

The entire car and its contents are soaking wet. Matt and Tony are shaking with the wind blowing in and the freezing water temps.

"At least for now, it looks like he's keeping us alive," Matt laments.

"Yes, now is the key word. I wonder where we're going."

"How are you boys doing? Why don't you turn on the car's heater?" Tragoon laughs.

"I didn't know dragons were so funny," Matt comments.

"Me either. He's hysterical."

"It's a beautiful night. Why don't you two sit back and enjoy this moonlit evening. I'd hum you a tune since I can't sing. You should be arriving at your destination shortly."

"He should be a standup comedian," Matt says.

"I have a feeling we're heading to the Hawaiian Islands," Tony announces.

"Great, I've been wanting to visit the islands for a while. You keep me working so much, I haven't had the time. You think he's going to drop us off at the Ritz?"

"Sure, Matt. I'm thinking the penthouse suite."

What a sight they must have been—a flying car being carried by a dragon.

"Hey, boys. Before you start dreaming of a nice night in a fancy hotel suite, you may want to think about a more rustic approach. I figured you two as nature lovers. Doubt you'll find turndown service. Buckle up, boys. Hope we don't meet again. If we do, I'll make it an eternal event."

They could hear Tragoon laughing hysterically into the quiet night.

"Oh no, hold on. He dropped us."

"Where do think we are?" Matt asks.

"It looks like we're in some type of lagoon. The good news is we are alive."

"Why do you think he didn't kill us?"

"I'm not sure. He had plenty of chances."

They swim out of what is left of the rental car.

"It's hard to see on this moonlit evening. I don't see a Hertz rental car return anywhere nearby." Matt scans the area.

"I bet not. All I can see is some trees, and it sounds like a waterfall nearby. Looks like we're in some type of rainforest. Plus, for the amount of time we were in the air, I doubt we're still in California. My guess may have been accurate. I think we're on one of the Hawaiian Islands."

"I hope you got the car insurance. This will be a hard one to explain." Matt smiles.

It seems someone doesn't want Tony and Matt at the big charity gala. They are both cold and soaking wet, along with inoperable cell phones. The first issue is to address the crazy terrain, and then to find a way off the island and back to San Francisco. It's 7:18 a.m. in California, and they have about ten hours or more to return to San Francisco.

It turns out Tony is correct. They are in Hawaii, on "the Forbidden Isle" called Ni'ihau. Population under a hundred, along with some US Navy contractors on the island. A helicopter goes flying overhead, and all the stranded men need to do is locate the helicopter launch.

Matt takes off running and returns completely out of breath.

"I have a good idea of where she landed. I'll try the mountain range. Looked like about two miles away. Not sure of the landscape," Matt explains, a little breathless.

"Show me the way, boss," Tony replies.

The launch is a couple of miles away, but when they locate it, the helicopter has left. They decide to wait for another. After a brief delay, another helicopter arrives. With some unusual stares and a few questions from the helicopter pilot, Tony and Matt hitch a ride back to Kauai.

Chapter 5

PALACE

The king of the kingdom is about to explode. Some confusion occurred while the king's son, Prince Mako (Michael), was being transported to the concrete country. The king has yet to be notified that his son is safe. The transporters are still malfunctioning.

"I send you to find my son, and you bring back a little girl who has beat up half my guards, and you expect me to be happy. The queen may be right. You're all morons. Get out of my sight before I have you beheaded. Bring in the girl!" the king demands.

Alessandra walks into the room between two giant beasts called Kondos.

"Well, well. I wanted to see for myself, what little girl is causing all this trouble for my guards. And how you could be mistaken for the prince is beyond me. You're one little young girl with short blond hair. You look harmless to me. Why is she here wasting my time? If she is that skilled, maybe I should have her replace my current guardians." The king laughs.

Alex is standing there not saying anything, remembering the stories Grando told about the king. *Never talk to the king unless he asks you a question. And do not ever ask the king a question. And if the king finds out where you're from, it could be trouble. He does not trust concrete-dwellers.*

"What is your name, young lady?" the king asks.

"Alessandra."

"Where are you from?"

With a little hesitation, Alex replies, "Rockland." She doesn't want to say Key West, Florida, nor use her last name.

"Why were you caged with Grando?"

"I was mistakenly captured by the rebels."

"So, you are not a rebel?" The king stares at her.

"I am most certainly *not*!"

The king is pleased. "Then, what am I to do with you?"

"Let me go. I will leave and—"

Screaming can be heard in the background, and people are running all over the place as the queen makes her grand entrance.

"Oh, great," the king mumbles.

She is screaming as she walks into the chamber hall. "*Who is this* and why is she here? She is wasting my time. Where is my son? You imbecile, I thought you said you found my son. This looks like a useless drifter. Where is my son!" The queen cries out again, "Where is my son!"

The queen knows the prince is with the Trefars, since she was the one who put out a kill order on the prince, which of course she hasn't shared with her husband.

"Calm down, my queen. We have found the prince. He is with the Trefars, and they are returning him at once," the king replies.

The queen turns away, screaming, "Socreen, where are you. You're a useless heap. Bring Siena with you."

If only the queen had taken the time to ask Alessandra's full name, she would have been alarmed indeed. But she didn't. Socreen runs into the chamber and catches a glance of the young girl, and stops in her tracks.

The queen looks at Socreen and says, "What, have you never seen a young girl before? Let's go. I need to make some travel plans. You are getting slow and dimwitted. Where is Siena?"

Alex turns around too late and only catches a glimpse of the woman. The voice sounds familiar. Alex isn't certain.

"Where *was* I?" the king asks one of his advisors.

"Oh, yes. You wish to leave. That can be arranged, my dear." The king waves a hand and says, "Take this young woman to the dungeon until I decide what to do with her."

Alex hears "the dungeon" and pleads, "I am not here to harm anyone. I don't want to go to the dungeon. Please!"

It's too late. A Kondo is dragging Alex out of the chamber as she is kicking and screaming. "Are you kidding me? You're a tyrant! Let's fight face-to-face, you wimp of a king." Alex starts screaming. The screaming gets louder. Alex feels a knock on the head and passes out.

Socreen has to confirm who and where the prisoner is being taken. "Siena, I have to visit someone in the dungeon. Please cover for me while I'm gone. I shouldn't be long."

Socreen has made a few special friends in this place. One is Siena, also a handmaiden to the queen. Siena is young, beautiful, kind, sweet, and full of life. Socreen, on the other hand, is getting old and frail. They work side by side, two principal handmaidens at the queen's beck and call every minute of every day.

Siena has lived in the palace almost her entire life. Both her parents passed when she was very young and, being the only child, she showed up at the palace doors all by herself at five years of age. And in a rare weak moment, little Siena was allowed into the palace. She started a friendship with the prince. She was five and the prince was four. They grew up playing together, and Socreen essentially raised them both. One night Siena confided to Socreen that she was in love with the prince. Socreen answered that she should keep it a secret. Most of the co-workers in the palace also cared for and watched over Siena.

"Of course, Socreen. I'll take care of the queen while you're out."

"For your own safety, do not tell her where I've gone." Socreen kisses Siena on the forehead.

"Not to worry, my lips are sealed." Siena smiles.

"You're an angel, my dear."

Socreen is preparing to depart her chamber when she hears a tap at her window, and in flies Carolyn. Carolyn is an 88 butterfly, and she is Socreen's only friend from outside the palace.

"I have some news for you, Socreen," Carolyn remarks.

"Good to see you again, Carolyn. I hope it's good news," Socreen responds.

"Some sad yet hopeful news. Rockland has been destroyed, and it seems the Trefars may be the next target. We need your help once again." She is looking around to make sure no one is nearby.

"I am alone. What help can I be? And what about your hopeful news?"

"We are aware that the queen is planning something on her own and no one can get close enough to hear her plans," Carolyn comments.

"What can I do? She tells me nothing."

"Can you unlock the east side palace gate door the day after next?"

"Oh my, that is the first day of the prince's birthday party. I'm afraid everything will be on lockdown. I will see what I can do. The prince is on his way back, and everyone is on high alert. Who is it that I am risking my life for?" Socreen asks.

"I would rather not say, since it will cause a problem within the palace if you are questioned. Better you not know for now. Sorry."

Socreen starts shaking uncontrollably. "Sorry, there is a lot going on around here, and none of it is good. I will not do it unless I know who it is for. I am not willing to risk my life for one of your troubleshooters," Socreen answers, almost in tears.

"Okay, I shall tell you, though it must remain a secret because a plan has been set in place, and she will need your help. You have been very kind to us, so I will tell you. You will not be harmed because we consider you an ally. Others may perish." Carolyn flutters her wings.

"Okay, tell me. I can keep more secrets than you may think," Socreen adds.

"Princess Xandra has returned, and she will soon attack the palace."

Socreen almost passes out when hearing the name of her daughter's alias. "I will be happy to help. She cannot do this alone. Will anyone be with her?" Socreen anxiously asks.

"I see concern on your face. Do not worry. She is a great warrior, and we will win, especially with your help. That is all I can say. If you could be sure and open the gate … sneaking the princess into the palace is the key to a successful takeover."

Socreen is so excited she can hardly walk out of her chambers. The day has finally arrived that she can possibly be taken back home and away from this awful place. Trembling, she departs for the dungeon to speak with the new prisoner.

The pitiful screaming is a reminder of why she rarely visits the dungeon anymore.

"I would like to see the prisoner in cell number 2875, per the queen." Socreen tells the guard.

The guard, not wanting anything to do with the queen, opens the door and lets Socreen inside. The odors reek and the heat is stifling.

The watch guard tells the other guard, "Take her to cell number 2875."

"Right away, sir," the young guard replies. "Follow me. This place is full of savages, so be careful. Take this lantern. It can get dark down here."

It has been a while since Socreen has been in this disgusting dungeon. It still smells. As before, most of the captives are innocent. Just because they disavowed the king or queen, they were put away—for no other reason. Some are very young, and it is sad to see all these children who have done nothing wrong. It is very disturbing. "Let me out," is all she hears.

The guard reminds Socreen, "Watch out for the prisoner in number 2875. She is aggressive and full of hate."

Socreen holds up the lantern and can barely make out a young blond girl in the corner of the cell. "Let me in the cell and leave us," Socreen demands.

"I suggest you stay outside her cell," the guard says.

"Leave us."

"As you wish, Socreen. She is a handful. I will wait for you at the end of the hall. If you need my help, cry out," the guard replies.

"Thanks, I should be fine."

When Socreen approaches the young lady, she hears: "Stay where you are before I kick your skull in, old lady."

"Let me see your face, my dear," Socreen asks.

"Who are you and what do you want?" Alex replies.

"My name is Socreen. And yours?"

Alex turns her head and stares for a while, before replying, "I am Alessandra Cabrella."

Hearing that, Socreen inadvertently screams and starts shaking. The guard comes running and yelling out to the young girl to stay put. He pokes the young girl with an instrument.

The guard says to Socreen, "You should leave at once. You are not safe."

"Stop it. *Stop!* Leave here at once, or I will have you thrown into the pit."

The guard, not wanting to argue with Socreen, departs.

Socreen composes herself long enough to say, "I'm Elizabeth Cabrella, and I haven't said that name in sixteen years." She breaks down and cries uncontrollably.

Alex jumps up and grabs her so tight, she almost squeezes the life out of her.

"Grandma, you're alive. What are you doing here?"

"I should be asking you that same question."

"Are you okay?" the guard asks.

"I am fine, and if you bother me one more time, I will inform the queen that you interfered with my interrogation," an agitated Socreen replies.

"Yes, Socreen. I am sorry."

Alex begins to explain. "I was unexpectedly brought here against my will. Actually, I've been imprisoned since my arrival to this horrible place."

"Oh my, that sounds awful. How did you get captured, and your mother escape?" Grandma asks.

"My mother is here? Where, when?"

"Are you telling me you came by yourself?"

"Yes, it was kind of an unintended consequence," Alex says, trying to recall her recent adventure.

"I was told your mother will be here tomorrow."

"Mom is coming here. That is not good. She will be very upset if she knows I'm here, and I'm fairly certain Dylan is also here."

"Who is Dylan?" Grandma asks.

Alex has forgotten that Dylan was born while Grandma was away.

"Dylan is my younger brother and a real troublemaker."

"How old is your brother?"

"Almost sixteen, I think."

"Oh my goodness, could it be?"

"Could it be what, Grandma?"

"Never mind. First I need to get you out of here. Do you remember visiting the kingdom when you were young, my dear?"

"Not really. I recall a few bits and pieces. I actually thought it was all a dream. Maybe we can all go back together. Grandpa misses you terribly."

"He is still alive, isn't he? I knew he was, that old goat. I need to get you out of here as soon as possible."

"Grandma, don't you work for the queen? Why not tell her who I am and it was a mistake. She will let me go."

"Sweetie, I wish it were that easy. See, the queen … how can I put it? Let's just say she's a bitch!"

"Grandma, really. That's quite the language, coming from you."

"I'm afraid living here for sixteen years has toughened me up, and not in a good way."

"Let's go now," Alex demands.

"Not so fast. I need a plan. This place is not safe for a little girl like you."

"Grandma, I can take care of myself. Can you sneak me out?"

"It's not that easy. This place is heavily guarded. Your mother will know what to do. I can't override the king."

"I don't understand. What can Mom do that you can't? You've been living here for years."

"I'm getting too old, my dear. Your mother has a unique quality."

"What are you talking about? She's a veterinarian. What's the big deal?"

"Oh, sweetie, she's much more than a veterinarian."

"Grandma, you've been away so long. What are you trying to say?"

"She's a legend here."

"A legend, you say. What kind of legend?"

"Her nickname is Princess Xandra, warrior for all the oppressed."

"Are you sure you're talking about my sweet and kind mother? She is some type of warrior? I doubt that!"

"Yes, she understands everyone, including the animals."

"That I believe. She is an animal whisperer."

"I can't explain, but take my word for it. She can wield a sword like no one."

"I, too, can wield a sword and knock a few heads. While you were gone, Mom sent me away to Hong Kong. I trained with the most accomplished instructors in the world, and I am quite skilled in martial arts."

"I believe you, my dear. All the guards are scared to death of you. You have made quite an early impression."

"So let's fight our way out."

"Slow down, sweetie. Let's wait for your mom. Can you hold up another day? Isabella will be here tomorrow. Together we will formulate a plan."

"Okay, I'll wait another day. Will you come visit me? This place is awful. No color palette. Damp and ugly. Not to mention the smell and the sounds."

"At least you have your mother's sense of humor. When your mother gets here, we will put together a plan. I'll think of something. Until then, stay put. Sorry, that was silly. Relax, I'll have you out soon."

"Okay, Grandma. You know where I'll be."

The hugs and kisses goodbye seem to last a lifetime. Then Grandma starts crying.

"Grandma, you're not helping."

"I feel sick leaving you here. I need a plan."

"I'll be fine."

"Okay, sweetie. I'd better leave before they get suspicious. This is the most wonderful day ever, seeing you again." She goes and calls out the small window grate, "Guard, I am ready."

When he opens the door she says to him, "If any harm comes to her, I will blame you."

"Yes, Socreen."

The guard is suspect since Socreen appeared so enthralled with the prisoner. Maybe he should alert the queen.

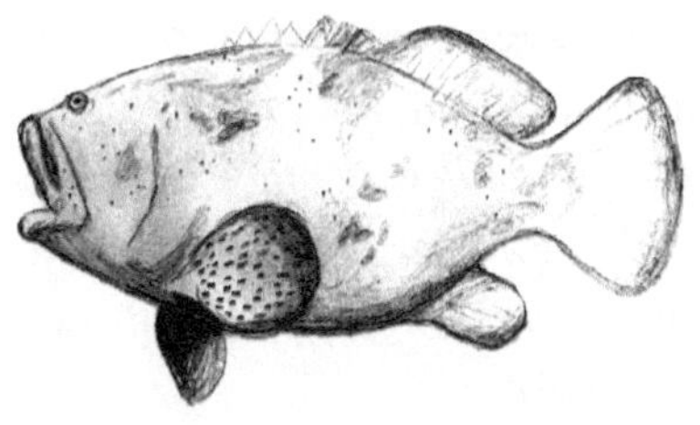

Chapter 6

SUBWAY

While Princess Xandra and Tabitha are traveling to the Trefars, Pup lands in front of the two of them, and they abruptly stop. He needs to speak with Tabitha at once.

Tabitha walks up to Pup. "What's going on?"

Pup says, "I have news from T that he would like you to go to subway station number 188. I will inform you as to why, once we depart. Do not alarm the princess. Tell her you have been called away. Do not mention T."

Tabitha says her goodbyes to Xandra and apologizes for her quick departure. She has something important to attend to.

"Goodbye, and thanks again for keeping my Dylan safe," Xandra replies.

"Anytime," Tabitha replies. "It was my pleasure to ride with the great Princess Xandra."

**

Pup explains to Tabitha that she is to meet up with Dylan the swimmer—me—at the subway station. The Trefars have finished the transformation of Dylan into Prince Mako. We look alike, so the biggest issues were to have me mimic the prince's mannerisms, speech, and facial expressions.

Tabitha thinks, *T pulled it off. That dysfunctional boy is now the prince. Well, good for them. I can't wait to see this.* She arrives at the subway station in time to meet up with Dylan, the prince impersonator.

**

"Welcome back, my friend." I am so excited to see Tabitha, I almost tackle her. I try to control myself. Wishing she was my girlfriend, I make a gesture to hug her, but that goes unheeded.

"My goodness," Tabitha responds, "you look more like the prince than he does. You sure have matured. I assume you are ready. You remember the last time we went out, so try not to stir anything up. We have much more to lose. Are you prepared and ready?"

The last time Tabitha and I were traveling together, we ran into a little trouble with a couple of Graeters. I may have upset one or two. Graeters are like bulldozers. Their nickname is "Excavators," and they can dig for miles. They have huge mouths and carry dirt and sand in their mouths as they dig. Big in stature, and stubborn, they love to argue, hate water, and love gum. They eat gum for breakfast, lunch, and dinner. Gum-chomping creatures is what I prefer to call them.

"Yes, I'm ready to rock and roll. Oops—yes, ready." I smile. *I've got to stop saying those phrases. Speaking like that may get me killed.*

The weather begins to turn cold and windy as we approach the subway station. I put up my hood, making sure I'm not seen. According to T, if I am spotted on a regular subway and not on the royal subway, it would cause complete havoc. Returning me—Prince Mako—back to the palace in one piece, unharmed, is of the highest priority. There are plenty of people who would take advantage of this situation. It's very unusual, or at the very least, rarely would you see a member of the royal family traveling without a huge entourage, and not on any subway other than the royal subway.

Tabitha waves her tattooed arm twice over the scanner device to allow us both entry onto the subway platform. Everyone at birth is supposed to be marked with some type of UPC code on their arm. It is only Tabitha and me, traveling by ourselves. T thought we would draw little or no attention if there are only the two of us. T doesn't trust the king, and prefers I am delivered back to the palace rather than allowing the king's men to encroach on the Trefars's compound. Trefars and the royals have never been companions.

Tabitha finds an empty semiprivate subway car so we can be undisturbed and hidden from prying eyes. It is my first subway ride, and I am thrilled. This thing is cruising at speeds far beyond what they do back in the States.

Then the car slows down, and I hear a big boom.

I look at Tabitha and ask, "What was that?"

"We are now going underwater, and it's one of the few waterways that hasn't dried up. It hasn't rained in over five hundred days," Tabitha replies.

"Wow, this is so cool."

"Could you at least act like you've ridden on a subway in the past?"

I have never seen a subway go underwater like this. I am staring out the window, with a huge grin on my face, watching the fish swim by and all the colorful coral reefs.

"Kind of reminds me of back home," I say. "And, by the way, T told me about you and Pup. That is an awesome story."

"What did he say?"

"You want me to tell you the entire story?"

"Yes, please. I'm curious to hear what T said."

"The story T told me went like this. One day, a little girl was working in the field with her father, and she found an odd-shaped, unusual-colored rock. She asked her father if she could keep the rock, and he said, 'You found it, it's yours. What are you going to do with such a big rock?' 'I will take it everywhere I go,' she told him. So she put the rock in her pull wagon and covered it with a blanket. She never left it alone. It was by her side night and day. She would sing to it and talk to it as if it were a real person. And one day the rock started to move.

"This little girl wasn't frightened. She was delighted that it moved. She told her parents about it moving, and they wanted to see her prize rock. It turned out the rock wasn't a rock, but an egg. It's extremely rare to find a dragon's egg. Her parents were afraid that the dragon's parents would come back and be upset. They said she should replace the rock or egg where she had found it. She didn't understand why she had to give back her prize rock. She had cared for this rock and it had been by her side every minute for many days. She was very sad, so she decided to depart from her family and hide deep in the forest.

"Right after she left, a tragedy occurred and both her parents perished. At the same time, her egg hatched. It was a beautiful dragon. She named her dragon, Pup. And they have never been apart."

"Yes," Tabitha says, "we have been together for many years. I would rather die myself than lose my best friend Pup. Just like Gaylok, I ..."

I see Tabitha starting to cry. I go to her and hold her for a few seconds, and soon her calmness returns.

"I am very sorry about Gaylok. I know you two were very close."

Gaylok, the leader of the rebels in Rockland, raised Tabitha after her parents perished.

"Yes, he was more than a friend. More like a father to me. Thank you."

"Did you get to see him?"

"Yes, he basically died in my arms with your mo—many around." Tabitha does not want to mention my mother was here, needing to keep me focused.

"How did he die?" I ask.

"The king's men ambushed his village and killed everyone in sight. It was a slaughter. Pup and I did not get there in time. I feel like if we were there, this would never have happened."

"Are you blaming me for your not being there?"

"I take back my comment about your maturity. You're still delusional. No, no one's fault but the king's, you dimwit."

Great, I am a moron. I'm making Tabitha upset again.

"Listen, are you ready for what's about to happen to you?" Tabitha asks.

"Sure, I am. I am more than ready. Why are you suddenly so concerned? Not long ago you were ready to throw me overboard."

"I am making sure you're ready. You do want to see your family again, don't you? Especially your mother."

"My mother! What does she have to do with this?"

"Nothing. Trying to get you prepared and focused."

"You're not helping by talking about my mother. I'm aware of the consequences. My initial quest or goal was to find my grandmother and take her home. All this other mess was not of my choosing."

Tabitha is getting frustrated, and looks away. Still dealing with Gaylok's death has taken its toll on her, and her temper is short.

All of a sudden, a huge fish swims up along the window. It seems to stop and gaze directly at me. While staring out the window, I lower my hood to get a better look. Not thinking anything can see inside the car all that well, I wave at this huge fish as it swims away. Tabitha turns in my direction, and—to me, what looks like slow motion—gets … up … and … grabs … me. She pulls me away from the window and throws me to the floor. It is too late. I have been spotted.

I look up at Tabitha and say, "It's not that big a deal. We are traveling in a subway car, underwater. Who can harm us down here? I don't expect anyone to recognize me underwater. Now, calm down."

It doesn't take long before something goes drastically wrong. The subway car begins to shake, and then I hear a big bang. It sounds like a crash, and then water comes rushing in. I think I hear an alarm or siren of some sort going off.

I look at Tabitha and ask her, "Can you swim?"

"Not very well, but I know how. We haven't had rain in so long, most of our waterways are dried up, so swimming is almost a lost pastime."

Within minutes, the entire car is full of water. Each car is equipped with a breathing apparatus in case of a crash. Only one apparatus is here, and I give it to Tabitha, who is happy to have the breathing element. Needless to say, she is not happy about the current situation. Her mission was to get me back to the palace, and if it meant her life, so be it.

I grab Tabitha and pull her towards the door. I point to an opening as I swim behind her, pushing her towards the opening. I can tell she's not a very efficient swimmer—a bit hesitant—so I make sure she keeps moving forward. I have been swimming my entire life. It should be an easy task to get us both to the surface.

I'm not sure how far down we have plunged into the coolish water. At least the water is clear and I can see Tabitha. I keep pushing her straight up towards the surface. The breathing apparatus helps her immensely. I'm not sure how much air is in those elements. I don't want to chance it running out. She would go into shock and suffer hypoventilation, which would make things more hectic.

As I am following her, two giant shark-looking creatures appear. These sharks look like they are smiling at me … as if I am lunch. Tabitha is too busy trying to reach the surface and, luckily, doesn't realize I am in jeopardy. Not that she could be of any help. I start to swim in another direction, to keep them away from Tabitha. She is no concern of theirs. Lucky for me, I am what they want.

Then I hear: "Hello, Prince Mako, it's good to see you down here. I am sorry to say, your days in the kingdom have come to an unforeseen end."

I look up and see this giant shark smiling at me, exposing its huge teeth. Telling me it's time for me to die. I think, *Oh no, here we go again.* I was attacked by a couple of sharks back in Key West. *This time they think I'm Prince Mako. Does everything want to eat me? Do I put out an odor or something?*

My plan is to swim towards the subway car and possibly hide somewhere inside. I doubt I can get to it in time. Those sharks are so fast they are almost on top of me. I am not sure how long I've been underwater, but now one of the sharks dives towards me for the kill. At the same time the shark dives down, something pushes me from behind. I lurch forward just in time to see another giant shark heading directly towards me.

At that exact moment, out of the corner of my eye I see a bus-sized grouper fish swimming towards me. I'm not sure what happens next. I think I am scooped up in the grouper's massive mouth. The shark bounces off the grouper as if it was made of rubber.

The shark curses out loud, adding, "That is one lucky prince."

I'm about half freaking out, seeing that I am possibly inside the grouper's mouth. Now what do I do? This is a first for me, being inside a fish's mouth. I'm usually the one catching the fish. Wasn't there a book about a guy name Jonah, who got swallowed by a whale. What was that outcome? I can't remember. Will anyone find me to tell my tale? Not sure how I'm still alive. I'm real delighted, though.

Where is that light coming from? I step towards it. It seems extremely dry in here. I must be dreaming. I know I'm dreaming because I see a lantern and someone sitting on a chair, smiling from ear to ear.

"Hey, Prince," Igagbee announces loudly, "did you think I would let you down?"

I can't speak. I can hardly believe my eyes. I'm fairly certain I'm dreaming or seeing things after I've drowned.

"How did you find me?"

Amused, Igagbee answers, "I told you I would protect you. So what are you quivering about?"

"You can't swim."

"I never even got wet. Not sure why you're so concerned about me. My only job is to keep you safe."

"Better yet, how did you both find me? The subway crashed and it was impossible to know where I was."

"Improbable, most likely. Not impossible," Igagbee responds.

"Did you see Tabitha? Is she okay?"

"She is fine."

Igagbee informs me that fortunately for Tabitha, Pup was following her every move and when she was almost to the surface, Pup dove into the water and plucked her out. Pup had mentioned a shark or two were in the water. They were too deep for Pup to attack.

"Did they give you any trouble?"

That is the last thing I hear from Igagbee, before I collapse.

**

Is that a dragon flying overhead? Wait! There are too many to count. Where am I again? All I see is an ocean of water. I have to duck down because one of those dragons swoops over, and I can see someone riding on its back. Why would a dragon attack me? What have I done? I don't even know where I am.

Suddenly a dragon lands and lowers its head as if it wants me to ride it.

Then I hear: "You need a ride?"

I hesitate, and mutter, "Sure, why not."

"Where would you like me to take you?"

"How about the mall, to get something to eat?"

"Come on. Hop up and hold on. We will be there shortly."

Now, this is awesome. Soon we are high in the sky. I look down and can only see water. We are flying at magnificent speeds. We are above the clouds and now I can see nothing, we are so high up.

"Hey, um, Mr. Dragon. Where is the mall?"

"My name is Skulleater. The mall is over the next cloud."

Skulleater, that sounds morbid. Hope he knows what he's doing. Better yet, what am I doing?

"Hey, Mr. Skulleater, I am no longer hungry. Can you drop me off at my house?"

All I hear is laughter. The clouds start to clear, and I can see the ground below me. Big birds are flying everywhere and it looks like we are heading straight to the crater of a volcano. The volcano is still active; lava is flowing from the crater.

I quickly realize I am no longer riding on the dragon's back. I am falling into the active volcano pit. Nooooo ….

**

I open my eyes and see Igagbee shaking me.

"Wake up, Prince, wake up." Igagbee turns his head and says, "Hey, Brian, take us up."

"Will do." Brian glides towards the surface, saying, "This made my day. I'm bored and lonely swimming around all by myself. I'm proud to have saved the prince."

"You were brilliant. Thank you again."

We surface, and Brian the giant grouper seems to spit Igagbee and me onto land.

I am fully awake now and ask, "Wow, what happened? Where am I?"

"You are on dry land, and soon the king's men will be here to take you to the palace. Let's clean you up and get you prepared," Igagbee states.

"Where is Tabitha?" I ask.

"She was last seen with Pup," Igagbee replies.

"She is supposed to take me to the palace," I remind Igagbee.

"That plan has changed. They will not let me enter the palace. I will wait with you until the king's guards arrive. You will be safe in their care. They are almost here. It's best if I am seen with you and they get a look at my lost hand."

"Again, I am so sorry about your hand. I feel like I have caused devastation everywhere I've been."

"Don't think like that. All this has been foreseen."

"Are you telling me you know how this story unfolds? Tell me, how does it end?"

"It all ends well, I am told," Igagbee comments.

"I bet it does. Why doesn't someone fill me in on the story, so I may feel better about our scheme?"

"You will know soon enough."

I start changing into the dry clothes Igagbee brought me, when I realize that the potions T gave me are lost. Before I can say anything, Igagbee is handing me a pair of shoes and additional vials of T's potion.

Igagbee smiles and says, "T is prepared for any catastrophe."

"How does he know?" I ask, bewildered. "It would be impossible to know that I was going to be eaten by a shark and then gobbled up by a grouper. There is something you are not telling me about T."

"You are aware that Tara, his mother, can see the future. If you recall, she saw yours."

"I don't remember that."

"It was while you were meeting with T."

"That explains it. I was unconscious. He's a little rascal, that one."

Igagbee turns a bright green and says, "I wouldn't say that too loud. Now let's get you ready for your task and focused on your mission."

Trefars can change colors, like chameleons.

Soon, hundreds of the king's finest trained guards surround us. One of the king's guards jumps off his huge horse and confronts me.

"Your Highness, I am glad you are safe. Welcome back. My name is Tazer, and I am ready to take you back to the palace. Say your goodbyes. Are you okay to travel?"

"Yes, indeed. This man saved my life. Thank you, Igagbee."

"My pleasure, Your Highness. Until we meet again." Igagbee grins.

Tazer looks at Igagbee and smiles.

I'm not sure if Igagbee is smiling because he lost his hand, or why.

"I have brought you the coach for your transfer," Tazer says, taunting the prince.

"I am ready to ride and not on that coach. I am not injured, you fool," I reply loudly. *Tazer must think I'm a wimp, that I need the coach, which is used for the injured.*

"Yes, Your Highness."

I am lucky the prince's horse is not here, so I ride another.

"Let's get going. I want to get back as soon as possible. This has been quite an adventure, and I am very tired and hungry."

"Yes, Your Highness. Welcome back."

Tazer barks out some orders and all the guards jump to attention.

"Did the Trefars treat you well, Your Highness?" Tazer asks.

"Very well. They are a strange group of people."

"There are very few that have walked away from their village."

"I never felt threatened. It is lucky for them that I did not. Otherwise, Father would have to wipe them out."

"You are correct, they are fortunate indeed. The king and queen have been very worried."

"They always worry. I am no longer a child."

"Yes, I can see that, Your Highness."

I ride up ahead and think, *It's official. I am the prince. Here we go. Game on, let the adventure begin. I may have fooled Tazer, so now I have to fool the king and queen. That will be another huge hurdle. And as T reminded me, it will take every day—*

not just the first day, but every day. Everyone will be watching and testing.

I wonder what Mom is doing right now. If she could only see me now, a prince. She will never believe me. Neither will any of my sisters, especially my older dingbat sister, Alex. Will Elizabeth, or Socreen, recognize me? Oh no, she may blow my cover. We have never met, so I will need to explain to her what's going on.

Chapter 7

KONDOS

Xandra and Hari arrive at the Trefars village without any trouble. Not many are suicidal enough to attack four giant galloping zebras and a warrior riding at full speed. After she has taken a brief rest, T summons Princess Xandra to join him for a moment.

"Hello, my dear friend," T says. "It has been a long time. Sit down and tell me how life has been treating you. We can have a smoke." The Trefars are not very affectionate, so a hug is not in order.

"I prefer not to have a smoke, thank you," Xandra replies.

Xandra acknowledges to T that her journey was uneventful, and Tabitha was unexpectedly called away. After a short discussion about Gaylok, Xandra has some questions of her own.

"T, it is very pleasing to see you. Where is my family, especially Dylan and Alessandra?" Xandra knows T well, and rushing him will be a challenge. However, she needs answers, and quick. She trained with and got her title of Princess Xandra because of T. He made her the warrior she is today. She needs to find her children. The Trefars are not known for being compassionate, so getting T to understand her predicament may be problematic. Trefars are even-keeled and show little emotion. That's why it is so humorous that they can change colors. To them, death is a way of life, not a tragedy, and only an event they all prepare for.

T responds, "Right to the point. I expected nothing less. I will get to that, but for now I need you to look at something and give me your opinion."

"Really. Can't it wait?" Xandra says.

"No. It's too important, and it won't delay you for long. You will be on your way in no time. Recently we have been in a state of high alert. Much more than usual. I do have something that may be of interest to you. Follow me, please," T says.

Xandra fears that "in no time" for a Trefars is relative. It's best not to question T about his affairs. It will get you nowhere.

They enter a large room with a Trefars standing guard. The guard sees T and allows everyone to enter. Xandra sees a rather large beast or creature lying on the ground, larger than a school bus—looking very much dead or sleeping soundly.

"My goodness, what is that?" She has never seen one of those huge beasts before.

"That is a Kondo, one of the king's new toys. There are not many and they are quite difficult to kill. This is a cadaver for you to do an autopsy, and to tell me where one would start if one wanted to take one down," T says to the princess.

"How did you get this one?"

"Fortunate! I would feel more confident if I had more info, so if you would, please?"

"How big is it?" Hari asks.

"She's only a baby, at twenty feet tall. Her name is Puddin," T replies.

"A baby, you say. That is some big baby. How large can they get?" Xandra asks.

"Eighty to ninety feet."

Xandra says, "How do you stop a ninety-foot Kondo?"

"That is why you are here. When you are done with the autopsy, we shall discuss your findings." T nods and departs.

Xandra has treated many creatures in this land. That's how, if needed, she knows where to strike for the kill and make it count. That's another reason why she is such a good warrior; she knows where to aim. This beast is so big, Xandra isn't sure where to start.

"What do you think, Hari? Can you see any wounds that caused her death?"

"Good luck, you're on your own. I'm not up for this type of thing," Hari replies.

"I don't see any wounds. I'm going to start at the top. I'll call you when I'm finished. No need for you to see this poor girl. And by the way, all you men are scaredy-cats."

"True. Goodbye." Hari trots away.

A beast this large could take a full week for an autopsy. Fortunately, T only wants vital organ locations. She may be able to get it done in a day or two. T did give her some helpers, which makes it much easier. The helpers don't even flinch when Xandra cuts into the beast. Xandra is getting curious as to the cause of death.

"Okay, Puddin, let's find out what happened to you."

There are no brain injuries of any type. It isn't a head wound. Next is the heart, though she has no heart—or at least an organ where you would usually find a heart. *Maybe she died at birth because she was born without a heart.*

After a thorough and painstaking analysis, Xandra finally finds the cause of death. Xandra should have started at the feet instead of the head. This Kondo has two hearts: one in each foot. That is why the arrows or spears to the chest do nothing against these enormous creatures. Stab both their feet, and they go down in more ways than one. Puddin has a kind and sweet face. This poor thing has two huge blood clots on both her feet, and that is her issue. She probably toppled over and never knew what hit her.

Xandra is so tired she can barely make it back to her cabin. As soon as she awakens, she wants to be taken to T at once.

"I have found their weakness. Somewhere you'd never look." She explains to T, "First, this one has two hearts, one in each foot. The quickest way to take them out is to stab both feet."

"That does explain a lot. Thank you. That information is valuable to me." T smiles.

"I also gave a copy of my findings to your assistant. I think my work here is done. Now, may I see my kids?"

"Yes, of course. As usual, you have done well. One more small favor? If you could say hello to my mother, Tara?"

"How is Tara? I wasn't sure she was still with us."

"She is still feisty as ever, for a four-hundred-year-old. She would like to see you. Her time is almost over."

"Okay, and I am not letting her read my mind. Any information on my mother?"

"Your mother is fine. She goes by the name of Socreen now. She is one of the handmaidens of the queen and lives in the palace. I can assume she is ready to get back to her homeland."

"I bet she is more than ready. I have been trying to get back this way, but to no avail."

"Working for the queen can be perilous, one would presume. She knows you're here," T says, smiling.

"Great. Can I see my son Dylan now?"

"That might be awkward," T replies.

"Why is that? You said he was here."

"Yes indeed, he was here."

"Was? What have you done? Where is he now?"

Getting angry at T will solve nothing, Xandra thinks, as her voice starts quivering. She's about to lose it.

"He is at the palace," T replies.

"Why would you send him to the palace?"

"Your son, daughter, and mother are all at the palace."

"How am I supposed to get them out of the palace? Isn't that place like a fortress?"

T explains his plan about transforming Dylan into Prince Mako. T has to enlighten Xandra as to who this Prince Mako is, and that Dylan is a spitting image. Xandra is not pleased.

"No, I don't like your plan at all. How do you suppose he replace this prince? After that, I guess he is supposed to murder the king and queen, perhaps?" Xandra asks half-heartedly.

"That could be part of my plan." T smiles.

"Are you kidding me! Where is the real prince?"

"I'm not entirely sure. He is somewhere in your land, America, as you call it."

Isabella recalls her conversation with her brother. Tony told her that someone who looked similar to Dylan was seen in the San Francisco airport. And soon after, Hari informed her that someone who looked similar to Dylan was in her Key West house.

"What happens if my son is found out to be an imposter?"

"That will not happen."

"That is easy for you to say. Have you met my son? He is only fifteen and only has girls on his mind every minute. His focus is very limited to any task at hand."

"He has been well trained," T states.

"Are you kidding me? You haven't had enough time to train my son. It would take many days. Oh, I don't think this is a good idea at all."

"You will see. It will be fine. I have no choice," T answers.

That does it. Xandra loses it. "You have no choice but to *kill* my son!"

"You need to calm yourself."

"I am going to visit Tara before I say something I'll regret." Isabella storms out of the room, ready to explode.

**

"Hello, Tara, how are you doing?" Xandra asks.

"I am fine, dear. It is good to see you. I can see my son has upset you."

"He has no idea what a mother goes through to protect her children. I could strangle him with my own hands."

Tara decides to tell Xandra a story about T, as a youth.

"When T was young, he found something and wanted to keep it for himself. His father would not allow him to keep this thing, and that infuriated T. He was so upset with his father, he decided to go against his wishes. And to go against your father's wishes as a Trefars is unheard of. T was very stubborn. So he didn't tell anyone he was keeping this thing, hidden far away in the forest. T kept this thing alive and raised it as if it was a brother or a sibling. You know T is my only child. Well, T took care of it for years, without his father's knowledge."

"Did you know?" Xandra asks.

"Of course. We mothers know more than most. As this thing started to grow, it became a burden for T to keep it well-fed and hidden. However, he did. Even though it had grown to over six feet tall, T loved it, and named this thing Buddy. It was part man, part animal. T had built a cage and kept him in it. As Buddy matured, he became furious that he was caged. He eventually escaped, and when T went to visit Buddy he was nowhere to be found. He was ready to attack T, since he didn't like being caged. In a wild rage, Buddy, holding a huge boulder in his hand, jumped in front of T. T's father had followed T that day, and shot an arrow into Buddy's head. T and his father never discussed it. Buddy would have killed T if his father had not followed him."

"That is a horrible thing for a young child to endure," Xandra says, almost in tears.

"Yes, dear, it is. T doesn't understand individual families. The entire village is his family and that is all he knows. Go save your family, dearie."

"Thank you, again." Xandra bows.

**

Xandra needs to depart at once. She needs her own plan because as time goes by, more can go wrong.

"And where are you heading?" T asks.

"The palace, to rescue my entire family. They all seem to congregate there."

"Who, may I ask, is going to let you inside the palace—the king, perhaps?" T smiles.

"I haven't figured that one out yet."

"Forgive me when I say this, but you and Hari will be annihilated. I have a few friends within the palace, along with the floor plans. Let me see what I can do. Otherwise, you both will be defeated."

Xandra was hoping for T's help. She didn't want to ask. The Trefars like to do things on their own.

"There is a big birthday event planned for the prince, and that would be an ideal time to sneak you inside. It is a three-day event. And Socreen, your mother, has agreed to open the east palace gate for your entry," T explains.

"May I ask, when does this event start?"

"It's the day after next."

"Thank you. In that case I shall stay here, and go over the palace floor plans that you somehow have in your possession," Xandra replies.

Hari looks at Xandra and says, "Isn't that the same day as Dylan's birthday?"

"Yes, it is. Let's go over these building plans, and see if we can come up with a plan."

Xandra and Hari are going over the palace layout when a Trefars approaches and introduces herself as Tic.

"I have been in and out of the palace many times, unnoticed. I know the palace like the back of my hand." Tic expands her arms.

Tic is very small, and Xandra can see how Tic could maneuver in and out so often.

"Thank you, your help is much appreciated. Can I ask you a question?" Xandra looks perplexed.

"What is T building outside? It looks like a ditch of some sort."

"It is a defense."

"A defense from what?"

"More like a moat."

"A moat. I have been told it hasn't rained in many days and water is sparse," Xandra replies.

"We do whatever T tells us to do. He said water will soon be upon us and it is best to be prepared."

Prepared is what the Trefars are at all times. They are ready for every event possible, at any moment.

"So where are the prince's chambers? And what areas should I avoid?"

"Stay away from this area," Tic says, pointing to some lines on the plan. "This is the queen's quadrant. She has more patrols and security than anyone, including the king. We have a statement from our insider that the east gate will be opened for your entry. That is located here. It will be open the day after next."

"Are we sure we can count on that information?"

"Yes, I am sure. Socreen is the insider. We are confident she will do this for you."

Isabella almost breaks down when she again hears her mother's new name, Socreen.

Chapter 8

JELAB

The palace is on high alert. Everyone is on edge since the king is not happy that the prince's subway train was sabotaged. The king commanded that the culprits be found and killed. The king is wandering around the palace, trying to figure out why the prince didn't take the royal subway. Everyone is walking on eggshells, waiting for the prince's return to the palace.

Korey is a tough servant and head of the palace. She is extremely loyal to the king. No one messes with her. Rumors are that even the queen stays out of her way. That would be the first and only person the queen ever avoids.

"Welcome home, Your Highness." Korey bows to the prince. "Jelab waits for you in your chambers, with some food, and a drawn bath so you may clean up, and rest. The king wants an audience with you right after you have bathed and are properly attired. I am sure this adventure has tired you out. We have all been so worried."

"Thank you, Korey. It has been an adventure that I prefer never to go on again. I welcome a bath and some of my favorite foods," the impostor prince proclaims.

"Of course, Your Highness. At once." Korey departs.

The palace is remarkable. From the outside it doesn't look like much: it's big and gaudy. Inside, it is full of gold, diamonds, emeralds, rubies, paintings, statues, pretty much everywhere I look. My jaw drops open, and I soon realize it and close it. The surroundings are crazy nice, too extravagant for my taste. That is the first room I entered. *How big is this place?* I wonder. *This room alone would be worth millions back home.* Hoping someone will show me to my quarters, I slowly pace around the room to show that I'm still tired from my journey.

Finally, someone shows up, and bows and says, "Follow me, Your Highness."

Thank goodness, I think. *Would be a rocky start if I didn't know where my room is located.* Everyone we pass stops and bows, but no words are exchanged. I could get used to this bowing and ordering people around crap. "It's good to be king" is a real saying.

I finally get to my room. Seems like a quarter-of-a-mile walk. It's even more beautiful than the entrance. What in the world do these people do for a living? This is senseless. Luxury on steroids.

"Is everything okay, Your Highness?" Jelab, the prince's valet, says inquisitively.

"Yes, yes. I am very worn out and hungry."

Before I can finish my sentence, ten people come in and place plates of food all along a table. They bow and depart.

"I am sure you are," Jelab says. "Being held by those pesky Trefars. I am so glad you are safe. Please eat something. I am so delighted you have returned unharmed. I have been very concerned."

Great. I attack the food with vengeance. *This stuff is delicious, even better than what the Trefars prepared.*

"Your bath is ready, Your Highness. Afterwards, the king awaits an audience with you."

"Yeah, yeah, okay," I reply.

As I undress I hear some voices coming from the next room … giggling and playful laughter.

"Hey, Jelab, what is that commotion?"

"Your bath, Your Highness. You need to clean up before you see the king. Are they making too much noise? I can have the water nymphs removed."

The water what? You better not have them removed. What is a water nymph? I wonder. "No. I'm tired. Sorry."

"Yes, Your Highness. I understand you have had quite an adventure. You are safe now. I am joyful you have returned."

Jelab actually really does like the prince. The prince has always been nice to him. Jelab is also good friends with Socreen and Siena. Jelab is so happy that the prince has returned, he doesn't recognize any changes in the impostor. Jelab's father, Zhann, worked as a valet for the previous king. Jelab was raised in the palace and was groomed to become a future valet for the royal family. When the prince was born, it was a perfect transition for Jelab.

"Your robe, Your Highness."

I put on my robe. Jelab opens the door to my bath, and I almost pass out. I count six young ladies in this huge bath, waiting for me. Six. I think, *How lucky is this prince! This guy has it made. Why would anyone ever leave this?*

I turn around, and Jelab says, "What is it, Your Highness? Is something wrong?"

"No, no, everything is fine. Thank you."

I walk down the steps. I am completely naked, and I see the girls all have some type of skimpy outfit on. I start thinking this isn't going to work. I don't remember T or Igagbee mentioning this part. I should have asked more questions. This is insane. I wish Jonny could see me now. Jonny is my best buddy back in Key West. The girls move towards me and start to wash my body. Well, it doesn't take long for me to have an "issue." This makes the girls giggle.

"What is wrong, Your Highness? Is the water too warm?" Jelab asks.

I guess Jelab is concerned since I have stopped smiling and have a disconcerted look on my face.

"Get out, get out now," I hear someone screaming.

The girls rush out of the pool and depart quickly. I stay in my bath while the queen comes barging into my bathing room.

The queen barks, "You too, Jelab, out!"

"Hello, Mother."

"My son, I have missed you, and we were all so worried about your safety."

"Sure, Mother, but as you can see, I am bathing. Can we discuss my return after my bath, please? I am a grown man."

"Oh, yes. You are not my little boy anymore. I realize that, but you will always be my little boy. I continuously sent out troops to look for you. I don't know what I would do without you."

"Mother, please, I am taking a bath. Can't we have this discussion afterwards?"

"I just wanted to see you. Your birthday is coming up, and I want everything perfect. You will come visit me soon?"

"Yes, Mother. I have to see Father first."

"Oh, I am so happy you are home." The queen laughs as she leaves the room.

"Jelab, my robe," I yell out.

It figures my new mom would ruin my bath with six hotties. It's as if I'm back home. I think about my mother and how I could see her running off these girls. Jelab comes hurrying in to give me my robe. I think, *What a sweetheart the queen is.* I start to feel sorry for the real prince. This is the same woman who tried to have me killed—loving mother that she is.

**

The queen departs, and in her chambers, starts bellowing out commands, which is not unusual for her.

"Socreen, get in here. The prince has returned. Has Trigon arrived yet?"

Siena runs in and says, "Trigon has arrived."

"Great. Send her in, now. Where is Socreen, that old witch?"

"Socreen had to see the nurse." Siena bows and departs.

"Whatever. Send in Trigon. You both are useless. Go away. Do something."

The queen is agitated that Trigon has again failed her. The queen needs to use Trigon one more time, and if she fails again, the queen may have no choice than to kill her. Killing a dragon is not an easy task. Trigon must not let the queen's secret out.

Trigon is worried about being summoned. She has failed all her recent assignments. Trigon knows your life is in danger anytime you make the queen unhappy. Trigon enters the queen's chambers. Clearly shaking, Trigon is bowing down and begging for forgiveness.

"So, so, sorry, my queen. I am sorry for my failures. The Trefars are very sneaky and have spies everywhere. I will not fail again. My queen, what is it I can do for you?"

The queen hisses at Trigon, and asks, "Why was your mission such a failure? You failed me again and again. Why do you think you can complete my next mission? I should have you slaughtered."

The queen leans in and whispers to Trigon, "What is your subway excuse?"

"The prince had help." Trigon bows.

"What kind of help?"

"A friendly grouper helped him before the shark brothers could pull him apart."

"Pitiful excuse. I have a new plan. We have work to do. I am not sure what the Trefars are up to. It is time they are wiped out." She scans the area to make sure they are alone. Again, the queen leans closer to Trigon and whispers, "I am fairly certain that this prince is a fraud, and he will be dealt with soon. Either that, or they have hypnotized my son. Why else would the Trefars so easily give me back the prince? Something is improper." The queen smiles.

Trigon's eyes get wide. "If it's not the prince, who is it, then, my queen?"

"Not sure if it is or not. I don't care, either way. Convincing the king will not be an easy task, so we will have to get rid of both of them. The prince's birthday party is upon us, so that's where we shall strike."

"I have more bad news, my queen."

"All you ever have is bad news. What is it now?"

"There is talk that Princess Xandra has returned."

The queen appears surprised. "Are you sure? I need to know if this is a rumor or a fact. You know these people are always conjuring up myths and such untruths. I need to know at once. Where was her last location?"

"Her last location was the Trefars." Trigon was not wanting to share that information.

The queen screams out, "*I hate those pesty people!* I want them eradicated. Now, this is what I recommend. It will be difficult to blame the Trefars on the prince's demise, yet we can use it against the king."

"Why would the Trefars attempt to kill the prince, after returning him to the palace?"

"Because they are tricky that way. Abscond with a few arrows of the Trefars, so we may use that against them. Can you at least steal some arrows without being caught? Or is that too much to ask."

"Yes, my queen. I will at once."

"I need this done yesterday."

**

I was not happy that my awesome bath was ruined, especially by my new mother, no less. Somehow, I may have duped the queen as to my true identity. I'm all cleaned up and ready to greet the king. I need to remember his first duty is being king, and being my dad is secondary. *Okay, Dylan, you can do this. Let's go!*—peptalking myself with every step.

Eight people are escorting me to see the king. I walk into this grand room to greet the king. It is beyond glamorous.

"Welcome back, my son. You must tell me all about your adventure. I have taken care of the people who have mishandled your transportation and mission." The king leans in as we slightly hug each other.

"It was very exciting, to say the least," I respond. I'm less nervous than I expected.

"How did you survive by yourself, all those days and nights in the wilderness? Your survival skills must be excellent. I need to thank my guard Tagot for all his training with you. Tell me, son."

"I had lots of help from many people. First, I was attacked by the rebels in Rockland. Not sure why I was sent to Rockland in the first place. Then—"

The king interrupts. "The rebels in Rockland have been dealt with. That place has been destroyed. Continue."

"I escaped, and was later aided by the Trefars. They are disgusting cretins, though they did help me."

"Did you meet the disreputable T?"

"Yes, Father, I did."

"I bet you wanted to take off his head."

"I did, Father. I felt it wasn't the time nor the place."

"Very wise, son. He would have killed you. I have heard his warrior skills are unmatched. Did you witness his skills?"

"No, Father, I did not. I was in the care of a Trefars named Igagbee."

"A commoner, I presume. That's disgusting. Igagbee has no royal blood, and T should be reprimanded for his insolence by having you in the care of a commoner. Continue."

"He also saved my life."

"Who, this Igagbee commoner?"

"Yes. While I was in the village, someone attempted to kill me. Igagbee stepped up and took the arrow instead."

"Are you sure it wasn't staged to make it look like you were being saved?"

"He lost his hand, Father."

"Yes, that would be an unusual sacrifice."

"When I departed the Trefars village, I was escorted to the subway. The subway crashed while underwater, and I was attacked by two giant sharks. I did not get their names."

"Which subway station was it?" the king demands.

"Station number 188."

"Why did you not use the royal subway?"

"Trefars did not want to take me to a royal subway."

"Figures. They are cretins. How did you escape the shark attack? That must not have been an easy task."

"Fortunately, a large grouper was swimming by and scooped me up."

"That was convenient. How can that be?"

"And inside this grouper was the Trefars, Igagbee."

"Ahh, I was informed that T can see the future. The one and the same commoner, I presume?"

"Yes, Father, he saved me twice."

"Tazer already informed me of Igagbee's missing hand."

The king calls over one of his guards and tells him to get him the names of the sharks that attacked his son, starting at station 188. And to find one large grouper, name unknown.

Dylan likes Brian, and has not divulged his name to the king, hoping they won't locate him.

"I am so glad you survived this treacherous journey. I need to personally thank this Igagbee for saving my son," the king proclaims.

"Yes, the Trefars saved me and the Rockland rebels were bad. T and I discussed that criticizing the Rockland rebels would do no harm. They have already been wiped out."

"Then, I will have to thank T for all his help," the king announces.

The king is thinking twice if it is wise to invite any Trefars to the palace. Probably not … maybe too dangerous. The king needs to discuss this with his council. As a rule, Trefars are not allowed in the palace.

"You must be famished. Go and rest. I have three days of celebration planned for your birthday events. Welcome home, son. I am so pleased you are safe and back home. Now I have work to do."

"Yes, Father. It is truly a miracle."

I think that went well. The king looked pleased. I told T I could fool these people into believing I am the prince. I'm smiling as I am escorted back to my chambers.

**

A sentry tells the king that Prince Mako has been found and is safe with Grull, back in concrete country.

Confused, the king wonders how that can be. He figures it must be old news that his son is home. *Then, who is this imposter and why does he look and talk like my son? My queen may be correct. The king is surrounded by fools.*

The king tells the sentry, "Investigate further. I want positive proof."

**

Jelab greets me at my chamber door. Once inside, I fall upon one of the many couches.

"Your Highness, you have a visitor. I know you are extremely tired, but knew you would want to see Socreen."

Jelab likes Socreen, so it was easy for her to obtain an audience with the prince.

"Not now, Jelab. Maybe la—. Who did you say?"

"Socreen, Your Highness."

"Yes indeed, show her in and leave us."

"Yes, my prince."

Socreen enters my chambers with her arms spread wide open. We have a nice long hug.

"It is so good to have you back, Michael. Everyone has been so worried about your safety."

Socreen is the only one who calls the prince "Michael." That is his given name, and she has been with him since he was born.

I look at Socreen with a Cheshire cat grin, and say, "It's not Michael, Grandmother. I'm Dylan, your grandson. I would recognize you anywhere. Mom has been showing us photos of you for years."

"Oh my goodness! You look so similar, and sound like Michael. Dylan, that is a sweet name. How did you …? What are you doing …? This is a very dangerous place. If you are found out, they will kill you," Socreen says.

"I'm here to take you back. I took Grandpa's place."

"Grandpa. I love hearing that name. Is he well?"

"He is alive and well."

"How did you get here?"

"I lay down on your old blue pillowcase." Thinking: *It's a case, alright. A pillow case for the detectives.*

"Do you … have it?"

"Umm, no."

"How do you expect to get us out of here, then?"

"Haven't thought that through yet. I got dropped off in a rock hut."

"Grock! You came through Grock?"

"Yes."

"This is good news. Okay, sweetie. I'm so happy to see you, I'm at a loss for words. You've put yourself in a dangerous place. Have you seen the queen?" Grandmother asks.

"Yes, and I have her fooled," I reply.

"Hmm. Don't be so eager to believe that. She is a cunning and ruthless woman. And she has spies everywhere. This does change things. If we can fool everyone that you are the prince, we may be able to make an escape. Now, where is the real prince?" Socreen inquires.

"I don't know, nor do I care. My plan is to get you out of here ASAP."

"What if the real prince returns?"

"That will be a problem, for sure."

Socreen says, "What about your sister? You can get her released."

"Released from what? What does my sister have to do with this?"

"She is here and is a prisoner in the dungeon."

"What are you talking about? Alex is back home."

"No, sir. I saw her, and she is most definitely not at home."

"She is so stupid. What is she doing here? I have everything under control. This does complicate matters," I reply in an irritated tone.

"That's not all. Your mother is on her way here."

"My mother. Are you kidding me? She will never survive this place."

Grandmother smiles and says, "You don't know your mother very well, do you?"

"Does she know I'm here?"

"Probably. That's why she's here."

"Have you seen her?" I think, *She's probably going to kill me.*

"Not yet. I heard she's coming to the palace."

"Oh my, what is she doing? Doesn't she understand this place is not cool?"

"I assure you, your mother can take care of herself."

"Is anyone not here? Is Chloe here too?"

"Who is Chloe?" Grandmother asks.

"She's my obnoxious little sister, and she never leaves my mother's side, so I bet if Mom is here, so is Chloe."

"Oh, this is bad news. Everyone is here because of me. I think I'm going to be ill."

"Don't worry, Grandmother. I will think of something."

"How is my old goat, anyway?"

"You mean Grandpa. He misses you every day. At least now he is out of jail."

"What, jail?"

Oh no, I shouldn't have mentioned that.

"You know, mental jail. Not real jail or anything like that," I say, trying to backpedal.

"How old are you, Dylan?"

"I am going to be sixteen tomorrow, I think. The days are kind of running together and over here I'm not sure if it's night or day."

Grandma mumbles to herself, loud enough for me to hear. "No, it can't be."

"What is it, Grandmother?"

Jelab taps on the door and speaks through it. "Your Highness, Socreen has been summoned by the queen."

Socreen whispers to me, "We will talk soon. I have been gone too long and do not want to draw attention. We shall devise a plan. Your mother will be here tomorrow. Goodbye, my angel."

"Goodbye, Grandmother."

"You'd better use my new name, Socreen."

Chapter 9

SOPHIABEE

Xandra is ready to go, and suspects that T will not let the Trefars be part of her attack on the palace. T summons Xandra for one last visit before her departure.

T says, “It is time. I wish everyone well. Word that you may be attacking the palace must have spread quickly because you have a huge contingency awaiting your orders. I will not commit any Trefars to your advancement.”

T walks outside and shows Xandra the large crowd of followers, and when they see her, they start to chant, “Xandra, Xandra, Princess Xandra.” An unusual array of humans and nonhumans are all chanting.

“You certainly have a lot of followers.” T smiles. “I usually don’t allow outsiders on our land. I wanted you to see all the support behind you.”

“T, I cannot thank you enough for all you have done for me in the past. Taking me in, training me as a warrior was the greatest gift I could ever have received, and I am at your disposal at any time. I need your Trefars to help me take over the palace and save my family.”

"It seems your secret is out, so the palace guards will be ready for an attack."

"Even with this huge contingency, we will be annihilated without your help." She knows he has his own agenda; pleading with T would be to no avail. "What do you advise?" Xandra asks.

"I do have a suggestion. Enter under a disguise and attack from within. Who knows? By the time you get to the palace, it may already be in disarray."

"You mean by the time I arrive, my son, your planted impostor, may have already killed the king and queen?"

"No. If it were that easy, I would have taken the king and queen out myself. It is best to attack from within the palace, than outside the walls. Those walls are impenetrable. Alas, inside it's a different story."

"Let's say I take you up on your suggestion. Do I walk up and ring the front doorbell?"

"Ha, again you jest. It has been a while since you have visited our kingdom, and times have changed. I'm more cynical these days. Not the affectionate soul you've known from our previous gatherings. Every day becomes more difficult. I do have some good news for you. Tic has confirmed that the east gate palace door will be unlocked when you arrive."

"What kind of disguise do you suggest?"

"Palace personnel. Sophiabee will accompany you on your journey and she will explain in more detail."

"Will it work?" Xandra asks.

"If we can transform your son into a prince, I am sure we can turn you into a common palace worker."

"Okay, I can't argue with that logic. I'm in. What do I need to do?"

T explains to Xandra that Sophiabee will transform her into a common maid. He also informs Xandra that he has spoken to Lightner, and it will be pitch-black outside upon her arrival, plus a cool wind will keep the guards inside.

Lightner is the main moon. There are four moons in the kingdom, and Lightner and T are good friends.

T hands Xandra Dylan's backpack.

"Everything you need is in the backpack. The rest of your gear will be hidden in the palace. Tic will meet you and give you the specifics. You will be maid Olive."

"Olive is my new name."

"I think it fits you. Are you not pleased with that name?"

"Yes, I like it. Thanks for everything."

**

Hari, Sophiabee, and Xandra depart. Sophiabee and Xandra are riding the giant zebras.

While riding Jacob, one of the zebras, Xandra watches Sophiabee walk around on her zebra's back, as if it's standing still. Trefars are trained to ride on elephants, so riding a zebra is no different. She's knitting something and singing. They are going so fast—like flying. It's easy to get knocked off at this pace. Sophiabee has no concerns and keeps on knitting and singing. Sophiabee tells Xandra that T thought it best if someone wasn't seen riding an elephant. It might have caused a panic. As T predicted, it is pitch-black out, along with a cool breeze. Xandra doesn't give it a second thought.

When they land, she thanks Jacob and Hayley for everything they've done. "I could never repay you."

"You already have, just by being here, Princess. Your appearance has given everyone hope."

The zebras take off in a flash.

"Wait! Aren't you going back with them, Sophiabee?"

"No, my friend Py will be taking me back. Let's start the transformation," Sophiabee replies.

"Thank you for all your help."

"It is my pleasure. My son Igagbee is getting a big head. I needed something else to talk about. We are getting tired of his story about saving the prince."

Igagbee was in charge of transforming Dylan into the prince. He blocked an incoming poisoned arrow with his hand; otherwise, it would have been fatal and probably killed Dylan. Igagbee lost his hand, so it may become a legendary tale that Igagbee saved the future king.

"These kids today are so full of themselves," Xandra remarks. "Aren't they, though?"

"When I was growing up, I was happy to have a nice meal in front of me. Now they want everything at all times. You've got to love them. Again, thank you for saving my son and myself. Someday I will repay you."

"Here, try this on. I knitted it on the way. It's a bonnet that the maids wear."

"Oh, that was sweet of you. Thank you. I'll always cherish it."

"It was nothing, for the great Princess Xandra. I will have my own stories to tell and maybe it will slow down Mr. Braggart."

They both break out in laughter.

Sophiabee works on Xandra until Hari hardly recognizes her. The hat Sophiabee knitted matches her outfit perfectly. All the workers in the palace wear a particular color, depending on their assignment. Today Xandra is in all gray.

"Let's bury your backpack," says Sophiabee. "I'll remember where it is."

Hari looks for a place to hide the item.

"Good idea," Xandra replies. "I doubt my cover would last long while carrying a foreign backpack."

Hari stops in his tracks, which usually means someone is nearby. Tic steps out from behind the wall. It is dark and extremely quiet, except for Sophiabee singing into the night.

"Hello. Sorry I'm late, but everything is in order," Tic says.

"How did you beat us here?" Xandra asks.

"I hitched a ride with Py. He needed to pick up Sophiabee.

He is exceptionally fast. All your gear is stored in the wall, in the last stall, in the south washroom, next to the ballroom on the fiftieth floor."

"How did you get my gear up there? Oh, never mind, I know the answer. Thanks, Tic."

"Good luck. We're all counting on you. By the way, you look like a palace maid."

Isabella and Hari are now officially in the palace, and are not surprised to find the east palace gate unlocked. The next door they open, they see a lot of people walking around. Hari takes off running, and Isabella walks into the flow of the maid brigade. This is much easier than a battle—to get inside. No one even glances her way. She grabs an empty basket and starts to wander around.

"Hey you, what are you doing? What is your name? Have you checked in with Jena?"

Before Isabella can answer, the same woman yells at someone else.

"Hurry along, everyone. It's check-in time, and time's a wasting while you're all standing around. You. Jena is on the fourth floor. Hurry, I don't have all day."

The woman yells at someone else. Isabella has a feeling this goes on all day and night. She bows, then takes off towards the fourth floor.

On the third floor, Isabella hears: "Hey you, come here." A rather large woman is pointing right at her.

"Yes, ma'am," Isabella answers, hoping she's not busted so soon.

"Are you new here?"

"Yes, ma'am."

"I thought so. You look lost. Have you reported to Jena?"

"Not yet. No, ma'am."

"What's taking you so long?"

Isabella doesn't want to say "Because of being stopped," so she replies, "I got lost, ma'am."

"Yes, that's easy to do. Especially with the prince's birthday celebration, everyone is in a rush. Now follow these stairs, and she is off to the right on the fourth floor. Hurry along, we have a lot to do. You look too scrawny to be wandering around. You may keel over before your shift starts." She belts out a hearty laugh.

"Yes, ma'am. Sorry."

The large woman walks off, mumbling to herself, "It's pitiful the undernourished type they's a-hiring around here."

There are patrols everywhere, so it's best to check in at once. Isabella arrives to report in to Jena. She's massive and is barking out orders faster than most people can speak.

"Next, name?"

"Olive is my name. I—"

"I don't care, I have you on the washroom detail on the fiftieth floor. Go. Next, name? Wait! Come back here. I've changed my mind. You're on stairwell cleaning duty."

"I am okay with—"

"I don't care what you're okay with, now you're on stairwell duty, floor thirty-five. You'll join up with Kaci. Next, name?"

All of Isabella's gear is on the fiftieth floor. Behind the scenes, it is quite amazing. All these people tending to the three royals—the king, the queen, and the prince. This army of helpers seems like a waste. Isabella takes off, starting down the corridor to the stairs, and catapults forward like a gazelle to the sixteenth floor. As she rounds a corner, there is Hari.

"What took you so long?" Hari asks.

"It's chaos, at best."

"For sure, this place is busier than your office back home. People screaming orders and others running around." Hari smiles.

"Not funny, Hari. How is it that you haven't been yelled at?"

"No one seems to bother me. I have tried to avoid any contact." He grins.

"Lucky you. I've been yelled at more than I prefer. Instead of working on the fiftieth floor, I've been moved to the thirty-fifth-floor stairwells. Not sure if we work up or down. It may be okay. I can go up the stairs at my leisure. I have to check in with a Kaci. Hopefully, she will be tolerable when I depart. Now, where is everybody?" Isabella inquires.

"Alex is in the dungeon. Dylan is getting ready for his birthday celebration. Or, should I say, Prince Dylan. Not sure about your mother. Haven't located her yet. Since she works for the queen, it will be hard to get in and out of her chambers without getting harassed."

"The dungeon. What did she do, I wonder?"

"Didn't get that information. It's a ghastly place."

"Poor thing. Should we get her first?" Xandra frowns.

"Let's stick with the plan and see where it takes us."

"So, Hari, do you think Michael is the real prince?"

"Yes, I do."

"This continues to be more and more complicated. I had a bad feeling about that. Now all we have to do is smuggle Elizabeth, Alex, and Dylan out of the palace. If we can do that, I can get us to Grock unharmed. We can pick up Chloe on the way to Grock. Who would have thought getting out would be harder than getting in? I'm sure stealing the prince will not be an easy one."

Hari says, "Quiet. Someone is coming."

Xandra walks back to the hallway, towards the cleaning supply room. It's complete chaos—nonetheless, organized chaos.

"Hey, you. What are you doing standing around here? Pick up that pail and follow me. Did you check in on the fourth floor?"

"Yes, ma'am. I am on my way to meet up with Kaci, and help clean the stairwell. I was on my way."

"Your name?"

"Olive."

"You're supposed to be on the fiftieth floor, washroom duty. And for some reason you're just standing around. Are you mentally disadvantaged?"

"She changed my work detail to work with Kaci on the thirty-fifth stairwell," Isabella replies.

"Kaci. Oh yes, she's starting on thirty-five. This is number sixteen. Can't you count? You need to climb nineteen more. Or are you too tired to climb that far? *Hurry, go now!*"

"Yes, ma'am."

It is like running through a maze blindfolded, as Isabella takes off up the stairs. Hari is again waiting.

She tells him, "I found out you can make changes to your work detail, and not everyone has the updated work schedule. That should work in my favor."

"Where do you want me? Most people haven't bothered me, even though it's still not easy sneaking around this place."

"Why don't you stay close to Dylan? I'm sure Mom and Alex are secure enough. I'll try and get back to the fiftieth floor later tonight. I suppose we will eventually end up on the rooftop. All my gear is up there. I have a feeling all the action will be at the rooftop ball." Isabella smiles.

**

Dylan is having a curious thought.

"Hey, Jelab, I was curious as to when is my next bath time."

"Why do you ask, Your Highness? Are you dirty?"

"No, no. I was wondering, since my last one was cut short."

"I can have one ready for you shortly, my prince. If that is what you wish," Jelab answers.

"Okay, that would be nice. I could use a nice long soak." I smile widely.

"Certainly, it would make you feel better before the events begin."

I will be ready for the water nymphs this time. At least I hope so.

"One more thing, Jelab."

"Yes, my prince."

"Can I have some *sakkuka, sakuca*, not sure how to pronounce the name. It is delicious. I ate some of it at Trefars camp, and it has become my new favorite food."

"You must mean *sadkuraka*. It is grown deep in the Trefars's forest. It is a rare delicacy."

"Yes, that's it."

"I will see to it that we have it at your birthday feast."

I begin to think how many will die trying to obtain this delicacy, so I say only, "Thank you, Jelab."

"Anything for you, my prince. Your Highness, your bath is ready."

Great, I can use a nice long soak. I put on my robe and open the door to my bath, and see no girls in the bath. I stop.

"Is something wrong, Your Highness?"

"No, nothing. Thinking about something."

I slide into the nice bath all by myself, thinking the first time must have been a dream. Who in the world bathes with six girls in the same tub? I probably shouldn't tell Tabitha about the girls.

"As you can see, I knew you wanted to be alone, so I ordered the bath with no disturbance," Jelab announces.

I mumble, "Thanks, thanks a lot."

My luck. No water friends. I need to get the hang of this prince thing sooner rather than later.

I can't come out and ask Jelab outright, can I? I need more time. I didn't see this coming—me, a prince. The soak does feel good, though.

Chapter 10

TRIPOLEE

Prince Mako wakes up in his San Francisco penthouse suite, with an annoying headache. This is probably Michael's first hangover. Certainly, at his young age he has never had this much liquor at one time. There is no such thing as an aspirin or any such pills in the kingdom.

The prince shouts, "Someone get in here. My head hurts."

Flobak comes running into the prince's room. "What is it, Your Highness?"

"My head hurts!"

Flobak leaves, and comes back with a drink or a potion of some sort.

"Drink this, Your Highness. It will help."

"Did you get my friend Kayda back to where she needed to be?"

"Yes, of course, my prince. She is back where she needs to be."

"Good. She was very nice. I would like to see her again."

"Yes, she was—is," Flobak stutters.

Flobak does not want to tell the prince what really happened to poor Kayda. It was all Grull's idea, so Flobak thinks he should not be the one to explain her fate. Plus, the prince is not in a great mood to begin with. Further upsetting the prince is not a good move.

Entering the room, Grull announces, "Good day, and happy birthday, my prince. Tonight will be a night to remember. Between the big gala event and your birthday, it shall be a delightful evening."

"I need to rest. I need a good soak, and I do not want to be disturbed," the prince laments. "This is not the way I wanted to start my birthday."

"Yes, my prince. Flobak will run you a nice soak. You need to rest up. There will be plenty of dignitaries who will want to meet with you."

The soaking tub is much smaller than the prince is accustomed to. It is comfortable enough, with its water jets and bubbles. This place is heaven compared to the kingdom. He has so much more freedom. The prince can't wait to tell Socreen what he has accomplished. The biggest question is: Why does he look like this Dylan guy? Why is Socreen in so many pictures? Who are those people in the photos? No wonder the king has outlawed twins. Too much confusion.

**

Tony and Matt arrive in Kauai. And as quickly as they arrive, they book a direct flight from Kauai to San Francisco, which should land at 8:42 p.m. It doesn't give them much time, but it's the best they can do. Matt isn't sure why they're going back to a place that's about to go kaboom. They both look and smell awful; no one comes near them. Soon they are sound asleep, slouched into their seats.

After arriving at their San Francisco hotel and scrambling to get ready, they head to the event. With so little sleep, Tony is nearly comatose.

"Is there anyone not at this event? I still feel like a penguin!" Matt exclaims.

"You look like one, too," Tony responds.

"Let's look for Dylan. We don't have that much time. That timer goes off tonight at midnight. Did you talk to your folks?"

"Yep, Mom and Dad passed through Sacramento, heading for Carson City."

"Great. Oh, there's the governor. I have something to ask him." Tony starts walking away.

"Yeah. You may want to tell him to get on a plane ASAP," Matt replies.

"Oh, wait a minute," Tony comments, "is that Grull, with Dylan? We've got to get him away from Grull."

The speeches start, and go on about how people are being abused by the current environment, and how great Tripolee is. They are the best answer to fix the environment. If it wasn't for this wonderful company, our world would be upside down. Clapping erupts. Grull takes the podium to show his face. The crowd groans and moans, and then cheers for the Tripolee group.

Grull's speech begins. "Tripolee has done more than all the other environmental companies combined. The only future America has is with the Tripolee group." Grull talks about his mishap due to environmental issues, and that is why he works for this great company—to save others. And the clapping and the cheers get louder.

Tony and Matt stop listening and start looking for the Dylan look-alike.

Grull spots Tony and Matt in the crowd and gives them a grin.

"Well, he knows we're here!" Matt exclaims.

"He doesn't look like he's in a hurry, does he?" Tony says.

"It's possible those explosives are meant only for the warehouse and nothing else. Maybe a fireworks display." Matt winks.

"I doubt it. Why all the secrecy and trouble to blow up a warehouse?"

"Probably right. I'm sure Grull is going to hitch a ride out of town with his buddy Tragoon. Wonder how Dylan is getting out of here?" Matt asks.

"With us," Tony replies.

After his speech, Grull confronts Tony and Matt.

"Hello, my good friends, so happy you could attend. I was hoping to see you both here. How was your flight to the islands? Comfortable flying first class, isn't it?" Grull smirks.

"First class. Is that what you call it?" Tony replies.

"How about I take your head off right here and now?" Matt smiles.

"Now, now, calm down. It's going to be explosive enough, so there is no reason for any additional violence. I want to apologize for absconding with your package. If it's any consolation, you did make me work for it. In the end, the best man won."

"What are you planning, Grull? We did find your warehouse and my empty crate," Tony admits.

"Let's say it's going to be a grand Fourth of July explosion. You Americans can never get enough fireworks." Grull laughs uncontrollably.

"What if I get up on the podium and announce your plans?" Matt turns as if he's going to the podium.

"Be my guest. The floor is all yours." Grull smiles.

"By the way, thanks for my going-away present at the San Francisco airport. One can never have enough dynamite," Matt reminds him.

"Oh yes, that was my idea. I thought it was brilliant. It seems you got off easy." Grull looks pleased with himself.

Tony asks Grull, "Where's Dylan?"

"What's a Dylan?" Grull replies.

"The fellow Matt was following, that Dylan."

"I don't know any Dylan. He was following the prince. Not smart. Big mistake."

As everyone continues to talk, the prince walks over. He is eager to meet any acquittances of Grull.

"I wasn't aware you made any friends, Grull. Please introduce us," the prince says.

"Dr. Anthony Rome and Mr. Matthew Robertson, let me introduce you to Prince Mako, or in your country, Prince Michael."

Matt and Tony stare at Michael, both not believing he's not Dylan.

"Welcome to America, Prince Mako. Where are you from?" Tony asks.

"It's a small country," the prince replies.

"Try me. I'm very good in geography," Tony answers.

Grull intercedes for the prince. "Take his word for it. It's a small country that you have never heard of."

"How about I take a guess?"

"Go ahead, I like this game," the prince declares.

The prince puts up a hand to stop Grull from intervening.

"The kingdom," Tony replies.

"The kingdom," Grull says with a grin. "There are plenty of kingdoms."

Tony responds, "No, there is only one Kingdom of Bonita, that I know of."

There is some concern in the prince's eyes. He has yet to respond, and only listens.

"The prince has given you two more than enough of his valuable time. So, if you would excuse us, we have more hands to shake that actually want to contribute to our fundraiser." Grull and the prince walk away quickly.

"What is the fundraiser for, to buy more explosives!" Tony yells at their backs.

"That was fun," Matt says. "You must feel like a loser uncle, since he didn't even acknowledge your existence at all. Are we still going with plan A?"

"Yes, plan A is a go."

"Okay, Houston, we have a green light." Matt smiles.

In the background they hear loud laughter and clapping.

"Okay, folks, gather around for our great senator, who is about to take the podium. So please welcome Senator—."

The roar of the crowd is so loud the name is unrecognizable.

"Thank you, thank you all. This has been one of the best events I have ever attended. What can I say about the Tripolee Emerald Green Environmental Enterprise and all it does for us in California, and soon, the rest of the country!"

The speech continues: "We have campaigned and collected over three hundred million dollars for this great cause." The same senator is spouting on about how great the green company is and that the company's goal is to build locations all over the country.

The crowd's clapping and cheering, chanting, "*T-R-I-P-O-L-E-E, EEE.*"

The fundraiser is the place to be. Anybody and everybody with their giant ego wants to be seen at this big gala event. From movie stars, athletes, governors, politicians, singers, game show hosts, comedians, ex-presidents, every news station, and the list keeps going.

**

10:59 p.m.

Grull is nowhere to be found. Michael departs the main ballroom.

"Okay, you're on, big boy," Tony says to Matt. "Meet you downstairs, out back. Keep the van running. Time is of the essence. I hope he doesn't give me a hard time."

"Do you want me to take your place?" Matt smirks.

"No, thanks, I'm trying to avoid any violence."

Tony enters the men's restroom, looking for Michael. Did he go to another restroom? Tony starts calling "Michael," hoping he's in one of the stalls. The restroom is quite large.

Amazingly, one of the stall doors opens, and Tony hears, "Yes, I am Michael. May I help you?"

"Yes, you may. We don't have a lot of time, and you're going to have to trust me on what I'm about to say. First, may I suggest you do not drink from the vial Grull gave you. It's poison."

"How did you know about my vial?" He walks towards Tony.

"I know more than you think. It's most likely poison, not a transport supplement."

"I doubt that," the prince says, and grins.

"If Grull gave it to you, it's poison."

"Why would Grull want to poison me?"

"I have a lot to explain. You will have to put your trust in me, and leave with me," Tony pleads.

"Why should I leave with you?"

"One reason, so you may meet your real mother."

"My real mother. What are you talking about?" Michael replies, getting curious.

"Your mother is my sister, and I have a lot to explain."

"With accusations like that, you had better be prepared to clarify that information."

"I have been to the Kingdom of Bonita. Now I need you to come with me," Tony says in a beseeching tone.

"So you have said. Do you also know my father, the king?"

"I know your real father, and he is not a king. I also know your real mother, and I think you should meet her."

"Listen, you seem like a nice man, but I don't plan on going anywhere with you." Michael heads for the exit.

Tony blurts out, "Can you explain the photographs from my sister's house, back in Key West?"

Michael immediately stops and turns towards Tony. "How do you know about those photographs?"

"We don't have much time."

"How do you know this?"

"Come with me, and I'll explain. I have a plane waiting to get us out of here, before the explosion at the Tripolee warehouse."

"I cannot leave Grull."

"Grull is long gone, my friend."

Michael is contemplating things.

"I also know it's your birthday, and we have to get back to my plane before midnight."

"How and why do you know so much about me?"

From his inside jacket pocket Tony pulls out an emerald golden bracelet, hoping it will have some effect. It is his last gasp, a gamble. "Does this look familiar?"

"How did you get that? That's a friend of mine's bracelet."

"Have you spoken with her recently?" Tony asks.

"No, I have tried to get in touch with her. I have yet to get a response. I wanted to bring her to this event. Give me that."

"Okay, it's yours. Most dead people don't answer the phone."

Michael grabs Tony's tuxedo jacket. "What did you do to her?"

"You may want to ask Grull. I found this at Tragoon's sleeping quarters. And if I was to bet, I would say she was an appetizer for Tragoon."

Michael loosens his grip of Tony's jacket, and looks despondent.

"Come on, son. We have to go. I'll fill you in on everything I know. Just hear me out, and then afterwards you can do as you wish," Tony implores.

11:08 p.m.

"Not sure if we can freely walk out of here. Let's give it a try," Tony suggests.

"You know I liked that girl. Why would Grull have her killed?"

"Because he's a monster, that's why. We have to go. Can you at least tell me what's going to blow at twelve o'clock?"

"I guess it's okay to tell you since you can't stop it. It's rigged to the San Andreas fault, and will be seen as an earthquake."

"Are you aware of the catastrophic event that will result after that explosion? Did Grull not inform you of the impact of this destruction? We need to move, now!"

"Not really. I was told some minor casualties. My plan was to be back home in the palace before the explosion."

"Minor. This entire city could vanish."

Tony pulls out his cell and phones Matt. "We're on our way to you. What's happening out there, Matt?"

"I'm beginning to get a few stares, sitting in this white van. I don't think I've got the attention of the Secret Service boys yet, thank goodness." Matt sounds unusually worried.

Tony says, "I've got more than looks. I may have a tail. We're heading for the back steps."

"That's Flobak and a few of my guardians," Michael explains. "They will not be happy that I'm departing with you."

"We don't have time to get their permission. We're going to have to make a run for it," Tony tells Michael.

Finally, Tony and Michael run into the van, which is surrounded by two security cars. Matt accelerates and rams into the first car. The heavy white van almost smashes the security car to pieces. All the local security services use the smaller electric cars.

"I'm afraid if I hit it any harder, we would roll right over it. Luckily, I probably only destroyed its intercom system, along with causing a few headaches." Matt smiles.

Tony looks back to make sure none of the security guards were injured.

"Do you guys drive like this all the time? I thought the objective was to avoid hitting other automobiles." Michael grins.

"Who brought the comedian?" Matt remarks.

11:22 p.m.

"It's eleven twenty-two," Tony announces.

"Thanks, Mr. *Time Keeper*," Matt replies.

Tony calls his pilot, Torch. "Get the plane ready to go. We're heading in hot, with a few folks pursuing us."

Matt glances at Michael, saying, "Hey, Michael, I bet you didn't know we were this much fun."

"I drive better than this and I've only driven once," Michael responds.

"Is it okay if we call you Michael, and not Prince?" Tony asks.

"Certainly, and thanks for asking," Michael replies.

"Lucy In The Sky With Diamonds" is Matt's mother's ringtone. Matt answers, even while driving like a maniac. "Hi, Mom, I can't talk now."

"Son, we made it to Carson City. Your dad is tired out. Tell us again why we had to leave so quickly?"

"Can I call you back? I'm kind of busy, Mom."

"Okay. What's that noise, son?"

"It's a police car. Gotta go."

"Son, pull over and see what they want."

"I know what they want, Mom. Can I call you later?"

"Your dad wanted to say hello."

Matt throws the phone to Tony, and shakes his head.

"Hello, Mrs. Robertson, how are you guys?"

"Who is this?"

"It's Tony Rome, Mrs. Robertson."

"Oh, hi. Are you with Matt? You guys are always together—getting into trouble, I bet. Where are you guys?"

"We're trying to get out of San Francisco."

"What are you doing there? You made us leave, and you guys stayed. I really don't understand."

"Mrs. Robertson, we are trying to leave, almost to the airport now. Can Matt call you back?"

"I guess so, but his father wanted to say hello."

"Please?" Tony pleads.

"Okay, call us back. If you don't call us back right away, we may not answer because we're asleep."

"Sure, we understand. Bye."

She's still talking when Tony ends the call. They go screeching into the private airport, with a trail of police cars.

11:51 p.m.

Matt and Michael jump out. Michael follows Matt as he starts running towards the plane. Tony goes back to talk with the police.

After multiple phone calls to some heads of state, the police finally decide to let Tony go.

12:09 a.m.

The runway is clear, and they take off. The plane banks off to the right. They all look out the windows and see the entire runway peel away as if it disappeared into the darkness.

Lights are flicking in the city and it's mainly dark. Soon it looks like a ghost town.

Michael is staring out the window in disbelief.

Torch asks, "What happened?"

Tony replies, "It must have been an earthquake."

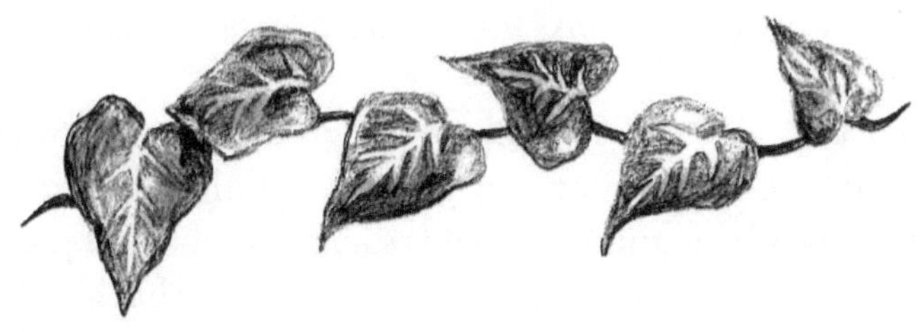

Chapter 11

DUNGEON

The queen is apprehensive about the prince's return from the Trefars. She is suspicious by nature and is constantly up to no good.

"Siena, summon Ivy to my chamber, *now*."

"Yes, my queen." Siena takes off in a run.

A minute later the queen is saying, "Ivy, so kind of you to come. I need you to do me a favor."

"Yes, my queen. Whatever you need, I am at your service," Ivy replies.

"I would like you to search the prince's chamber for any unusual artifacts that he may have brought back from the Trefars. You know how devious they are. I don't want the prince to think I don't trust him. Otherwise, I would ask him."

"If I find anything, I will have it brought back to you."

"Only if you think it is important. I will let you decide," the queen says with a smirk.

Ivy knows this means to bring everything to the queen, or die.

"I will have the prince summoned to my chambers and Jelab sent out on an errand so that you can conduct your search."

"That will make my search much easier. Thank you, my queen."

Ivy is sneaky; she moves like an ivy plant. She knows where to look for hidden objects. Ivy goes through the room, trying not to disturb anything. She finds some type of liquid potion in a vial. Impossible to say what it is for, but she has a feeling this is what the queen is looking for. It was well hidden. Then again, Ivy can get anywhere and see everything.

Ivy has returned and is announced to the queen.

"I think I found what you are looking for, my queen."

"I am not looking for anything. Very curious, is all. What is it you found?"

The queen's eyes gleam when Ivy shows her the vial.

"Well, you have done better than I imagined, and you will be richly rewarded," the queen remarks. "Not a word to anyone. Begone."

It is very difficult, extremely unlikely, to smuggle any potions or poisons into the palace. Between the taste testers, thorough food and drink inspectors, it is almost impossible to get any poisons into the food supply. Getting them into the palace is completely unheard of and just plain doubtful.

The queen is very pleased. She knows that the prince would not have been searched. She needs to find out what's in the vial—confirmation as to its contents. If it is poison, she could taint the king's and prince's food. Who will be her tester? Since Xandra is back in the kingdom, it is time for the queen to implement her plot. She decides to test it on Socreen.

"Siena, get in here, *now*," the queen calls out.

"Yes, my queen," Siena responds quickly.

"I assume Socreen has returned from the medic station?"

"Yes, my queen. She is resting in her room."

"Good, she needs to rest. Poor thing is so overworked. Take this to her and make sure she drinks it. It's from the medic station. It will cure her," the queen says in an unusually sympathetic tone.

"Yes, my queen." Siena bows.

Siena takes the goblet and wonders when the queen began to care about Socreen's health.

In Socreen's room, Siena expresses her concern about the fluid in the goblet.

"Siena, I don't think the queen has any poisonous potions," Socreen notes.

"She said it was from the medic station. I don't believe her," Siena comments.

"Siena, you are too sweet. Let me drink it. I will be fine, I'll show you. I do not want you to be in any trouble with that witch."

Siena puts the goblet to her own lips and gulps down the liquid. Within seconds Siena is lying down, gasping for air.

"*Ohhh* my goodness, my angel!" Socreen exclaims. "This was my time, not yours."

"Will I ever see this other kingdom you have been telling me about and writing stories about?" Siena asks.

"My sweet one, you will be in God's palace, and nothing can ever harm you ever again. You will be with your family soon," Socreen replies, in tears.

"Is it as pretty as this palace?" Siena is smiling.

"It is more beautiful than this place. Everyone there is sweet and kind, just like you. You will see rivers and lakes and waterfalls, blue skies, and the birds will sing to you every day. There is no yelling or screaming. Only love and kindness."

"It sounds so beautiful. Why haven't we ever visited it before now?"

Those are Siena's last words. She dies in Socreen's arms.

"Help, help!" Socreen is so upset she starts to tremble uncontrollably.

She storms into the queen's quarters. The queen is shocked to see Socreen alive.

"What is it you want, you old hag? How dare you barge in on my chambers."

"You killed the only sweet thing left in this world—Siena."

"Guard, get in here. As I see it, you killed her. That was meant for you. Take this woman to the dungeon," the queen commands. "She killed Siena."

At hearing this, the guard is taken aback because everyone likes Siena. The guard knows better than to argue. "Yes, my queen."

"Take her out of my sight. I don't want to see her ever again."

Four other guards come in and whisk a screaming Socreen away to the dungeon.

Once everyone departs, the queen smiles and mumbles, "Now I know what's in the potion. Too bad it killed the wrong person. Oh, well." She laughs out loud.

**

The dungeon has many levels and each level is determined by the crime committed. The higher brutality of a crime, the lower the level. The head of the dungeon, Buffalo, has a big job. Unless the king specifically announces where a prisoner should be placed, it's up to Buffalo to place the victim within the dungeon; he decides which prison cell fits the crime. This can be one busy place since a minimum of twenty per day are thrown into the dungeon. Sometimes more, sometimes fewer, but on average, twenty, and it's doubtful or rare that twenty are let out on any given day.

Socreen has been kind to all the guards, so she is hoping they take pity on her. Most of them despise the queen. Knowing that Buffalo can be reasonable, Socreen starts her pleading. She wants to be put into the same cell as prisoner 2875.

"Are you crazy? She will kill you," Buffalo remarks. "The guards dislike going near prisoner 2875. She has knocked out almost every guard I send in. We only feed her through the bars. No one will even go inside to get her empty plates." Buffalo leans closer to Socreen. "Listen, you have been very kind to me, so I will put you in a much better cell. Not that we have many. Some are better than others."

In a loud voice he says, "Take her to number 1007."

"Yes, sir." A guard grabs Socreen's arm.

Knowing that cell is nowhere near Alex, Socreen lashes out with a punch.

"Settle down, or I will put you with prisoner 2875."

Socreen bites the guard, and he knocks her to the ground.

"What is wrong with you? I heard you killed Siena. Okay, you can have your death wish."

Buffalo, visibly upset, announces, "Take her to number 2875, and let her perish. I am done trying to be nice. Next."

Socreen doesn't speak another word as the guard takes her to cell number 2875. He opens the cell door and throws her in so fast that the prisoner does not have time to kick him. Alex turns to greet her new cellmate.

"Oh my God, child, what have they done to you?" Grandma sees blood all over Alex's face and clothes.

"It's okay, Grandma, you should see the other guy. What are you doing here? You were supposed to get me out, not join me."

"Yeah, well, that didn't work out as I had planned. That wicked queen killed the sweetest person in this world and blamed me. Siena was like my own child. I am so upset I can't think."

"Oh my, that sounds horrible. It's okay, Grandma. We can both work on our escape plan."

"That won't be easy. You haven't made many friends around here. They are afraid to even open your cell door. Let's clean you up," Grandma says, wiping the blood off Alex's face. "I am so sorry you came back for me. I feel like I got you into this mess." Grandma starts to cry again.

"Don't worry, I'll get us out of here."

Alex hugs her. Grandma cries even harder.

"What made you stay behind all these years?"

"That's a long story."

"I think we have plenty of time, Grandma."

"You're going to find out eventually, so I should go ahead and tell you." Grandma sits on a board that serves as her bed, and Alex sits on it, facing her.

"Do you remember the stories Grandpa told you when you were growing up? It all sounded so strange and unreal, and you always asked for more stories. They were all real—this place and the strange stories. Your mother, your grandpa, and I used to visit this place. Not the palace, but the kingdom itself. Uncle Tony would come, usually on his own. Sometimes Isabella would bring you by herself. You were so young, I'm sure you've forgotten."

"I remember a few things. I actually thought it was a dream," Alex replies.

"In the good days, thirty years ago, this place was different. It was like a paradise. Everyone was kind, no battles, no evil. The past king and queen were different. Everyone appeared happy and kind."

"So why didn't you come back home when Mom came back? Why did you stay behind?"

"It wasn't on purpose. Things changed quickly when the king passed away and his son replaced him. The son took over as king, and his young bride suddenly passed away. After that, this place went into a downward spiral. Rumor is that the new king's wife killed the young bride. That has never been proven, and having worked for her for sixteen years, I believe she is capable of killing anyone that stands in her way. And since she killed Siena, I do believe she would destroy anyone in her path."

"Grandma, you still haven't answered my question."

"Your mother may get mad at me for telling you, but one day you all should be told. Especially now that you're all here, and older. Maybe you can also fill in some of the blanks for me."

"You're starting to scare me."

"Oh, sweetie, that's the last thing I want to do. Your mother was pregnant, and she wanted one last visit. She loved the kingdom. As you now are aware, all the animals can be understood, so your mother was intrigued, being a veterinarian. She treasured her time here, and everyone loved her. She helped all the inhabitants—animals, humans, young, old, she didn't care. She hadn't been able to visit in a while and wanted to come back one more time before her next baby. I also bet you never knew your mother is extremely accomplished in martial arts, archery, and swords. This is where she learned most or all of her skills. She was trained by the Trefars. They are the most advanced warriors in the world, or at least in this world."

"Mom is a trained warrior! What are you talking about?"

"Yes, honey, she was—or is. She is a feared warrior and became known as Princess Xandra. If a battle started up, which there were very few, Xandra terminated the battle quickly. Against all odds, she has defeated many opponents, including a few Graeters."

"What's a Graeter?"

"A Graeter is a wild, uncontrollable beast. You never know what sets them off. It can be a look or the way the wind blows. Huge beasts, they work for the king as excavators, which is like a bulldozer. Their only source of food is gum."

"You still haven't answered my initial question. And, by the way, I'm also skilled in martial arts. I guess I take after Mom, after all."

"You do take after your mother, sweetie. You look just like her."

"Grandma, the story, please?"

"Okay, okay. I see you're getting restless. Your mother and I came back while she was very pregnant. Your grandpa Vincenzo wasn't aware that we'd left. At least we didn't tell him, since I am fairly certain he would not have allowed it."

"Wait, I have another question. How did you get here?" Alex asks.

"Oh my, that's another story."

"Then start with my first question, and then we can come back to that question."

"Where was I? Oh, yes. We sneaked out early in the morning, hoping to return before your grandpa was even aware of our departure."

"Oh my, I realize now Grandpa is innocent—he didn't kill you."

"Why do you think he did?"

"Umm, Grandpa got put in prison for your disappearance. The authorities never found your body. He was still put away for murder."

"What are you saying? My husband was put in prison because I was foolish?"

Grandma starts to cry again, uncontrollably. "I knew it. What a fool I was. Is he okay?"

"He's fine, and was recently released from prison, and he misses you dearly."

"Thank goodness. What else have I missed?"

"I have a little sister, Chloe, and one brother, Dylan. He's a moron, and she's a clone of Mom."

"How old are they, dear?"

"Chloe is ten and Dylan is fifteen. No, wait. I think he turns sixteen soon. I've lost track of time."

"You have two brothers, then." Grandma grins.

"No, I have one brother, Dylan," Alex assures Grandma.

"No, dear, you have two."

"Grandma, I think I would know if I had two brothers or not. I am the oldest."

"Maybe, dear, but you have two. I have met them both. It may be confusing, because they are identical twins. It is hard to tell them apart. And by the way, Dylan is here in the palace."

"I think you have been in here too long. Why do you say Dylan is here?"

"I spoke with him right before they threw me into the dungeon."

"What's he doing here? How is it that moron is not in the dungeon and I am? Is he coming to get us out of here or what?"

"I did tell him you were in the dungeon. He could be of some help."

"How in the world is he going to help us get out?"

"He is the prince."

"Prince of what? Prince Dingbat, maybe."

"Nope. Somehow, he has replaced the real prince of this kingdom. I'm sure his life is in danger because soon, when they realize he is not the real prince, they will kill him. No dungeon. Only a quick death," Grandma says, agonizing over the words.

"Sounds like him. Always getting into trouble of some sort. This place must be nuts if Dylan is the prince." Alex isn't sure what to think.

"He is the prince and he can do almost anything. He has to be extremely careful."

"This is kooky talk. Let's get back to the twins."

"Your mother and I came back for a quick visit, and her water broke while we were here. We couldn't get back home, so she had her baby, Michael, here. Your mother realized we were being tracked and we needed to return home. We both couldn't get away, so she left me behind with Michael, and as I now understand, she had Dylan when she arrived back home. She had to be one strong woman to have identical twins to be born at two different birth locations. Actually, your other brother's real name is Michael Dylan."

"That's amusing," Alex says, "because Dylan is Dylan Michael. How is it no one knew she was carrying twins?"

"She didn't tell anyone during her pregnancy because she was having complications. She didn't want you to be upset if she happened to lose both babies. One would be a tragedy, so she couldn't comprehend losing both. She was always protecting you."

"You're telling me you were left behind with Michael, while Mom came home to have Dylan?"

"That sounds right. I didn't know they were identical until now," Grandma responds.

"How did you get to the palace? How did Michael become this prince? Does Mom know about all the prince stuff and whatever else? I'm so confused," Alex says, shaking her head.

"Right after Michael was born, the queen tracked us down. I wasn't letting Michael out of my arms. I was slower than your mother, so at that time only one of us could get back home. We decided to leave me behind, with Michael. The queen captured Michael and me. Little did we ever realize it would be sixteen years until anyone could return. I am still astonished that your mother did not have the second baby until she returned home."

"So, the queen captured you and a newborn baby. Did she hurt you guys? How cruel can one be?"

"That would be the queen. She had lost her own baby, and substituted Michael as if he was her own. No one knows this except me. She warned me she would kill the baby if I told anyone. No harm has come to me—other than working for the tyrant."

"Does Michael know?"

"No, dear, no one. Not even the king. As far as the king knows, Michael is his child. That is why I am sure she has plans to kill both the king and the prince, so she can become queen over the land. While either is alive, she cannot become the authentic, ruling queen."

"Why did she keep you alive?"

"I think it was to torture me."

"Oh my goodness, I think I'm going to throw up. She must be something evil to substitute him as her own child like that. I did see her for a brief minute, and she sounded like a wicked witch."

"With your mother coming back, the queen is terrified the truth will come out, so all our lives are in danger. The queen doesn't know who you are yet. I assume she will, soon enough."

"Is Mom here already?"

"Yes, dear. She may be already in the palace. I have a feeling she's coming to take her family back. I'm afraid that our trip years ago was not smart. However, it's too late now."

They both start crying.

"You're telling me my poor mom has been carrying this around all on her own. Does anyone else know?"

"I guess not. She doesn't know anything about Michael being the prince. I assume she remembers having a baby and I doubt she told anyone back home."

"Why didn't Mom come back for you sooner?" Alex asks, in tears.

"Oh, my dear, I'm sure she had her reasons. Probably the transporter failed."

"Transporter?"

"So, you're still not sure how you got here?"

"Not really. I'm not a hundred percent sure how I got here. I awoke in a rock hut."

"Oh, that's Grock. Did you lay your head upon my blue pillowcase, by any chance?"

"Yes, I did find a blue pillowcase, and put it on my bed. It was so unusual."

"Well, there you are. If that thing is working again, it's a transporter. It's because of that miraculous—or evil—blue pillowcase that all these events have unfolded."

"Are you saying that blue pillowcase I fell asleep on caused all this?"

"Yes, sweetie."

"How did you figure that out?"

"That's for another day."

"If it was that easy, why didn't Mom come back sooner?"

"I'm sure your mother can answer that question."

Alex tries to figure it out. "Mom, Dylan, you, and I are here."

Grandma says, "You may as well add Chloe. I think I heard she is also here."

"Perfect. We are all here to take you home, and now we both are imprisoned. With no hope of escape. Great."

"You've got the first part right. I have hope we will escape. I don't think the Good Lord has placed us all together so we could die here."

"Let's hope not. At least we will go down together."

"He's always watching, even in this place."

"If you say so," Alex comments.

Alex remembers finding Michael at Jimmy Johnson's house. "Grandma, I'm pretty sure I met the real Prince Michael!"

"How and when?"

"It's a strange story. Grandpa got robbed by a bunch of high school punks. Of course, the police were taking their time, and I had to jump into action. I found all the stuff that was taken from Grandpa. Interestingly enough, when I found the stuff I also found Dylan, which was odd. He was tied up, drugged, and gagged. Now I think it was Michael." Alex smiles.

"Did he have blond hair?"

"Yes."

"Tied up, drugged, and gagged, why?"

"Because the guys that took him are pigs. I met him for a minute. I took him home, along with Grandpa's paraphernalia. I stuffed everything into the blue pillowcase. Before I knew it, I awoke in a rock hut. Never saw Michael again."

"I hope your stubborn grandpa doesn't come."

"No, he's hiding out. The police think he had something to do with Dylan's disappearance since he has a history of those types of things."

"Oh my. How does he look?" Grandma asks.

"I hear he looks fine. I was coming home from college to welcome him back. When I arrived, no one was there. Everyone was gone. I do know he wants you home very badly, so we need to stop yacking and find a way out of here," Alex remarks with a determined look.

**

Beginning to get nervous about my fake prince predicament, I ask Jelab to bring Socreen to me.

Jelab informs me that Socreen has been imprisoned by the queen.

I think, *Oh no, now what does that mean?*

Jelab announces that the queen is entering my chambers.

Her timing is impeccable. Great.

"Hello, son, how are you? Are you getting ready for the big party tonight? I have everything planned, so don't you worry your little head. Sixteen is an age you'll never forget, and I have a feeling you'll never forget this one." The queen puts on her evil smile and departs, laughing.

"Jelab, I did not like the sound of that."

"Me either," says Jelab.

Jelab and Socreen are good friends. Jelab is concerned about his own safety. Socreen has been working for the queen for over fifteen years, and then, for no reason, she is thrown into the dungeon.

"Prince, have fun, and be very careful tonight."

"I will, Jelab. I may need a favor from you." I'm not sure who to trust, so I figure Jelab is my best bet.

"Anything, my prince," Jelab replies.

Word about Socreen's imprisonment and Siena's death have already spread quickly throughout the palace.

Chapter 12

KACI

With Socreen in the dungeon and Siena poisoned to death, the queen needs some new attendees. The maids are scared to death of the queen, so they jump when she beckons.

"Have Anchor come see me."

"Yes, my queen."

Anchor is a beetle, another spy for the queen, that is programmed to repeat everything it hears. One of the guards has told the queen about Socreen's interest in prisoner 2875. This is enough information for the queen, so she sends Anchor to bug cell number 2875.

"Okay, Anchor, start talking. I want to hear everything. Leave out nothing."

"Yes, my queen."

Imitating the two voices, Anchor recites:

"Oh my God, child, what have they done to you?"

"It's okay, Grandma, you should see the other guy. What are you doing here? You were supposed to get me out, not join me."

"Yeah, well, that didn't work out as I had planned. That wicked queen killed the sweetest person in this world and blamed me. Siena was like my own child. I am so upset I can't think."

"Oh my, that sounds horrible. It's okay, Grandma. We can both work on our escape plan."

"That won't be easy. You haven't made many friends around here. They are afraid to even open your cell door. Let's clean you up. I am so sorry you came back for me. I feel like I got you into this mess."

"Don't worry, I'll get us out of here."

"What made you stay behind all these years?"

"That's a long story."

"I think we have plenty of time, Grandma."

"You're going to find out eventually, so I should go ahead and tell you."

The queen continues to listen and smiles her evil grin. She knows that Anchor cannot have this information, so Anchor will have an unfortunate accident very soon.

**

Hari and Xandra are standing in the stairwell. Xandra starts heading up the stairs. She isn't sure, but thinks she hears a noise behind the door on the twenty-first floor. She stops for a few seconds to listen, and hears nothing. She keeps climbing and hears it again, and stops.

"Hello, Princess Xandra. I wanted to come by and see how everything is progressing."

Xandra almost jumps out of her skin, hearing her name come out of thin air. Tic scares Princess Xandra again with her sudden appearance.

"You startled me! So far, so good, with one minor dilemma."

"Oh, we don't like dilemmas. What's wrong?" Tic asks.

"I have been transferred to the thirty-fifth floor, and all my gear is on the fiftieth."

"That's not a dilemma. I thought something was wrong. Everything has been brought down to the thirty-fifth floor. Come with me, I'll show you."

Xandra recalls that the Trefars are amazing creatures. How in the world did Tic know? Xandra herself was just told. She will never figure them out. She had forgotten how impressive were their instincts or clairvoyance or whatever it is they do.

They arrive on the thirty-fifth floor. Tic shows Xandra the spot in the wall, and she sees nothing.

"Princess, here is everything. No need to worry. Everything is on schedule."

"I don't see anything, Tic. Maybe my eyes are deceiving me."

Tic pushes against the wall, and a secret door opens: all the weapons and her outfit are neatly displayed.

"Thanks, that is great. You're the best. How did you …? Never mind."

Before Xandra can finish, Tic turns the exact color of the wall, blending in perfectly. She disappears into thin air. Xandra knows Trefars can change colors like chameleons. She wasn't aware they could blend into their background or become invisible.

"That's quite the trick, Tic. Not sure if you are still here or not, but thanks."

"No problem. We shall meet again. Goodbye," Tic replies.

Xandra ponders how many times Tic was secretly following someone, and they didn't have any idea. Finally, Xandra arrives at the southeast corner stairwell on the thirty-fifth floor and introduces herself.

"Hello, you must be Kaci. I am Olive." Xandra offers her hand to shake.

Kaci stops cleaning and looks at Xandra for quite a while before she says, "You're late. We have a lot of work to do, and I would rather not be here all day and night. You don't look like an Olive. What is your real name?"

This catches Xandra by surprise. Kaci is probably around twenty-five years old. Tall and skinny. It is hard to guess someone's age around here.

Olive says, "I will tell my parents that they gave me an incorrect name."

"Yes, I'm telling you they gave you the wrong name," Kaci replies.

Xandra needs Kaci on her side since she will no doubt leave her to finish the cleaning. Xandra decides to keep talking and smiling. She has to save her family and may have to depart at any minute.

"What should they have named me?"

"You have the face of a princess." Kaci glows.

"Thank you. So do you."

"I know you're a liar. I look more like a toad."

"Well, you're the prettiest toad I've ever seen."

This makes Kaci smile. Kaci is so young, it's hard for Xandra to imagine hard labor like this for Alex or Chloe. A supervisor comes by to see how they're progressing.

"What are you two squawking about? Work slows when people talk. Get to work, and no more chitchat." Off she goes, mumbling to herself.

"Speaking of toads." Xandra points at the supervisor.

They burst out laughing.

Xandra is having a bearable time talking and working with Kaci, though Xandra can tell something is bothering Kaci. But Xandra needs to get moving upstairs.

Snap, crack. Kaci's mop snaps in half.

"Oh my. I will get in big trouble. Do you mind if I use yours, and you could get another one from the closet downstairs? I'm afraid they will fire me, or even beat me for my clumsiness. I have broken others."

"Sure, dear. I doubt they will beat you. I'm sure mops break all the time."

"You being so new and all, they will give you some leeway." Kaci sulks.

Not knowing any better, Xandra hands Kaci her mop. Kaci closes her eyes, and looks to be in deep thought.

"Are you okay, dear?" Xandra asks.

Slowly, Kaci opens her eyes, and smiles. "You know, it's not right to make you get a new mop. I'll get one. I broke it. I'll be right back." Kaci is gone in a flash.

Okay, that sure was odd. What made her take off like that? Xandra wonders.

"It's time we depart," says a voice from out of nowhere.

"Who said that? Is that you, Tic?"

"Yes, it's me. We have to leave now."

"I should wait for Kaci."

"She's the reason we're leaving. She went to get the guards. I have to hide you."

"She's only getting a new mop. I-I think. Oh no, what did I say? I told her nothing."

"It's not what you said. You gave her your mop. She can read your past from the mop handle you touched. She is telepathic for the past. She is what you would call a *pastpathic*. Most people would like to know their future. We have some that can only read the past, not predict the future. You might call it being clairvoyant."

"Well, I didn't see that coming."

"It happens."

"It must be difficult for her to have any friends." Xandra tries to imagine what it's like for poor Kaci.

"They prefer to read palms or foreheads, but any article touched by their unknowing victim will provide enough information. And most *pastpathics* have no friends," Tic notes.

"That is sad."

People probably avoided her because she could see into their past, good or bad. Most everyone has made some mistakes in the past and would like a do-over.

"We need to go at once," Tic reminds Xandra.

"What about my gear?"

"All your gear has been relocated to the fortieth floor, in the same location as I showed you. When you get there, you should change into your warrior gear and stay there until the time has come. Your time will be soon."

"What does that mean? I have to go upstairs and protect my boy."

"I assure you, you'll be more useful on the fortieth floor. Hide here and wait."

Xandra knows it's useless to argue with a Trefars. They take off in opposite directions. On the fortieth floor, Xandra finds the secret door and, sure enough, her gear is stored inside. That is one tricky Tic. Isabella changes into her Princess Xandra outfit, along with her sword, bow, and quiver of arrows.

Kaci tells her story to anyone who will listen. She wants and needs friends. Word has gotten back to the queen that Princess Xandra is inside the palace and disguised as a cleaning woman named Olive, and the queen wants to release the mongrels. Only the king can command their release. No one is willing to argue with the queen.

The queen tells the guards, "I have spoken with the king, and he doesn't want any scandals before the birthday party, so he is okay with a few mongrels being released to find the culprit. Release them *at once*!"

The siren has sounded so everyone may take cover. Everyone has to stay inside their rooms. Cleaning personnel have to go back to their quarters and wait to hear the all-clear siren.

Everything is at a standstill. The four mongrels are huge beasts, and clever. It doesn't take long for the large hounds to scour the palace since they have a good idea where to start. If you are found in the wrong place, they may maul you to death.

The issue for Kaci is that when she returns to her station, she does not hear the first siren which alerts everyone that the hounds have been released. While walking fast to the stairwell, Kaci sprains her ankle and falls to the ground. She screams out for help.

Xandra hears someone screaming and runs towards the cries.

"Kaci, are you okay?" Xandra asks.

"Not good. I think I sprained my ankle, and I can't walk." Kaci is almost in tears from the pain.

"Where did you run off to?"

She looks at Xandra and says, "I'm sorry. I know who you are, and I had to warn them."

"Who am I, then?"

"You're Princess Xandra, and the palace has been alerted of your presence."

"And why did you do that?"

"Because you're a killer. Look at you, in your warrior killing outfit."

"I was never going to harm you."

"Possibly. I couldn't have you destroy the king or queen. You have killed so many."

Before Xandra can respond, they both turn and see a huge mongrel staring at them.

"Hello, ladies. I could use a nice meal today. Who will be first? How about the lame one?"

"I don't think so," Xandra tells the huge beast. "If you want to live, you should turn around and go back where you came from."

"You are funny. You and what army?"

Hari comes running around the corner and confronts this massive hound. The beast is almost twice the size of Hari, and Hari himself is huge.

"You're not getting past me," Hari tells the beast.

"Oh, but I am. Either you let me by and live, or die fighting for these two."

"What is your name?" Hari asks.

"David. And yours?"

"I'm Hari, protector of the great Princess Xandra."

"Then it will be my pleasure to pull you apart in front of your charming princess."

Within seconds, Hari and David lunge at each other. Xandra takes out an arrow, aims, pulls back the bow, and lets the arrow fly directly towards David's chest. David falls to the ground. Xandra runs over to see if David is dead.

"I didn't want to kill him. I only meant to hurt him," Xandra says.

"Isn't that nice. He was going to kill all of us. I owe you my life," Hari says.

"You owe me nothing. I owe you. You have saved me and my kids multiple times, so now we're even."

Kaci is crying her heart out.

"What's the matter, dear?" Xandra asks.

"You just saved my life, and I turned you in as a killer. What kind of killer saves little ol' me? I'm so confused."

"I'm not a killer, dear. I'm here to save my family, that's all. I don't want any harm to come to you, or anyone."

"I read about your past, and you have killed so many," Kaci remarks.

"I had no choice. It was either kill or be killed. I chose to kill."

"I don't understand. I wanted you to be captured, yet you still helped me."

"It's what we do, where I'm from."

"I see you have also saved many animals from death."

"Yes, I am a veterinarian back home."

"Oh my, you're a veterinarian and a princess? How do you find the time? I can hardly finish one task per day."

"I'm only a princess when needed. Mostly, I'm a mom when I'm not taking care of animals."

"I like animals. Do you think I could be a veterinarian one day?"

"Indeed. You would make a great veterinarian. You could see how a wound or how an issue begins, and treat it."

"That's what I'm going to do. Save as many animals as possible." Kaci smiles.

"I think that's a grand idea. Can you control your clairvoyance?"

"Sometimes it's hard. I'm scared."

Xandra examines Kaci's foot and determines it's a sprain. "You should be okay."

"Wow, you know everything."

"Not really. I'm also scared. I've lost my entire family."

"How did you get here?" Hari asks, perplexed.

"I was told to stand by and wait. Tic told me to hide out here until I'm needed. Do you think this was the reason?" Xandra asks.

"It sure was reason enough for me. That beast was huge. I didn't have a chance," Hari replies.

"Yet you still attacked. My hero, Hari."

Kaci says, "Thanks, Olive, or Isabella. Or should I call you Princess Xandra? Sorry, but I think you're the hero in this situation."

"Considering where we are, let's stick with Princess Xandra."

Xandra says to Hari, "What should we do with Kaci? I'm worried about leaving her by herself."

"I'll be fine," she says. "I don't want to cause you any more trouble. I feel bad enough turning you in."

"In case another beast comes this way, I'll stay by her side until help arrives," Hari replies.

"There are probably more of those things running around inside the palace. Once they find this one, they will call for more than mongrels. The guards will be everywhere. At least we should try and hide David."

Hari and Xandra drag the huge beast into a back corner room.

"Kaci, I have to depart. I wish you well. Hari will stay by your side until help arrives."

"Princess, I don't know how to thank you. Again, I am so sorry. This gift, or curse of mine, causes many friendships to go awry."

"I consider you my friend, Kaci. And please pursue the veterinary career. I think it would be a perfect fit for you."

"Oh, that makes me feel so good, Princess. Thank you. Can I tell my parents I'm friends with the great Princess Xandra?"

"Yes, of course. If I had more time, I would go home with you and meet your folks."

"Then I shall. My papa will need some convincing. I'm sure Mama will believe me. It is far away, and I doubt you would ever travel that far for me."

"I would indeed."

"That will be another dream for me."

Xandra is afraid to hug Kaci. She doesn't want her to have any more visions; they would only scare her. She waves goodbye.

"Hari, I'm going back to the fortieth floor, and stay hidden. Once she is safe, you'd better do the same. Why don't you try to get up to the fiftieth floor and see what's going on?"

"Okay, will do. See you soon," Hari replies.

In the background, voices can be heard, and they both take off.

A guardsman finds Kaci sitting on the steps.

"Did you find her, the intruder?"

"No, sir, she wasn't around when I returned. I sprained my ankle and cannot move."

Another two guardsmen come around the corner to confront Kaci. Then the all-clear siren blasts.

"Pick her up and take her to the medic station."

"Yes, sir."

Chapter 13

BIRTHDAY

Jelab notifies me as to the reason Socreen is in the dungeon: she is accused of poisoning Siena to death. Socreen told me that Siena had a sweet soul, inside and out, so I know Socreen would never have poisoned Siena. Fortunately, I was also informed that Siena and I were very close, so I act the part of a dejected friend.

I yell, "Poisoned, poisoned by Socreen, are you kidding me? This is outrageous! Jelab, this is ridiculous, ludicrous."

"Calm down, my prince," Jelab responds.

"How can I be calm? Who will be next? Me, perhaps!"

"My prince, you needn't talk like that."

By now everyone in the palace will have heard about Siena's untimely death.

"Jelab, I need some air. All these sirens and all this noise. It's making me uncomfortable."

"You cannot leave the palace now, my prince. I think it's safer for you to stay in your quarters."

"I need to get away. What is the issue? It is my birthday party. This is foolishness."

"Someone has infiltrated the palace. It seems we may have an intruder."

"What kind of intruder?"

"I have heard it is a rebel, disguised as a maid. She may be here to harm you."

"She doesn't sound like such a big threat. I need to get out of here."

"How about a swim, my prince? I can get you to the pools."

"Yes, perfect. That sounds like a great idea. Let me go change."

"All your swim attire is at the pools, Sire."

"Yes, of course. Let's go."

We arrive, uninterrupted, at the pools. Jelab knows every hallway and secret crevice in the palace. He has been working at the palace for more than forty years, and is well trusted. I see a beautiful blue sparkling pool that looks endless, plus another two lap pools. This is the most awesome thing I have ever seen. I doubt anyone else around here has a swimming pool.

"Be careful, my prince. Do not swim too far and tire yourself out. You have a big party planned for this evening."

I don't respond, and dive right into the pool, holding onto my swim goggles.

"My prince, you need to wait for the swim guards. Oh my, where are the guards?" Jelab sighs.

I don't hear another word. *Aahhh, that's more like it.* I need a good long swim—it's been a while. *Now let's see where this thing goes.* I wonder if the entire water supply for the kingdom is being allocated from these waters. I'm so wound up, I feel like a crank: out at record pace for the first five thousand feet and I keep swimming as fast as I can go. *How far out does this pool extend? Where does it end?*

I slow up and dive down to look around. I find something that feels like locks. I wonder if these locks are preventing water from going into the surrounding lands. Is this some type of dam? I try to open one. The lever is impossible to turn. I swim farther down, and it's too dark to read what's on the locks. I feel some lettering, which may spell out *LD*. I find other locks, but can't decipher the lettering.

What Dylan doesn't realize is that *LD* stands for Lake Demise, and these locks do control most of the water flow for the kingdom. It does work like a dam.

The large swimming pool gradually turns into a small swim lane. *Who builds a single swim lane this long? It must have taken them years to build.* I come upon a split in the waterway. Do I go right or left? One sign reads, PALACE, the other, DANGER – Do Not Enter Without Guardians. I see no reason to stir up any trouble, so I head towards the palace sign. As I start swimming, the water begins to get extremely dark, almost black. I wonder if I went the wrong way. I don't remember the water being this dark. Since I was swimming so fast, maybe I overlooked it.

In a sweet, calming voice, I hear someone say, "Are you lost, Mr. Prince? May I help you?"

"No, I'm not lost. Just going out for a short swim. Thank you."

"Now, now, I think you are lost. Why else would the prince be venturing out towards Lake Demise?"

"I need to get away for some fresh air."

"Take hold of my hand, and I will pull you to safety."

"I can't see you. Where are you?"

Both the water and the air are pitch-black. I can't see much. I hold out my hand, and grab hold of a hand or a tail or a fin. It feels slimy. In hindsight, grabbing an unknown thing in the dark is a critical mistake.

Sometime later, I awaken, dazed and confused, on dry land. I realize Tabitha is giving me mouth-to-mouth resuscitation. She is trying to revive me! And I do the unthinkable—I start puking up water.

"Where am I? What happened? How did you find me?"

"We are not sure. Lucky for you, Pup and I were flying around. Pup saw something floating in the lake. As we got closer we realized it was you, and Pup pulled you out before you were someone's meal. What in the world are you doing out here?" Tabitha is shaking her head.

Still dazed, I say, "I'm not sure. I went for a swim, and I thought it was a shortcut back to the palace."

"A shortcut to death. Nothing good comes from Lake Demise. You have more lives than anyone I know. T asked me to watch the lake for anything unusual. Fortunately for you, Pup can see for miles, even on this dark day."

"Sorry. I was actually following a sign. It pointed this way, to the palace."

"Really. Are you sure?"

"Yes, I think so. Then I was told to grab on."

"Grab on. Didn't that seem a bit suspicious? Grab on to an electric eel, most likely. I would assume everything is going well, since you're still alive. I suggest you stay away from Lake Demise."

"The voice sounded so sweet."

"What did you expect, a blood-curdling voice?"

I slouch down, knowing she is right.

"Do you think anyone suspects foul play?" Tabitha says.

"I don't think so. I'm fairly certain I have convinced everyone that I am Prince Mako."

"I wouldn't be so sure. Watch out for the queen. She cannot be trusted. Have you seen your mother yet? She was disguised as a maid."

"No, I haven't. Oh no! I bet she's the intruder. A siren sounded to alert everyone that someone or something infiltrated the palace. I was later told the intruder is disguised as a maid. I had no idea it would be my mom! I'd better get back."

"Do you think you're okay to swim? It would be very dangerous for Pup and me to take you back."

"Yes, give me a minute. I'll be fine, thanks."

"We will follow you to the split. There is supposed to be a sealed gate with guards standing by, so no one can exit or enter. This time, swim towards the palace, for all our sakes. I will point you in the right direction."

"I didn't see any guards."

"I bet they were pulled off duty. Not many could order that. It had to be either the king or the queen."

Before I depart, Tabitha pulls me close and plants a big kiss on my cheek.

"Happy birthday, my prince."

I must be turning beet-red. I am dazed, for sure, plus I haven't forgotten the mouth-to-mouth. All I can say is, "Thanks."

Grinning, I open the gate and jump back into the pool, and start swimming. I make sure it's the correct direction … far away from Lake Demise.

When I return, Jelab is waiting for me.

"You were gone for quite a while. Is everything okay, my prince? You look drained."

"Yes, I am fine. I would like to go back to my chambers and get ready for the events."

To my dismay, I later find out the direction signs had been switched.

While Jelab is running my bath, I pass out.

**

"I now pronounce you wife and wife. You may kiss the bride."

What am I doing at this wedding? Why is my best friend Jonny here?

I am going to kill him. He knows I'm in love with her.

Wait, is that Violet and Tabitha holding hands? Are they getting married? Oh no, that's a problem for me. That's not possible.

How do they know each other? Have they talked about me?

Tabitha did tell me she likes everyone. I still am so confused on how they would know each other. This is not good. Now what do I do?

Both girls turn and point in my direction.

Oh no, they see me. I'm a dead man. Plus, I think we are all underwater.

"Hey, Jonny. What are you doing here?"

"I was invited. Why are you here?"

A little clown fish swims by and says, "They have been living together for years. What is wrong with you?"

"I am not sure. How do they know each other?"

Suddenly, Jonny disappears. It looked like something pulled him deeper underwater, because all I heard was "What?"

Then, again both girls point at me and motion that they want me to visit with them.

This can't be good. I slowly walk towards Violet. I see them raise their hands, and then I see each girl is holding a machete.

I start screaming, Noooooo ….

**

I awake to Jelab shaking me.

"Wake up, my prince. Wake up."

"Oh my, that was crazy. I'm okay, Jelab."

"Do you remember what caused you to yell out, my prince?"

"Yes, and it's something I'd rather not discuss." I figure it's best I don't mention that dream to anyone. I haven't thought about Violet since I left Key West. I wasn't sure that was even possible. I used to spend every waking moment thinking of Violet. Now all I think about is Tabitha. I must be a mental case of some sort. Is it common to disregard one girl after years and years and years of pursuing? Probably not. However, I'm not normal. I'd better focus on this prince stuff.

**

The king is extremely upset that one person, a lone woman, is the reason the siren alert was sounded. He starts berating Crate, one of his assistants.

"Are you telling me we shut down the palace right before my son's party because of one woman? This is ridiculous. No further alerts unless approved by me. I thought we were under attack."

The queen arrives and shoos Crate away with her hand. "Go away," she bellows.

"My king, we should celebrate. We are finally alone and we can properly toast that amazing boy of ours. He is turning sixteen and soon he will become a fine boy." The queen smirks.

"You mean, man. He turns sixteen and will become a man. I think he will be ready when the time comes to take over my reign. You should be pleased that we have an heir to take over my throne. That way, you will not be burdened with such a task. It shall be fun to see him take over. I of course will be there to help him, if I live that long!" The king glows. "Yes, my love, he will make a great king. And we should be proud of our wonderful son. Let's toast! Tonight will be the biggest celebration ever in the kingdom. I am proud of my son."

Koper enters and bows. "Excuse me, my king. I have some urgent news to share with you."

"Not now," the king replies. "Can't you see I am about to toast with my bride, you fool?"

"Yes, my lord. But I do have some news of the utmost importance."

"If I deem it unimportant, you shall lose your head right here and now. Are you willing to take that gamble, Koper?"

Koper thinks for a moment, and replies, "Yes. It's that important."

"It's for the king's ears only. Sorry, my queen." Koper is visibly shaking.

The queen screams, "If it is so important, may I not also hear, you fool?"

The king knows how conniving his wife can be. "Koper, whisper it to me. If I deem it acceptable to share, I shall."

The queen, not very happy, grunts. Koper whispers, and the king's eyes get big. Koper whispers to the king that the prince has been located and is safe in San Francisco, with Grull.

"Tell no one of this," the king responds.

"Yes, Sire."

"Are you sure this is accurate and current information?"

"Yes, my king, one hundred percent."

"Very well then. You may keep your head." The king's attitude changes at once.

"What is it, my king?" the queen asks.

"Nothing to worry yourself with. Now, I have to depart."

"But my king, what about our toast?" She has filled the king's goblet with poison.

"Not now. I have some important business to take care of."

"But my king …."

"Be quiet, woman. Not now." He stomps off.

The queen is upset her plan did not work. Now she has to find another way to kill her husband.

**

Jelab announces, "It is time for me to prepare you for the upcoming events, my prince."

When I finish dressing, I take a deep breath. "Okay, Jelab, it's showtime."

"What is that, my prince?" Jelab asks, not familiar with that word.

"Nothing." I try to shake off that weird dream. *How in the world would Violet and Tabitha ever meet?*

I arrive at the palace's fiftieth-floor rooftop. One of many rooftops. I think this one is the tallest. My birthday bash looks outrageous. An overabundance of everything. I see food, wine, mead, beer, dancers, trapeze artists, jugglers, glassblowers, fire-breathers, and clowns. I can assume more will be arriving soon.

I turn and bow to the king and the queen. "Father, Mother, thank you for all of this. It is marvelous, and I am having a grand time."

The king stands and claps his hands, and soon the music and dancing commence. The king stares at me, trying to figure out who the imposter might be and how it is I look so similar to his son. Maybe Koper was wrong. The king sees no reason to interrupt this joyous occasion.

"Son, aren't you going to dance? This party is for you," the king says.

"Yes, Father. I couldn't decide who to dance with."

"Would you prefer for me to choose a partner for you?" The king chuckles.

"No, thank you. I'm choosing one now." *I wish Tabitha were here.*

I spot my prey. She has beautiful black hair, lots of curls, and dark eyes. I do not know her name. Who would dare turn me down? I am the prince. I eventually find enough courage to walk over. I approach her with an authoritative strut. I keep saying to myself, *I hope she doesn't say no, don't say no. Please say yes.*

She bows and says, "Good evening, my prince. My name is Regina."

She puts out her hand, and I grasp it. We head to the dance floor, and everyone moves away. I'm feeling rather energized now that I am dancing with Regina. *She said yes! Ha. I'm the man.* I have this big grin on my face. I have to remind myself to slow down. No one would say no to the prince. *Calm down, big boy.* There is so much going on in my mind, I almost step on Regina. I bet Tabitha would be jealous if she could see me now. *Concentrate, before I trip both of us.*

As we are finishing our first dance, someone walks right by me and towards the king. I hear him scream, "Down with the king and his reign!" He pulls out a knife. I am so close to the gatecrasher—I hurdle in front of the perpetrator before the king's guard can step in. The guards' archers can't get off a clean shot with so many people around. I bet a Trefars could place an arrow through this crowd.

I wrestle with the intruder until we both fall over the edge of the roof. Not sure how we both go over. It's as if he tried to pull me over the side.

The crowd is aghast at the sight of the prince tumbling off the roof. All at once the crowd runs to the side and looks down to see if anyone survived. As if in slow motion, we are falling to the next rooftop ten floors down, to the fortieth floor.

Confused, the king ponders why this imposter of a prince would risk his own life for him. He orders his guards to get down to the fortieth floor at once. The king can only assume that his actual son would have protected him, and Koper's information must be inaccurate.

The queen is smiling from deep within while trying to keep a straight face. "Someone, save my *boy*," the queen yells.

Now everyone is running around screaming—complete havoc and bedlam everywhere. Out of nowhere an arrow appears in the sky. It hits the king directly in the chest. The defense system is down since all the attention is focused on the prince. The arrow attack was timed perfectly and with precision. Talk about mayhem; now it is total chaos run amuck.

The queen is yelling for help, but she is thinking her plan is working perfectly.

The king is whisked away on a gurney, and all anyone can hear is screaming, crying, and yelling. This wonderful event is now a complete catastrophe.

**

Princess Xandra hears a loud thump outside somewhere. She is still waiting on the fortieth floor for something to happen. She is trying to figure out what made that noise and where it came from. She also hears a lot of voices in the upper stairwell.

Hari comes running around the corner in a panic and says, "It's your Dylan, the prince. He has taken a tumble off the roof. He's outside on the terrace. I'm certain he survived."

The prince and the assailant are both alive. The assailant realizes he is in grave danger, and limps to the side, and again jumps off the roof. This time a large bird catches him as he falls, and takes off into the sky. Arrows are shot from the palace defense system, but it looks as if the perpetrator has gotten away.

I am understandably shaken, though unhurt after falling ten stories. I groan and look up to see what caught me. I half grin. I am in the arms of a giant Graeter.

"Hello, I'm Greg," the Graeter says.

What are the odds of a friendly Graeter being on this rooftop? I look out and see my mother. Thank goodness, this whole thing must have been a weird dream. What comes out of my mouth next is, "Am I dreaming? What are you doing here and why are you dressed like that?"

"It's not a dream, sweetie. It's me. I've come to take you home."

In a matter of seconds, we are surrounded by many guards with arrows, spears, and swords drawn.

Princess Xandra stands, ready for battle. I'm still dazed as Greg slowly lets me down.

I command the guards, "Lower your weapons."

The guards are befuddled as to why Princess Xandra is protecting the prince. She is a dissident and usually fights against the palace.

"It is a trick," one guard yells.

Another guard yells, "Prince, you are in danger. Do not trust her!"

An arrow comes flying towards Princess Xandra. Hari jumps in front of her to block the arrow and takes it deep into the neck.

Xandra screams, "No! Oh, Hari!"

Hari smiles. "I told you I would save you one day. Tell Teri I love her and I will see her in doggie paradise."

Xandra runs to Hari and starts to cry. Xandra is so upset she is not sure how to react. Hari and Xandra have been close friends for many, many years.

"I am not going to say it again, *lower your weapons*," I yell at the guards.

No way anyone wants to dare undermine the prince, so they do as they are told and back off.

"Happy birthday, my angel," Xandra (Mom) whispers into my ear.

"Thanks, Mom," I whisper back.

Greg, T's Graeter, scoops me up, and we head back inside the palace. Greg is a spy.

**

"Chloe, I cannot thank you enough for all you have done for me. Now I must depart. I have to go to the palace to find out why I was left to die!" Grando exclaims.

"You promised my mother that you would protect me, and if you're not here, how can you protect me?" Chloe says.

"For the ninetieth time, I have to go to the palace alone. It is not safe there."

"You said you would protect me, and if you're not here, how can you protect me?"

"It is much safer here than in the palace." Grando is getting exhausted arguing with a tiny child who is annoying.

"The journey will be treacherous," Grando repeats.

"Not with you. I would feel safe. Please. I miss my mommy." Chloe starts to cry.

"She will come back for you, I promise."

"Mother said you would protect me, and you promised—"

"Okay, okay, I'll take you. I have warned you many times." Grando grimaces.

"Warned me about what?" Chloe asks.

"I give up. We will leave in the morning, so get all your chores done." Grando walks away thinking maybe he can sneak away. She is a strongheaded, determined little girl, but she did save his life. It would be a shame to take her to her death. The palace is no place for children.

Chapter 14
DEATH

"I want to see my son," the king demands.

"Yes, my lord."

"Bring him to me at once," the king murmurs, barely able to speak.

While coughing up blood, the king looks around and notices that the queen is nowhere in sight.

"What is she doing here?" the king comments as he sees Xandra.

Kati replies, "She is with me, my lord, and unarmed. She has something to tell you." Kati is one of the Kondos that guard the king. She is more than sixty feet tall.

"Can she be trusted?" the king mumbles.

"Yes, my lord."

The king decides to hear what she has to say—he is going to die, anyway. If she attacks, it would only speed up his likely demise. He has nothing to lose.

Xandra bows to the king. She gets close enough to whisper so only the king can hear.

"My king, you need to be made aware of something. It will probably upset you. I think it's time you know the truth. It's a long story and I will try my best to keep the story short. And you will have to trust me that everything I tell you is a fact," Xandra clarifies.

"Can I assume it has something to do with the imposter prince? Because my son, the real prince, is in the concrete country?"

"Yes, Sire, it does. If I may explain, Your Highness?"

"I would like to know before I expire. Why didn't this imposter let the assailant kill me? Why save me? Wasn't the imposter hired to kill me? I am a bit confused," the king replies.

Princess Xandra begins her story. "It all started long ago. Approximately fifty-seven hundred days have passed since I gave birth to two boys. One was born in your kingdom and grew up here. You refer to him as your own Prince Mako. The other boy, who is here now, and saved your life from the intruder, was born in my world—as you call it, the concrete country. Both Prince Mako and the boy in front of you are my sons. They are identical twins. Until recently, I did not know they were identical twins. I have not met my other son Michael, or Prince Mako.

"My unexpected birth while visiting your kingdom was indeed untimely. The queen has fooled you all these years and kept this a secret from you—allowing you to think that the prince was your child with her. You raised him as if he was yours. That is all a child needs, to be loved. And you accomplished that. No one can take that away from you. The boy in front of you, who saved your life, is also my son."

"Why would your son save me?" The king rubs his chin.

"He was not sent here to harm you."

"Then why impersonate my son? What deception are you up to?"

"It wasn't deception. It was to keep the queen from overtaking the kingdom." Xandra does not want to implicate the Trefars; that would only infuriate the king.

"Where is the queen?"

"I do not know, my lord." Xandra frowns.

The queen is nowhere near the king. She is packing her things, wanting to depart the palace while she still has a chance. The king is not surprised by this information. He realizes that the queen is evil and capable of anything. She's undoubtedly hiding. Tears are filling his eyes.

It is sad for the king to die all alone, with no one to take over his reign. A very long legacy gone. He is the last of a long line of royal families.

**

When we finally arrive at the king's chambers, Greg lets me down to the floor.

"Son, come closer," the king states, pointing to me.

I approach. "Yes, my king?" I gulp.

The king whispers in my ear, "I knew you were not my son, long before you saved my life. Since you look and act just like my son, I wanted to see what your plan was to be."

The king rises and announces, "I want to make a statement."

The king's scribe runs up to the king, "Yes, my lord?"

"Let it be known that I announce the prince as my successor, effective at once. Now, bring me the queen," the king expresses with very little energy.

**

The queen is packed and departing the palace. Word has already come back to the queen that the king is dying or dead, and he has announced the prince as his successor. The queen knew she was not going to be crowned ruler of the kingdom.

The queen says to her dragon, "Go down to the dungeon and grab prisoner number 2875. Not Socreen. Take the young one. Bring her with us. Put her in the caged wagon."

"Yes, my queen," Trigon replies.

**

The guard yells through the door, "Hey, you, get up. You have a visitor. They're going to take you for a bath."

All the guards laugh. Alex and Socreen are not amused.

"That's okay, I'll stay here. I like being dirty," Alex replies.

"Get up! Not you, old lady," the guard shouts.

Alex replies, "Why don't you come get me up, you little weasel?"

"Open the cell door and let me in. I can handle her."

"She's tricking you," one guard comments.

"I don't think so. Let me in. I have to get her to the queen's caravan at once."

"Okay, it's your funeral."

Alex and Socreen hear the queen's name mentioned, and look at each other.

"Oh no, she knows who I am, Grandma." Alex holds Grandma tightly.

"This cannot be a good thing," Grandma comments.

The guard walks cautiously into the cell. "Okay, you be nice, or it will be a nasty ride for you."

"Ride? Where are we going? I thought it was bath time," Alex says.

"You don't get to ask questions. The queen has summoned you …."

In a flash and while he is talking, Alex kicks the guard square in the face, and says, "Tell the queen I don't like rides."

Another guard rushes in and says, "I warned you."

The struck guard screams, "Get that witch and bring her downstairs." He is holding his head as blood is flowing from his nose.

Six giant guards appear, and grab Alex as she is kicking and screaming … but to no avail. The guards are so large she has no hope of hurting them. They tie her feet and hands so she cannot kick them. Next they gag her.

Socreen screams, *"Do not hurt her! Do not hurt her!"*

"Shut up, old woman, or you will be next."

The dungeon door slams shut.

Socreen is a wreck—crying, shaking, and talking to herself.

"Take her down to the queen's caravan," the guard commands. "She is departing in minutes."

**

I take my mom back to my quarters and introduce her to Jelab as Princess Xandra. I don't think it's wise to tell anyone she is my mother. That would cause some unknown issues.

Jelab bows. "You were only a legend until now. It is my honor, Princess Xandra."

He explains to us, "The word spread rapidly that the king has passed on. Now that Prince Mako is in control and the queen has departed, most everyone in the palace, including the guards, will be committed to whoever is in charge. There is very rarely any infighting, and a coup from within the palace is rare."

"Okay, Jelab," I say, "take Princess Xandra to Socreen, and bring her and her cellmate back to me."

"Yes, Your Highness. At once."

I jump twenty feet in the air when, out of nowhere, I hear: "Congratulations, Prince, job well done."

"Who said that?"

I see Tic standing in front of me, smiling.

"Tic, what are you doing here? You've got to stop sneaking up on me. I thought the Trefars are not allowed in the palace."

"I brought Princess Xandra, and decided to stay close by in case things went erratic."

"They went erratic, alright. The king is dead and the queen has departed," I reply.

"Yes, and your mom is here with you."

"Indeed, and I would keep that a secret for now."

"Of course. I also came to warn you," Tic says.

"Warn me. Warn me about what? What else can happen?"

"It's going to become extremely wet outside, very soon."

"I know you Trefars well enough. So when you say something like that, it usually is worse than it sounds. Wet outside. Meaning what? Why, it hasn't rained in over five hundred days."

"Stay inside if possible. If you do go outside, have your swim goggles in hand." Tic smiles.

Jelab returns with Princess Xandra and Socreen.

"I have to go. The queen took Alex!" Mom exclaims.

"I'm coming with you," I reply.

"Not this time. You have to stay here and make sure there is not an uprising from within," Mom reminds me. "I have to travel fast, and alone."

"I am the prince—I can do whatever I want."

"Listen, Dylan, you'd better get this prince thing out of your head. As soon as I get back with Alex, we're getting Chloe and we are all departing."

"But Mom, I'm the prince."

"Dylan, I don't want to embarrass you in front of your new friends, but if I have to, I will put you across my lap."

"Alright, alright, calm down. Hold on. Let me ask Jelab something."

"Jelab, can I send some guards with Princess Xandra?"

"Of course, my prince. You can do whatever you wish."

"Summon some of my best guards at once, and send them with my mo—Princess Xandra."

"Yes, my prince. I shall do so now."

After the door closes, Mom kisses me on the forehead. "Oh, my darling Dylan. You have grown so much in a short period of time."

"I am so sorry that Alex got taken away," Socreen says, wiping her tears with her handkerchief.

"It's not your fault," Princess Xandra says. "What could you do? You guys wait here. I promise you everything will be okay."

"Hey, Mom, be careful. Tic told me it's going to be wet outside. Must be getting ready to pour."

"I will, dear." She plants a kiss on her mom and another one on me.

As Xandra starts to depart, Kati the Kondo arrives at my door and says, "I'll make sure no harm comes to the prince."

Kati and Xandra have become close friends. Xandra had noticed an ankle bracelet on Kati. Any form of jewelry is forbidden unless you're a royal. The king allowed Kati to wear an ankle bracelet inscribed with her daughter's name, Puddin. Xandra had recognized the name, and they talked about her loved one. Once Kati heard that Xandra found the cause of her death, they were instant pals for life. It doesn't hurt to have a sixty-foot giant on your side.

"I feel better already. Thank you." Xandra smiles.

When Princess Xandra gets outside of the palace gates, she is accompanied by so many warriors she can't believe it. Jacob is there waiting for her. She hops onto Jacob the zebra, and he takes off, leading more than five hundred soldiers.

"I hope we can catch them, Jacob."

"We will, Princess. I doubt the entourage can keep up with us. We will catch them. That I can guarantee you."

**

Grande is in the lead of the queen's caravan. Grande is Grando's father. Grande left the king, and now apparently is helping the queen. Grande was the head of the king's guards. Loyalty has never been his strong suit.

The queen feels more at ease, the farther away she gets from the palace. Her exile will give her some time to regroup and come up with a plan to take back the crown that was stolen from her. One day she will be crowned the queen and take over this kingdom.

The caravan comes to a halt.

The queen screeches, "*Why are we stopping!*"

"I will check, my queen."

Grande and Grando, staring at each other, are blocking the road. Grando has grown considerably during his recovery. He is almost as large as his father.

"Well, well. Hello, my son. What can I do for you? I am so glad to see that you survived the attack at the Rocklands. I have been so concerned about your health and well-being." Grande grins at Grando.

"Yes, Father, I am sure there were many sleepless nights worrying about me," Grando replies.

"Aah, you were always so sensitive. Now step aside before I have you and your little friend torn apart," Grande commands.

"I don't think so. I'm not going anywhere," Grando announces.

One of the queen's guards comes riding up to the front and tells Grande, "Hurry along, and take care of the issue at once. The queen is in a rush."

"Okay. This will be as easy as your brother." Grande growls.

"Did you also kill my mother?" Grando asks.

"Let me think on that. Oh, yes. Your big-mouthed mother did die unexpectedly. She opened her mouth about your brother's death, shall I say, once too many times. Now step aside before I take you and your little friends' heads."

The queen is informed that Grando is the obstruction on the road. Grando is blocking the road, with Chloe riding on his back.

"I don't have time for family quarrels," the queen says, laughing.

"My queen, the road is completely blocked and we cannot move until they move."

The queen knows that Trigon has gone ahead to make sure her new accommodations will be ready for her arrival. "Then, move or kill the beast, I don't care. Hurry!"

"Yes, my queen."

Twenty guards take the lead and hesitantly walk towards Grando.

Grando perches Chloe high up on a tree limb. "Stay put, I'll be right back," he tells her.

"Okay, but he looks mean, and I don't want you to get hurt. I can't keep sewing you up."

"That's for sure, little one. You are not so steady with your big giant hands, anyway." Grando laughs. "It's a bit different when I'm not in a cage."

The first five guards attack at full speed, and Grando tosses them aside like rag dolls. The next five last even less time.

Grande says, "I can see you have been taught well. All those lessons with Kaptuk seem to have paid off." Grande clears the ground with his huge paws, while silently cursing Kaptuk, the 200-year-old cheetah who teaches the apprentices of the king's guards.

Alex, in a gated cage on the back of a wagon, spots Chloe in a tree, and screams, "Chloeeee, Chloeeee, it's Alex. Help!"

Chloe hears her name and can't see who or where the cries are coming from. She thinks it sounded like Alex. "Alex," Chloe screams.

The queen says to her guard, "Get her and bring her to me."

"Yes, my queen."

One of the queen's companions flies up to pluck Chloe out of the tree. Chloe is so far up she allows the bird to grab her. The giant bird places Chloe next to the queen.

"Hello, dear, and who might you be?" the queen asks with a smile.

"I'm Chloe, and that's my sister, back there."

"Oh, my. Would you like to join your sister?"

"Yes."

"Put her with her sister. I hate to break up families." The queen laughs hysterically.

The fight between Grando and Grande begins. It is quite a sight to behold. Trees, boulders, and anything in their way are demolished. The tigers roll off the path, and the caravan moves once again.

Chloe yells out, "Grando, you promised to protect me."

Grando hears his name as he is about to get torn apart. Soon the combatants are out of sight, and Chloe starts to cry.

Between sobs, Chloe says, "I like him."

Alex whimpers, "So do I."

"Where are we going?" Chloe asks.

"Not sure. It can't be good. This queen is evil."

A huge zebra streaking towards the caravan catches their attention. Riding it is Princess Xandra, and she is already attacking the caravan in the rear. With a sword in each hand, she wipes out four guards in one thrust. She is a mother on a mission, determined to rescue her girls.

Alex asks Chloe, "Who's that? Is that a woman?"

"I think that's Mom. She's some type of super warrior villain. Not sure how, but she is bad to the bone, I've been told. And they love her here."

"It is Mom! Are you kidding me? When did this happen? Grandma tried to tell me she was some type of warrior."

"That's her, alright, and she doesn't look happy."

The sisters look at each other and, in unison, scream, "*Mom, Mom*, we're over here."

Xandra hears the girls screaming, and picks up speed, destroying anything and everything in her path to get to her two daughters. The girls are mesmerized watching their mom wipe out anyone in her way.

Alex looks at Chloe and says, "I'm not upsetting her again. She's a beast. Holy cow."

Chloe's mouth is wide open and all she can mumble is, "Uh-huh."

But before Xandra can reach the cage holding her daughters, a huge amount of water comes flowing down the path, like a tsunami. Soon the entire caravan is underwater.

Trigon has returned in time to swoop down and pull the queen out of danger. They fly due east. Everyone else is underwater.

Chloe and Alex, hugging each other and crying their goodbyes, feel their cage plucked from the wagon … and they are flying in the sky.

Pup, with Tabitha riding her, has pulled the cage out of the water, and is flying west, back towards the palace.

"Chloe, are you okay?" Tabitha asks.

"Yes."

"Who are you?" Alex asks.

"We are friends of Dylan the swimmer. I thought you could use a lift."

"Dylan. You know Dylan, my brother?"

"I do indeed. We refer to him as the prince."

"That's Tabitha," Chloe says. "I like your friend," Chloe tells Tabitha.

Pup winks.

Alex screams, "Our mother is down there!"

**

With a firm grip on Grande, Grando starts dragging him deep into the water, knowing it's possible neither will survive. Then Grando realizes he will never find peace if his father is alive. Grando continues downward, even if it kills them both.

Grando can hear his mother whispering in his ear: *Sweetie, you'd better let him go, or you both will perish.* She adds, *Okay, I'll see you soon, my angel.*

The young tiger pushes Grande deeper into the water.

Chapter 15

CAITLIN

Chloe and Alex are holding onto each other, crying and mumbling, "Mom, we love you."

Chloe says, "Alex, what is that?"

"It looks like a giant elephant. Can we get closer?" Alex yells out.

Pup heads straight down. As they approach, they can see Dylan riding this elephant—an enormous elephant.

Tabitha says, "It's the prince, on Caitlin. It looks like he's heading towards Princess Xandra. Let's get you two back to the palace."

Chloe and Alex yell "*Dylan*," but he can't hear them.

"Is he going to save Mom?" Chloe asks.

Tabitha replies, "He's on Caitlin, T's magical elephant. Odds are he's going to try and save her."

**

The queen's caravan is in complete chaos. Anyone that couldn't swim would have surely perished. The water is flowing in like a raging river, and it could be one hundred feet deep in some areas.

"Okay, Caitlin," I remark, "I think we're getting close. I'll jump off here."

"Be careful. It's getting deep, and I'm losing my footing. I'll wait here for your return. Good luck, Your Highness."

I dive headfirst into the water. Thank goodness Tic reminded me to bring my goggles.

Caitlin, T's elephant, is approximately seventy feet tall. Most importantly, she's one of the largest creatures—and probably the smartest—in the kingdom. How and why she showed up at this time is nothing less than a miracle. I no longer wonder if T or his mother can see the future. It seems as if they can predict its outcome. After having no rain in many days, he builds a moat. How convenient. It's going to be wet outside? Really, this is beyond wet; it's a major flood.

Now, where's Mom?

It looks like Lake Demise has converged with this flooding water because I see so many unpleasant monsters of the sea swimming ubiquitously. This is deeper than I thought and much cloudier than I ever expected. I wonder, *Where did all this water come from?* It hasn't rained, and even if it had, it wouldn't have caused this much flooding. How will I ever find Mom in this cloudy water? I see a lot of dead bodies floating around. *Did T do this? If so, how? Doesn't seem like his style.*

I know she's down here and I need to find her soon. She can hold her breath a long time. Why is she staying down so long?

**

Xandra isn't staying underwater because she has a choice. As she is about to grab onto her daughter's wagon, that is when Pup grasps their cage and the giant cart falls over. It lands on top of both Xandra's legs, which are now pinned down.

She ponders whether the reason for her return was to drown. *I couldn't even save my little girls. What kind of warrior am I?* She hopes her mother and Dylan will be okay. They may not make it back to Key West, but at least they'll have each other.

Where did all this water come from? Did the queen release some reserves? It tastes like salt water. What in the world would they be doing with salt water? She tries and tries, but she can't budge the heavy cart. Xandra prays that her girls have a quick death and she'll see them both in heaven, possibly sooner rather than later. Her only consolation is that Alex and Chloe are together.

Unexpectedly, Xandra sees a huge fish swim by and it appears to be smiling at her. She realizes it's a great white shark, and it isn't a smile. Maybe it's a smirk.

"Well, well, well. Look who we have here." The shark sneers. "The miracle healer seems to be stuck, and I am hungry."

Xandra despondently answers, "Listen, I'm sure there are plenty of things to eat around here much larger than me. Please let me drown in peace."

"You are correct, but for some reason I like the taste of fresh human meat, and I see nothing fresher than you."

Xandra turns her head and can barely make out someone or something swimming towards her. She can't tell who or what it is. However, she estimates it may not be able to see the great white from its angle.

Oh no, it can't be! Xandra realizes it's Dylan and yells at the killer shark, "Come on, big boy, come and get me."

**

I stop swimming when I see this huge fish. *Great, it looks like a shark. How did I miss that thing?* Luckily, I don't think the shark sees me. It is so enthralled with Mom. It looks as if my mom's eyes are closing and she is about to expire. I need to get her out of here real soon. How?

"Hey, no sleepy time yet. You'll taste much better alive," the great white says with a laugh.

Something brushes by me, and I shriek. That gets the great white's attention.

"Hey, I am going to have to get a bib. This is going to be a feast."

"Oh, no," I tell the shark. "Listen, that's my mom, and I need to get her out of here before she drowns."

"That's so nice. I do like a family feast. Okay, this is what I'll do. I'll eat you first, so you won't have to watch your mom die."

"I have a better idea. Why don't you let us both go?"

"Let me think about it. No!" The shark smirks.

I'm not sure what it was, but something came crashing down on the great white. It had to be enormous to crush this huge shark. Dazed, the great white shark swims away, whimpering about something.

The next thing I see are giant tentacles everywhere. One tentacle grabs the cart, one grabs Mom, and then I get grabbed with a ton of force. Astonishingly, we are both rushed to the surface and tossed into the air. We land on Caitlin's back. It happened so quickly, I was caught by surprise. Mom still isn't moving. Now I know what came crashing down on the great white shark; it was a giant leg of T's elephant.

I tell her, "Caitlin, hurry. We've got to get back to the palace at once."

Caitlin takes off as fast as possible, considering the water level, which keeps rising. Even though Caitlin's legs are getting gnawed on, she doesn't stop. I try CPR on Mom. That doesn't work. I try everything I know to revive her, and then I start to cry hysterically. It is taking forever to get back to the palace.

When the guards see us coming, they open the gates. Greg the Graeter is here to meet us.

"Take her to the medic station at once," I shout to Greg.

"Yes, Your Highness."

Greg gently takes Princess Xandra and heads for the royal medical infirmary.

Inside the palace, I gather Grandmother Liz, Alex, and Chloe to the infirmary. Everyone is stunned to see the lifeless body of our mom. Chloe is almost catatonic.

"This is my entire fault," Grandma murmurs, and grimaces.

Then I hear: "Is she dead?"

"I think so."

I am so absorbed and shocked, I'm not sure when Igagbee arrived.

He comes up to me and says, "Administer the antidote T gave you."

"No. It's poison, anyway. Plus, I don't have any antidote T gave me. You're wrong. Leave me alone."

"I doubt I'm wrong. T gave you two vials."

"How do you know all this? Leave us alone," I reply, in tears.

"Who do you think brought Caitlin? T knows everything. Here are both potions."

"Where did you get these?" I ask.

"I brought them to replace the ones the queen stole. Hurry. Now that she is unconscious, you must inject her with an exact mixture of two milliliters each. It has to be exact. After she's injected, mix a batch of three milliliters each. When she awakens, have her drink the rest of the potion," Igagbee says.

"You're insane."

"Hurry, Your Highness. When have I ever lied to you?" Igagbee waves his arms.

Grandmother screams, "Stop! That's what killed Siena."

"Igagbee hasn't steered me wrong yet." I figure it can't hurt. Prospects look dismal at best. "I don't think we have a choice." After a precise measurement, it's put into a syringe. "I can't inject her. I'm too scared."

"I'll do it," Chloe says.

Mom's not moving. I grab Igagbee and start to strangle him.

"See, you poisoned her! Get him out of here before I—"

Mom coughs and spits out water.

Igagbee says, "It's vital that she drinks the rest of the potion."

Chloe hands me the potion, and I pour it down Mom's throat.

"Where am I, in heaven? I see all my family. It must be. Did we all die?"

"No, Mom. Dylan saved you first. Then we all pitched in," Chloe says, and hugs her.

"Um, you'd better call me the prince."

"Oh yeah, I forgot." Chloe smiles.

"Actually, T saved you," I inform Mom.

"That doesn't surprise me." She speaks slowly. "The last thing I remember was trying to get to my girls. And the rest is fuzzy. I do remember a river of water coming from nowhere. Does anyone know where all this water came from?"

"No," I reply. "I have people checking on that."

We all head back to my chambers.

"Jelab, we would like to be alone."

"Yes, Your Highness. I will take care of it at once."

Jelab ushers everyone out of the room.

For the first time in sixteen years, most of the Cabrella family are together again. Everyone is talking at the same time. There's lots of laughter, and crying, and just about every emotion a human can experience.

"We leave first thing in the morning," Mom announces.

"Mom, I've been thinking about that. I think I should stay."

"What in the world are you saying, Dylan?"

Jelab enters and says, "Excuse me. Your Highness is needed at once."

"What is it, Jelab?"

"There is an issue outside the palace that needs your attention."

"You're not going anywhere without us," Mom replies.

All at once, everyone says, "Yep, it's all or nothing."

We follow Jelab. He leads me to one of the palace balconies overlooking the kingdom. All I can see is rows and rows of elephants, with Trefars riding them.

Jelab says, "The guards have orders to attack any Trefars on sight. Fortunately, they thought it best to contact you first, now that you are in charge."

"Thank you, Jelab."

After seeing all these Trefars, I know it would have been a tragic mistake to fire upon them because it would have turned into a slaughter of the palace guards. Who knew that so many Trefars existed? The Trefars could overtake the palace at any time.

"There must be thousands and thousands of them. What is it they want?" I ask.

A huge elephant—not Caitlin—sidles up to the balcony. T is riding it.

"Hello, Your Highness. May I have a word with you inside?" T asks.

"Certainly." I call out to the guards, "Let him in."

Most people have only heard of the great T and few have ever seen him.

"Is he to be trusted?" a guard asks me.

The past king did not allow any Trefars into the palace.

"You would all be wiped out if they wanted to attack. Let him in, *now*."

"Yes, Sire."

Most of the guards have never seen T, and I can tell something is happening.

"He doesn't look that tough," one guard mutters to another.

And "I could take him with a flick of my bow and end his reign."

I overhear the guards talking and I yell out, "Do not harm T or any Trefars, or you will be held accountable." I mumble under my breath, "I hope you guards don't try anything, or T will cut you down in seconds."

Chloe grabs Mom's arm and asks, "Who are they?"

"They are Trefars, dear, and they are very nice."

"I like the elephants they're riding. I didn't know you could ride elephants that easily. They're so cute. I like their big ears."

"Trefars have been trained at birth to ride those huge animals."

"Can I pet one?" Chloe asks.

"Not now, sweetie, maybe later. Let's see what T has to say."

T makes his entrance alone, and greets the prince, who is now sitting on the king's throne.

The leaders bow to each other. "Thank you for seeing me at such short notice."

"Anytime, T. What can I do for you?"

"I see everyone is accounted for and well, I hope."

"Yes, we are well, thanks to you, and the antidote, and Caitlin. Everyone is fine, thank you."

"I'm glad it all worked out. I do need some help."

"You need my help? I'm listening."

"I actually need Princess Xandra's help."

"I do not answer for the princess. You may ask her yourself."

T turns to her. "Princess, I require your services. In reality, it's Caitlin that needs you. She has been badly injured, and you're the only person who can save her."

Knowing it is useless to argue with T, Xandra tries anyway. "I will be departing tomorrow, not to return anytime soon. Don't you have specialists who can treat her?"

"I am aware of your rapid departure. That is why I came so quickly. It will only be a moment. One evening, and then I will bring you back to the palace. No harm shall come to you." T smiles.

Everyone is looking at Mom, hoping she will decline his offer.

"Okay, I will come with you. Once I have finished, I shall come straight back to the palace so my family and I can depart for home."

"Agreed. I shall guarantee your quick return. Thank you, Princess."

"Mom, can I go with you?" Chloe asks.

"Not this time. I can take care of it myself. I need you here, to watch over everyone else."

After all the goodbyes and crying, Xandra departs on Jacob the zebra, with T at her side, surrounded by thousands of Trefars. Even the kid Trefars are out, riding their baby elephants. The Trefars are so much fun to watch. They jump from elephant to elephant while the giant animal is moving at top speed, and do not miss a step. In the darkness of night, watching the Trefars change colors when jumping from one elephant to the next is like a neon light show. Anyone else would fall and be trampled. It's an incomprehensible sight and much better than any planned circus act.

**

As soon as Xandra arrives, she is directed to Caitlin, and attends to her needs.

"Okay, T, what's up? There is nothing more I can do for Caitlin that already hasn't been provided. What do you want? I finally get my family back, and you take me away."

"I know, and I'm sorry. This is very important."

"More important than my family!"

"I'm afraid so. Tara wants to go back with you."

"Say that again?"

"Tara, my mother, would like to see, and expire, in your world. Everything is written down. She doesn't have long to live."

"Really. What am I supposed to do with your mother? She should be here with you when it's time for her death."

"We have said our goodbyes. This is what she wants, and I concur."

"Wow, I didn't see that one coming. Do I have a choice?"

"She can teach you plenty. It's her dying wish."

"I'm sure she can. Arguing with you is a waste of time, so I'll do it, under one condition."

"Yes. Your condition?" T smiles as if he already knows her request.

"If my son stays, which I'm guessing he will—for a short period—will you make sure he is safe?"

"I would have done that anyway. He will make a great leader."

"Not so fast. He's still in school. Okay, do we have a deal?"

"Deal. I'll bring Tara to Grock the day after next."

"Thank you for everything, and for saving my life, again."

"My pleasure. Maybe we will meet in the near future."

**

I try to relax, now that everyone's back together. Only Mom is absent, and she will return tomorrow.

"Okay, go through that one more time, Grandmother?" I ask.

"I wish your mother was here to explain it all."

"You're here, so let's hear your version. Start at the beginning, please."

"Here goes. Your mother and I would visit the kingdom often. Isabella wanted to come back one more time before you were born. She figured after the twins were born, her chances of coming back would be limited. So your mother and I came here, with her about to burst with twins."

I shake my head. "Twins. What twins? Oh, no wonder I'm having nightmares every night. Do you think it has affected my brain?"

"Yes," Alex replies, "you're mentally unstable for sure."

"In case you haven't noticed, I am the prince, and can have your head on a platter."

"Try it, and I'll kick your little a—"

"Okay, that's enough. I don't want to hear any bickering. You can bicker once we're back home."

"I'm sorry to interrupt. Please continue." I smile at Grandmother and stick my tongue out at Alex.

"Very mature, Mr. Prince," Alex comments.

"Stop it, you two. You both should be happy that you have a loving family. Now, behave. Where was I? Oh yeah, your mother loved it here. It used to be so different. We accidentally got in the middle of the queen's guards. Not sure how, but we were in the wrong place at the wrong time. We tried to hide as best we could. Your mother's water broke and out came Michael. How in the world that only Michael came out is something only your mother can answer. Michael was making such a racket, he let our location be known. Your brave mother got us out of there even after giving birth. Her strength had to be zero, but she never stopped. I couldn't keep up with her, and we had to split up. I guess she made it back to Grock. Michael and I were found, then taken back to the palace. That was the last time I saw your mother, until now. It's been sixteen long years."

Grandmother's tears overflow onto her cheeks. Chloe joins her, and soon everyone is crying.

"It's okay, Grandma. We're here to take you home. Grandpa is waiting for you, and as soon as Mom gets back, we're all leaving," Alex reminds everyone.

I think, *I'm not going anywhere.*

Grandma wipes her tears and resumes her story. "We named him Michael Dylan. I'm guessing she had her second baby, you,"—she points directly at me—"when she returned home."

"Hey, my name is Dylan Michael. That's cool. I have a brother. I knew it."

"Cool it, Prince Dimwit. Please finish, Grandma." Alex smiles.

"When we got back to the palace, Michael and I were whisked away to the queen's chambers. It turned out the queen had a miscarriage. She made a deal with me that she would take Michael and let me live as her slave, or what she called a handmaiden. If I told anyone, she would kill Michael first, then me. She did let Michael keep his name."

Chloe says, "That's not very nice, Grandma. She's so mean."

"Yes, sweetie, she is. She is gone, and we are all safe. The prince's given name is Michael. The king officially named him Prince Mako."

Jelab enters the room and addresses me. "I'm sorry to disturb you, Your Highness. You are needed for a brief moment." He smiles.

"Yes, I'll be right there. Maybe you can finish your story when I get back."

I depart, and Jelab guides me into another grand room. And there, lying on the floor, is an enormous saber-toothed tiger. It seems to be dead.

"Who's that?"

"That is Grando, son of the great Grande."

"Where is Grande?"

"We do not know. His loyalties are to the king. He was last seen with the queen."

"What shall we do with his body?"

"I'll let you know."

I depart and go back to my chambers.

Alex asks, "What was that all about?"

"I was shown the dead body of Grando."

"Whose body, did you say?" Chloe asks.

"Grando, son of the great Grande."

Soon Chloe and Alex are in tears once again.

"He … saved … my life," Chloe says between sobs.

"Mine too," Alex says. "He saved both our lives. Can we see him?"

"Are you sure you want to? He's dead."

"Yes, I'm sure. He was very brave, and too young to die. He saved my life."

"Mine too." Chloe solemnly smiles.

"His dad was an arrogant ass," Grandmother adds.

Chloe screams, "Grandma, you said a bad word. I'm telling Mom."

"I'm sorry, sweetie, but he is. Grande was the king's head guard, and rumors are he killed his own wife, and now, possibly, both his sons."

I say, "Grando kept me alive. He protected me from the king's guards, and he should have a nice send-off."

Alex sobs.

"Yes, he should, Dylan—oops, I mean, Mr. Prince guy." Chloe shrugs.

"I'm guessing the king never found out the truth about Michael not being his child," Grandma says.

"Mom told him the real story. I kind of feel sorry for the king," Alex responds.

"Alex, you may be right," Grandma replies. "It would be sad to find out on your deathbed that the child you raised was actually someone else's."

"Grandma," Alex says, "are you telling us that Mom has been aware of Michael this entire time?"

"I would think so. She didn't know if we were both dead or alive. And there is no way she knew he would become the prince. I'm not sure how she dealt with the situation all this time. Your mom is one brave woman."

"You're telling me. She's always been my hero," Chloe announces.

"Did anyone else know?" I ask.

"Her brother may have known. Your uncle Tony was coming here a lot."

I ask, "Why didn't Mom come back for you sooner?"

"I'm sure she had her reasons. The transporters have been sabotaged."

"Transporters," I mumble.

"My blue pillowcase is actually a trans-portal," Grandma says, smiling.

"Oh yeah, that thing. I really didn't think it would work. It should be a case for the feds to investigate. They could call it 'The Blue Pillow Case.' "

"There is a transporter in the palace, but it was destroyed," Grandma tells us.

Chapter 16

SAN FRAN

After watching all of San Francisco slip into the bay, Matt and Tony think the world is coming to an end.

"Do you think my explosion caused all this?" Michael asks while staring out of the window of Tony's plane.

"You can bet it did. What did you think it was going to do?" Tony asks.

"Like I said, I wasn't sure. Grull said, 'It will have minimal effect on the concrete-dwellers.' I had no idea how populated this area is."

"You call this minimal?" Tony points out the window.

"Tony, I actually believe him." Matt shakes his head in the affirmative.

Michael lowers his head and shakes it back and forth, mumbling over and over, "I really had no idea."

"Anything else you want to tell us that we may have overlooked?" Matt asks.

"Are you asking, did we plant any more bombs anywhere else in this country? Not that I am aware of. After a few aftershocks, the fault will close back up. Then the kingdom should be well replenished with much-needed water."

Tony asks, “Would Grull let you in on everything?”

“Yes, he reports to my father, and would not dare be insubordinate.”

“I’m not so sure of that. I guess we shall see. Can I see that vial Grull gave you?”

“Why not? Grull said, ‘It is your transport potion to get back to the kingdom.’ ”

“Do you mind if I test it? I have a mini-laboratory on board. I think it’s poison.”

Michael reaches into his pouch, pulls out the vial, and hands it to Tony.

Tony starts to perform a diagnosis of the vial’s contents.

“Anything else in your little purse?” Matt smiles.

“Nothing that would concern you,” Michael answers.

“I’ll be the judge.”

“Your friend here isn’t very nice,” Michael comments.

“I know. You’ll get used to him. Dump out your contents and make him happy, please,” Tony retorts.

Matt sifts through the contents. He finds a wallet, a golden emerald bracelet, a hotel key, a hairbrush, a bottle of cologne, and a picture of Tony’s family. In the wallet, Matt finds Dylan Cabrella’s picture ID.

“Botulinum toxin,” Tony announces.

“What’s that, Doc?” Matt smiles.

“Botulism is in the vial.”

“What’s that?” Michael wonders aloud.

“This stuff would transport you to another kingdom, alright. The kingdom of death. One nanogram per kilogram can kill a human.”

“In layman’s terms, please, Doc?” Matt pleads.

“It’s poisonous, and drinking this vial would kill you instantly.”

“That’s impossible,” Michael replies.

“I can assure you this test doesn’t lie. Your friend Grull and Tragoon have already left you. I wonder how Grull is going to explain where you are and why you haven't returned. When they realize you have not arrived back home, do you think they may come back looking for you?" Tony asks.

"Are you sure that it is a poison? You know that stuff is very complex. Maybe you are incorrect in your assessment." Michael tries to smile.

"I tested it twice. It's toxic, alright. Want to try it, have a go?"

"No thanks, I'll pass."

"Why would Grull want you dead? Does Grull work for your father?" Tony asks.

"Everyone works for my father, the king."

"Would Grull try and overthrow your father?"

"I doubt he would try. He has no army, that I'm aware of."

"Well, someone wanted you dead. Can you think of anyone close to you?" Tony grins.

"Are you suggesting my father wants to kill me?"

"No, I'm really trying to figure out who. Someone definitely wanted you out of the picture."

"My father and mother love me."

"Would your mother become queen if your father passed on?"

"Yes, possibly. So now you think my own mother would have me killed?"

"No, I'm trying to figure it out for you. If you died, would anything change in your kingdom?"

"No, not really."

"What if the king passed?"

"That's a different story. Someone would have to replace the king."

"And who would that be?"

"Me. I'm the prince."

"No, you're dead."

"Then it would be my mother, the queen."

"I see. And yet you don't think she would be the one trying to kill you?"

"I can't imagine. She does like power, but I don't believe your theory is accurate."

"What if she died?"

"Nothing changes. The king remains," Michael answers.

"Listen to this," Torch, the pilot, announces over the intercom.

"A massive ten-point zero earthquake may have been the cause of this unbelievable and most devastating sight we have ever seen. The entire San Francisco coastline is now in the ocean. We are only guessing on what happened, since no official reports are in. We are being told the entire coast, from San Francisco to Los Angeles, is underwater. There are so many dead, with so many unknowns. It is very difficult to make any comment. This is not a joke, this is real …."

Michael starts feeling nervous and sick because the devastation is so catastrophic, and begins to worry about his own life. He wonders who would want him dead. This trip has turned upside down and is very confusing. And his birthday celebration was not as expected.

"Holy Toledo!" Matt exclaims.

"Man, that's some crazy stuff," Torch says, and turns off the speaker.

Tony says, "Does that sound minimal, Michael? Why in the world would you need to blow up the entire coastline?"

"We needed water, or my people would have disappeared."

"By disappear, you mean die, I assume." Tony glares at him.

In a defiant tone, Michael replies, "Yes!"

"Seems like a lot of death and destruction for my country to keep your kingdom alive. Is it customary for your kingdom to destroy other lands?"

"No. My kingdom critically needs water."

"Your world must be underneath us, if you need water to flow into your kingdom," Tony comments.

Matt asks, "Where is your kingdom located? Maybe we can fly there and get some answers."

"You cannot fly there."

"Tragoon must have flown here."

"Possibly."

"I'm going to say, unquestionably, and Grull rode him the entire way," Tony responds.

"Again, very possible."

"Then why can't we fly there?"

"Can your airplanes fly straight down a narrow air shaft for approximately two thousand miles?" Michael asks.

"That would be a big no."

"Then, again I say you can't fly there."

"Where is this air shaft?" Tony says.

"I do not know. I have never seen it."

"Maybe this will jog your memory." Matt stands up, ready to fight.

While holding up Dylan's ID, Tony says, "Let's change the subject. How did you get this?"

Michael mutters, "It was loaned to me by a friend of mine."

"Really, you know this guy? It says here you're Dylan Cabrella. How in the world did you get this?"

"We do look alike."

"Not what I asked." Tony smiles.

"Okay, I borrowed his ID."

"And where did you find it?"

"While traveling around."

"Let me finish the story for you. You found it in Key West, Florida, while rummaging through my sister's house, along with a picture of my family. And before I forget, happy birthday. Sorry it's not what you expected."

"Your sister's house. That would be an illogical coincidence."

"Then explain how you got there. I have you on breaking and entering, stealing. The police would love your explanation. Or you can tell us, and keep the police out of it. The police are the ones that can put you in prison."

"Is prison like a dungeon?" Michael asks.

Matt says, "Yes, very similar."

"Okay, I shall explain all the unusual events prior to my appearance here. I was transported to this strange house. Someone knocks me out. I awaken in another house, with people talking, eating, and drinking. They gag me and keep me dazed. Then I remember some girl waking me up and taking me to her house. I awake the next morning to an empty house. I look around and find that ID, which strangely looks like me, and take it. Plus, many photos of a young-looking Socreen. I take an automobile and drive it to Miami's airport, and fly out to San Francisco. So, you tell me why it's my fault. I think the police would like to ask you people some questions. Was that girl your daughter?"

"No, sir, she is my niece, Alessandra."

"Ask her if she's the one that came and got me."

"As soon as we find her, I will."

"Hey, you don't think I had anything to do with her disappearance!"

"You were the last one to see her alive," Tony declares.

"I never saw that girl ever again. I woke up, and she was gone. The house was completely empty, other than a couple of dogs."

"Doesn't that seem odd to you?"

"Yes, it did. What was I supposed to do, wait around till someone returned and found me, lost in someone else's dwelling? I quickly departed. I had to be somewhere. Not my fault she left."

"For your sake, she'd better be okay," Tony remarks.

Matt says, "It's probably best you didn't mess with her. She knows martial arts and would have torn you up."

"Torn me up. What does that mean?" Michael looks confused.

"Beat you up, critically."

"Sure she would," Michael says, and smiles.

Tony says, "Who is Socreen?"

Michael points to a woman in a photograph. "Her, that is Socreen."

"You know this woman?"

"Yes, she raised me. And why do you have a picture of her?"

"It's odd that you would ask me about a photo that you're carrying around. You may not believe me … but we will talk more when we land."

"Where are we going?" Michael asks.

"Santa Fe, New Mexico," Tony answers.

They arrive at Tony's house in Santa Fe, and are welcomed by Tony's dad, Vincenzo. Vincenzo knows that Matt and Tony were in San Francisco, and he has been very concerned about their well-being, seeing what happened there.

"It's like a movie scene. The entire city fell into the ocean. A huge earthquake, a re—." Vincenzo stops in midsentence. "Hey, sport, where have you been?" He's looking at Michael.

"Who are you?" Michael answers.

"It hasn't been that long, sport. Come on, give me a hug."

"Listen, Mister, I don't know you, and a hug is the last thing you're getting," Michael answers.

Grandpa looks at Tony and says, "What's with him, son?"

"His name is Michael. He's not Dylan," Tony replies.

"I'll be! He looks just like Dylan to me." Vincenzo shakes his head.

Jake walks into the room. "Hey, boss, I watch over everybody."

Jake is a young boy Tony and Matt hired to help them while in Africa, and he refuses to leave their side.

"Thanks, Jake. I knew you would be a big help around here." Matt smiles.

"Who's he?" Jake asks, pointing at Michael.

"He is my nephew, Michael."

"Okay, boss, I watch over him too."

"I don't need anyone watching over me. I can take care of myself." Michael leers at Jake.

Tony interjects. "Everyone must calm down, and let's all get some sleep."

Matt's cell phone starts ringing, "Lucy In The Sky With Diamonds."

"Hello, Mom."

"Oh, dear, are you okay?"

"Yes, Mom, I'm fine. I couldn't talk last night."

"Did you see what happened? Oh my goodness, the world's coming to an end. I told you God was upset with us."

"Yes, Mother, you have mentioned that a few times."

"What else could it be, son? Go to church Sunday. It would make me feel better."

"Okay, I'll try."

"Your father says we might as well travel around the country for a while. He wants to stay inland, away from any ocean views. You want to join us?"

"Wish I could. I may meet up with you later in your trip. Have a few things to tidy up. Maybe one day I'll surprise you guys."

"Oh, that would be wonderful. Your father would be so happy to see you. He would like to say hello. Jim, Jim, come say hello to your son. …… Of course he's busy right now. By busy, I mean he's on the toilet."

"Okay, Mom, thanks for the play-by-play." Matt grins.

"Bye, son. Be careful, love you."

"You too, Mom. Kiss Pop for me."

In the morning the television is on in the background. The earthquake is the only thing on the news, on every channel: devastating pictures of the new coastline, about five miles inland.

"There is a new coastline. If your house was in the desert, it now could be waterfront property. This is CNN reporting …"

Tony says, "Good morning, Michael. How did you sleep?"

"It was more comfortable than I would have imagined," Michael responds.

Michael still can't believe the destruction, and Tony has concerns that more explosions are coming.

Michael says, "I didn't think it would be that devastating, for some reason. There should be one more big aftershock. That is needed to fill the gap. I was told minimal lives would be lost. I guess I wanted to believe them."

"Who is them?" Tony asks.

"The king, Grull, and a few others."

Tony and Michael are finally alone. Many unanswered questions need clearing up.

Michael says, "Before I meet her, could you tell me something about your sister?"

"I'll do my best. Soon you can make your own decision. My sister Isabella, your mother, is really sweet, loving, and kind. Everyone likes her, human and animals. She is a well-established veterinarian, which adds the animals to the equation. I think she likes animals more than humans, but you didn't hear that from me."

"That's a noble profession," Michael replies.

"Indeed. Plus, she is very accomplished and enjoys her profession. Going to your kingdom has assisted her immensely because most of the animals can be understood. She would have prolonged conversations in which she learned a lot from those experiences."

"It sounds like you both have been to my kingdom," Michael says.

"Yes, many times. It has been over sixteen years since our—my last visit."

"That's very curious. My father did tell me our transporters have been down for quite some time."

"My sister and I have been trying to get back to the kingdom. Sixteen years ago, our mother and you were reluctantly left behind. We had no way of knowing if either one of you was still alive. Simply a fact, nothing morbid. We just didn't know. Of course, we desired that you both were doing well. I find out that you're the prince. Sorry, that one is a big surprise. Now it seems everyone in my family is in the kingdom."

"It seems we both have a big surprise. Your mother, what's her name?"

"Elizabeth Cabrella. She's the one in the photograph that you call Socreen."

"Yes. If I'm not mistaken, this one in the photograph is Socreen, and she basically raised me."

"Are you sure that woman in the picture is Socreen? If so, that confirms she's alive."

"Yes, I'm fairly certain that's her."

"Okay, let me grab a few more photos to really confuse you. Is this the girl who found you?"

"Yes, I'm certain she is."

"That's Alessandra, my niece. And standing next to her is my nephew, Dylan."

"Dylan and I look alike."

"Indeed you do. That's because you're identical twins."

"That's impossible!" Michael blurts out.

"Is it? Look at the photo and tell me again."

He examines it a few moments. "You make a valid point. How did all this happen?"

"I would prefer Isabella to elaborate on everything. She has probably pieced it all together, now that she has finally made her way back into the kingdom. We are leaving for Key West soon, and await her return."

Michael's mind is going at full tilt. He may have another family in a whole new world. Add in Socreen, who raised him. He was aware that Socreen was from the concrete country. Michael never envisioned her being his authentic grandmother. Did the king know? It's obvious the queen did.

Michael has no idea the king is dead, and the queen has escaped and is in exile.

The plan is for Tony, Vincenzo, and Michael to take a flight to Key West. Matt and Jake will drive Vincenzo's car cross-country to Key West.

Chapter 17

GUS

Everyone is waiting for Prince Mako to make his first public appearance since the king's demise. Finally, the kingdom is calming down after the king's death and the queen's disappearance. Very few know the real story.

The prince is now in charge of the entire kingdom, which includes all the palaces. His coronation will be in fourteen days.

Princess Xandra returns from her consultation with T.

"Mom, there is no way I can leave here. This place will come crumbling down, and the queen will return and destroy everything." I start begging my mother that I must stay behind.

"Listen, Dylan—oops, I'm sorry—Mr. Prince. The kingdom was here long before you, and it will still be here long after you. How can I allow you to stay behind? What if the real prince reappears?" Isabella is shaking her head, trying to control herself.

I put on my "please" face. "How about I stay for the summer and see how it goes?"

Isabella looks at Igagbee. "Will you talk to him for me? He doesn't seem to understand the complication of the situation.

He might listen to you. It is insane that we are even having this conversation."

"What if we build a transporter that can go from the palace, directly into your house? And vice versa?" Igagbee asks.

"You both have lost your minds."

"Mom, that does sound like a good idea," Alex meekly comments. "I can't believe I'm saying this, but if Dylan leaves now, this place will crumble and many will surely die."

"That way," Chloe says, "we can come back anytime, and I can visit all my new animal friends. I'm sure they will need some of our services."

"Oh my goodness, has everyone lost their minds? What is going on?" Isabella shakes her head. "Mother, you're my last hope. I need someone with some sense. What do you think?"

"I think they are right," Grandma says. "This place would collapse. However, if you could come visit anytime, it sounds like a great option. I'm never coming back here—that I can guarantee you. You guys could and should," she says. "I like the transporter idea directly into the palace. It's much safer that way."

"Mom, it will just be temporary, until we can find a replacement," I plead.

"We, who's we? You're not going to be involved with that decision."

"Mom, duhhh. I am the prince."

"Don't you duhhh me, son."

"Mom," Alex asks, "what ever happened to your other son, Michael?"

"That's for another discussion. Let's take care of one boy at a time."

"He's in the concrete country, your world," Igagbee comments.

"I thought so. I've met him." Alex smiles.

Everyone asks at once: "What! When?"

"I told Grandma the story. I was—"

Kati the Kondo knocks and then opens the massive door. "Excuse me, Your Highness. What do I do with Grando's body?"

"Any sign of Grande?"

"No, Your Highness."

"I want Grando to have a proper burial."

"Yes, Your Highness. Only royalty have proper burials."

"Not anymore," I rapidly reply. "Grando deserves a proper burial."

"How about a proper burial for Grando, next to his mother?"

A proper burial in the kingdom is actually a cremation.

"Yes, Your Highness, at once." Kati smiles, happy with that decision.

Igagbee says, "See, your son is already acting like a prince."

"This is what you are going to do," Isabella says. "I am losing my mind, like the rest of you. If Igagbee can guarantee me that a transporter will be direct from the palace to my house, I'm okay with a transitory short-term engagement. And if at any time I decide it's enough, you must come home, no questions asked. It's my final and last offer."

"No problem, Mom." I grin.

"Hmm, this is no joke," she replies. "This is not a game. I must be crazy. Maybe it's catchy. Okay, kids, Mother, we depart in the morning. Off to Grock we go, but the next time we return, it will be to and from a different portal, right?" Isabella stares directly at Igagbee.

"Yes," Igagbee replies. "Working on it right now."

My entire chamber starts shaking. At first I think we are under attack. Then it sounds like a loud argument outside my door.

"What is going on out there?"

I get up and open the massive doors. The voices and the yelling are earsplitting.

"Yes, we are!" Kati shouts.

"No, we are not!" Greg shouts.

"Yes, we are!" Kati shouts.

"No, we are not!" Greg shouts.

"Oh, sorry, Your Highness. Did we disturb you?" Greg the Graeter uneasily inquires.

"Yes, you are both rather loud. What is going on?"

"It's nothing, Your Highness." Kati grimaces.

"It doesn't sound like nothing, with you two screaming at each other. The entire palace is shaking. What is going on?" I demand.

"It's kind of silly." Kati grins.

"I'm listening."

Even though I am the prince, it's still hard to get too angry with a huge Kondo that's well over sixty feet tall, or with a giant Graeter. I think I should tread carefully.

"I told Greg we were boyfriend and girlfriend. And he said, no we are not. It's silly. I'm so sorry to disturb Your Highness." Kati holds her head down, sulking and sad.

What no one knows is that Kati and Greg are secretly seeing each other. Which would be a unique and odd couple. That's why no one suspects they are together.

I motion Jelab to come closer, and I whisper into his ear.

"Okay, okay. I pronounce you boyfriend and girlfriend."

"Oh, thank you, Your Highness." Kati is so delighted she picks up Greg and takes off, out of the room. And I hear Greg reply, "Thhhanks!"

He sounds somewhat pleased, I think.

"Again, he proves himself," Igagbee pronounces.

Isabella exclaims, "Get the transporter ready!"

People and creatures are coming from all over to greet me, and to tell me how sorry they are about the king's death. Lines and lines of humans and nonhumans, to pay their respects to the king. No one ever mentions the queen. Even Kaptuk makes an appearance. He is devastated over both deaths, and mostly saddened about Grando's demise. Kaptuk thought highly of Grando and has contempt for Grande.

Jelab mentions to me that some of the palace guards would like an audience.

"Of course, Jelab, let them in. I also would like to meet with my guards."

I think, *I am great, aren't I. Is there anyone better than me?*

"No, Your Highness, they want to meet with Princess Xandra. Most have never seen her. Only heard stories."

"Oh yes, of course. Let them in." *Okay, maybe I should be more modest. My bad.*

Some of the guards bow down in her presence. Others just stare.

"She doesn't look so tough to me," one says to his mate.

"Yeah? She took down a whole regiment all by herself, so calm down," he whispers back to his mate.

One of the guards steps forward. "I wanted to introduce myself. My name is Gus."

Gus is a strikingly good-looking fellow. Probably in his early twenties, over six feet tall, short crew cut blond hair, bright green eyes. Built like a bulldozer.

"Hello, Gus, it's a pleasure to meet you." Xandra glows.

"The pleasure is all mine, Princess Xandra. We may have met in the past."

"We have? When?"

"Many years ago. I used to play with the youngest girl."

"Really? You know Chloe? Are you sure?"

"Sorry, Princess, if I recall, her name is Alessandra."

"Oh my, that was a long time ago. How do you remember that far back? Is Gus your nickname?"

"Yes, Princess. I rarely use my given name since I have grown."

"What is your given name, if I may ask?"

"Asparagus."

"I do recall a young lad named Asparagus. You and my Alessandra used to play at Rock Lake. She was only five and you were probably around seven at the time."

"Yes, that is correct. Is she with you?"

"Who?"

"Alessandra."

"Yes, she is. Give me a moment. I'll bring her over."

"Thank you, Princess Xandra." Gus bows when she passes by him.

Xandra returns with Alex. Both Alex and Gus look bewitched. Alex is not happy that her mother didn't let her primp herself. Alex is looking at her mother as if to say, What were you thinking? Why didn't you tell me someone was asking for me?

I turn and try to listen to their conversation.

"Hello, my name is Alessandra, and who might you be?"

"My name is Gus. We used to play together by Rock Lake years ago."

"Really, and when was that?" Alex asks in a light voice.

Xandra says, "Dear, you were five. This is Asparagus. Don't you remember singing songs about asparagus when you returned home?" Xandra smiles.

"Mom. I don't need your input right now, thank you." Embarrassed, Alex turns bright red.

I can hear only bits of their conversation, and walk towards Gus. "Gus," I say, "why don't you stay a while?"

"Yes, Your Highness, if you wish."

If Alex falls for this big dude, then she will want to come back more often, and possibly get Mom off my back for staying. "Then it's settled. You two have a lot of catching up to do."

I've never seen Alex smile so much. Alex and Gus disappear into another room, acting like two giddy kids in a candy store.

"Your Highness, you have a guest. Tabitha."

I almost fall over, and my mother may have noticed. In my grown-up voice I say, "Send her in, please. Thank you." I haven't seen Tabitha in a while. I begin to sweat. I wonder if she realizes I want her to be my princess. Maybe, probably … oh, I'm getting way ahead of myself.

Mom asks, "Prince, are you okay?"

"Yes, why do you ask?"

"You look pale."

"Leave me alone." I grimace.

"Your Highness, thank you for inviting me to the palace," Tabitha says.

"You are welcome here anytime. Where is Pup?"

Tabitha despises this place. She was originally invited by me, to my most awesome birthday party, which has now turned into a funeral gathering. Tabitha had been summoned to attend and wasn't aware that the celebratory party functions were cancelled.

"Pup is in the palace pen. Don't forget, I am considered a rebel. I'm surprised they let me in without incident. Since you invited me here, it was easier than I imagined," Tabitha explains.

"How have you been?" I ask, feeling lightheaded.

"Fine. I'm sorry to hear about the king."

"Thank you. I miss him more than you can imagine." I figure someone could be listening and I'd better make it look good. "Would you like to stay here for a few days?"

"I haven't planned on it," she replies.

A side door opens. I can hear laughter and see Alex with Gus. I watch Tabitha turn around to see where the laughter is coming from, and I notice her unusual facial expression.

"Gus, is that you?" Tabitha says as she stares at him.

"Oh, hi. Hello, Tabitha," Gus says, surprised to see her.

"You two know each other?" I ask.

"Yes, we have met, Your Highness," Gus replies.

"Isn't that special." I smile.

"Tabitha, is there anything you would like to add?" I ask, trying to determine how she knows this Gus fellow.

"No, Your Highness. Nothing to add, thank you."

My sister Alex, who has never backed down from anyone, comes right up to Gus. "Who is your friend, Gus?" she asks.

This makes Gus uneasy. "This is Tabitha." Gus sheepishly smiles.

"Oh yes, now I remember. I have met Tabitha. She and Pup saved me and my sister. Hello again." Alex grabs Gus's hand.

"You know, Your Highness, I will take you up on your offer to stay in the palace for a few days." Tabitha grins while staring at Gus.

"Perfect. It's a date, then. I mean great, great, not a date." *Oh no, she knows I'm an idiot. My true self is showing through. Snap out of it.* "Great, I am glad we all agree. I need to depart on some urgent business. Jelab, make arrangements for Tabitha's quarters. She's going to stay with us for a few days. And make sure Pup is comfortable."

"Yes, Your Highness."

Alex finally lets go of Gus's hand. She departs the chamber, almost yelling to make sure the entire world hears her: "Goodbye, Gus, I hope to see you tomorrow!"

What no one knows is that Gus is actually Tabitha's boyfriend. It's been secretive, since Gaylok probably would not have approved.

As I depart I pull Jelab off to the side. "Has anyone found out the cause of all this flooding?"

"It appears the king's men were successful. They have blasted a section of the concrete country's waterways and it has caused flooding in our kingdom."

"You mean this was done on purpose?"

"Yes, Your Highness. You were part of the mission, so I thought you would be aware of what caused this flooding. It came from someplace called San Francisco, California."

"Sure, sure, I know. I wanted to be certain. Thank you." I think, *I hope no one was hurt back home.*

I try to explain to Mom what has happened.

"Concrete country! What part of the concrete country?" Mom asks me.

"San Francisco, California." Then I lean over and whisper to her, "That's where the real prince was supposed to have been transported."

"Oh my. Do you think they blew up California?"

"Now, Mom, look who's talking cuckoo. No one blew up California."

**

"What are you doing here?" Gus asks Tabitha.

"*Why* were you holding her hand?" Tabitha responds.

"I wasn't. She was holding mine," Gus replies.

"Oh, what's the difference? You looked like you were about to kiss her."

"I haven't seen her in years. I . . . I . . . I was just being friendly."

"Friendly, I bet. You stay away from her. I saw the look in her eyes."

"What? Well, why did the prince invite you to stay here for a few days? And you said yes."

"I had to, so I could keep an eye on you two lovebirds."

"Lovebirds. What are you talking about? You're being ridiculous," Gus says.

Jelab enters the room and informs Gus that he has been summoned. Gus departs at once. And Tabitha storms off in the other direction, following Jelab to her chambers.

**

Chloe asks, "Mom, before we go, can Alex and I say goodbye to Pup?"

"Sure. Dylan—I mean, Mr. Prince. Can you get someone to show the girls where Pup is located?"

"Certainly. I'll have Jelab take care of it."

Gus is standing outside Alex's chambers, waiting for the girls.

Alex smiles radiantly at him. "It's a pleasure to see you again so soon."

"I was requested," a smiling Gus replies.

"Can we go, please!" Chloe exclaims. "I think you both are acting goofy. Let's go."

"Okay, we're coming," Alex replies.

When they arrive at Pup's location the guard reminds them not to get too close. "She's a handful," he says, and wanders off.

Without a care in the world, Chloe runs up to the giant fire-breathing dragon.

"Hello, Pup. I'm going to miss you. Thanks again for saving me and my sister."

Pup replies, "It was my pleasure, little one. You are always welcome at my home."

That is all Chloe needs to hear, and tries to hug the giant beast. Soon Pup is purring loudly.

Alex is not as frivolous with Pup. She is more skeptical, as most people would be.

"Thanks again, Pup, for all your help." Alex gives her a quick smile.

"You are welcome." And then more purring sounds when Chloe pets Pup.

"She's a magnificent beast, don't you think?" Gus asks Alex.

"Oh yes, she is marvelous. Tabitha is lucky to have her."

"I think they are lucky to have each other," Gus replies.

"You're probably right. What girl wouldn't want their own pet dragon to protect them?"

Alex leans into Gus, thinking, *He'd have to protect himself from me.*

Gus inquires, "What's it like in the concrete country? I have heard stories."

"Concrete country?"

"Yes, where you are from."

"Oh, Key West. It's awesome. You can see the sun shining and bright blue skies above. There is a lot to enjoy. Shopping is one of my favorite things to do."

"Shopping for what? We have everything here that you would possibly need." Gus scratches his head.

"You don't know what everything is until you come shop with me. We have everything and anything."

"What do you do in the concrete country?"

"I am still in college."

"College. We don't have that here."

"How does one get educated?"

"The palace teaches us everything we need to know."

"That sounds ridiculous and primitive. Have you ever been to what you call the concrete country?"

"No, but that would interest me." Gus smiles.

"Why don't you come visit me sometime?"

"I would like that."

"Okay then. Once the transporter is repaired, you should come and visit. I will take you on a shopping tour."

"What transporter?" Gus asks.

This conversation begins to get Pup's attention. Her friend Tabitha is dating Gus, so now Pup is listening to every word. The transporter is supposed to be a secret, but Alex is so excited about Gus, she's giving him way too much information.

"I'm ready, Alex, let's go." Chloe clutches Alex's arm and starts to pull.

"Okay, okay. Give me a minute," Alex quickly responds.

Gus walks them back to the prince's chamber and, as a goodbye, kisses Alex's hand.

Alex blushes all over, and Chloe rolls her eyes.

Chapter 18

TRANSPORTER

Everyone is really excited about heading back to Key West. I have been arguing with Mom the entire time because I do not plan to leave anytime soon. She finally gives in some more and is somewhat on board with my staying. You would have thought everyone is leaving the abyss and going to a place in paradise. This place is awesome. *What's wrong with everyone?* I wonder. It's an easy decision to stay in the palace.

I figure no harm can come to me while I'm in the palace. At least, I can't imagine any significant injury, with all these guards following my every move. All these funeral proceedings are bringing me down. There is so much unhappiness going on around here, I almost forget about Violet since I constantly think about Tabitha. Which I didn't think was ever going to be possible. *Could I possibly love two women at one time?*

"You know the rules. Build the transporter and any time I want you home, no argument. Right?" Mom reminds me.

"Right. I fully understand, for the one millionth time. Igagbee will have the transporter ready."

"Don't get smart with me. After summer break you are coming home. That will give them three months to find a replacement. You're coming home, with or without a replacement. Three months."

"Mom, why would they find someone to replace me? I'm the prince."

"See, that's where you are wrong. You are not the prince. If needed, they always have someone in mind."

"Mom, the queen will destroy this place. I need to protect it."

"Prote—three months! That is all you get. You kids ready?" Isabella is about to explode.

"Yes, we are all set. I am so ready to get back home," Alex responds.

Jelab announces, "The caravan is ready to take everyone to the subway."

Chloe runs up and hugs me. "I'm going to miss you this summer." She sheds a tear.

"I'm gone every summer anyway. I'll miss you too. Watch over Mom. You know she needs you nearby at all times. Keep an eye on Alex too." I see tears now dripping off Chloe's face. "Don't worry, you can come visit me anytime."

Chloe lights up and says, "Hear that, Mom? I've already been invited back."

Grandmother is crying so hard it's like another flood. "I just met you, but I feel like I've been with you forever. Stay safe and come back home soon, alright?"

"Yes, ma'am. I'll be fine. Tell Grandpa I'm okay and not to worry about a thing. I'll take care of everything."

"Okay, honey. You're a very brave young man," Grandmother says as she holds me, "and I'll pray for you every day."

Alex grabs me and squeezes me tightly. "Don't do anything stupid. This kingdom is in for a real roller coaster ride. I may be back, so keep my room clean."

"Okay, sis. You're welcome anytime."

"Thanks, little bro. I may have to give you a new nickname now that I have two bros." Alex grins.

"Mom, you look so glum. I'll be fine."

"I wish I could believe you. You're so young. I hope I'm doing the right thing. I want that transporter up and running tomorrow. You hear me, young man?"

"Yes, Mom. Igagbee is on it. He'll have it up and running in no time."

"Let's go, kids, before I change my mind." Mom hugs me so hard she won't let go.

"It's not the final goodbye yet. I'm riding with everybody on the subway," I remind them.

The caravan to take us to the subway is extremely long, even though the subway station is only a few hundred yards from the palace. If I were to pass on, no one knows who would replace me. All my advisors are having a spontaneous meeting to discuss the next in line. This, to me, could cause problems. If they don't like me and want to put in my replacement, I'm doomed. No election; it seems like it's the advisors' decision.

I make sure Gus is on the subway with us. I want him close to Alex. If Alex falls for this guy, maybe it will keep Mom off my back. And throw in the possibility of making Tabitha jealous. I tried to get Tabitha to ride the subway with us, but she declined. She wants to fly with Pup. I think she and Gus are fighting, which is okay by me.

We all board the subway. Chloe is leading the way while talking with Greg the Graeter, followed by Alex, Grandmother, Mom, and then me, plus a few hundred guards. The royal subway is like a traveling fortress. The cars are magnificently decorated: gold, diamonds, rubies, and emeralds everywhere. I am not sure if the royal guards are guarding me or the valuable trinkets. Chloe sits next to Mom, and I sit across from them both.

Chloe gets up and asks Greg, "Why are you so sad? I'll be back to visit."

"I know you will. I miss Kati. We are together so much, I miss her when we are apart. She cannot fit on the subway." Greg grins.

So far, no issues or problems while traveling to Rockland. The plan is that the Trefars will meet us at the Rockland station and from there they will take us to Grock. Mom didn't want the royal guards knowing that Grock is the actual transportal. Otherwise, they would destroy it for sure.

I depart the main car and walk around to another. When the subway goes under the water, I look out the window and see a huge creature swimming next to the subway. I have never seen anything that large in my life.

I ask one of the guards, "What is that?"

"That is Megan, Sire."

"She has a name?"

"Yes, Sire. She is one of the largest from the white shark family."

"I had no idea they could get that large."

"She protects the royal subway from any predators, my prince."

"I bet she does," I mumble. Then I think, *How do they know it's a she? She looks like a megalodon, and I thought they were extinct. Thank goodness that thing wasn't the one that attacked me.*

The subway departs the water and is now back on dry land.

The landscape looks dramatically different since the floodwater is covering most of the land. It no longer looks like a desert. The land looks more beautiful than ever, with water flowing in the creeks and the ponds filled up.

We arrive safely at the Rockland station, and all I can see is a wall of elephants. I guess T wants to make a statement. The royal guards get very nervous when Trefars are nearby, even though there is no reason for a battle. Gus and Alex moved to the back of our subway car and have been conversing the entire trip. Gus jumps up when he sees all the Trefars.

I'm not sure how I missed her, but as we slow down and pull into the Rockland station, Kati the Kondo is standing there. Greg sees her and runs out the door, knocking over a few guards. As our group departs the station, I see Kati's face, which wears a wide grin.

"How did you get here so quickly?" Greg asks.

"My new shoes are wonderful. The prince asked me if he could do anything for me, and I said my feet are always cold and a pair of shoes would be splendid. And lo and behold, see? I'm wearing them. They are a size sixty, 'specially made for me. I'll be forever in the prince's debt. I love them, especially this color pink, my favorite. So I ran here. I need to rest a minute."

I think, *That must have been a sight!*

I have had the royal guards remove Hari's casket from the subway.

An unknown Trefars walks over and says, "Thank you. I will take it from here."

Before I know it, Hari is whisked away. Mom had asked T if the Trefars wouldn't mind performing a proper burial for Hari.

"Well, did you ask him yet?" Kati questions Greg.

"Yes, I did."

"And what did he say?"

"He said, 'Enjoy your time off, and I will see you in six days.' "

After hearing the good news, Kati scoops up Greg and takes off running. The Trefars accompany us on our way to Grock.

"They are so cute," Chloe observes.

"Hari means a lot to me, and I cannot thank you enough," Isabella says to T.

"It's my pleasure. Goodbye, my friend. I'm sure we shall meet again, possibly very soon." T waves.

"T, thanks again for looking after my Dylan—I mean, Mr. Prince. I really appreciate it. Knowing that you will keep an eye on him does make me feel a little better."

"Igagbee will keep me updated. Tara is already inside."

"Great," Isabella says. "May I ask you a question?"

"Certainly."

"How did you know it was time to build a giant moat to protect your people?"

"Fortunate, I suppose." T smiles.

"Yeah, right. Fortunate. Is there anything I need to know about your mom?"

"She is very self-sufficient and has packed all the food she requires."

"What if she runs out?"

"She will not."

"If Tara passes, you want me to bury her at sea, correct?" Isabella raises her eyebrows.

"Yes, and here is a token of my appreciation."

T hands Isabella what looks like a small hand-carved knife.

"What is it?"

"It's a knife my mother made years ago. The blade is made entirely from a solid piece of crystal."

"I can't accept this. It's priceless. It's worth billions. It looks like a solid diamond."

"Worth nothing to me. I have plenty. Please accept this. Tara wants you to have it and she will be very upset if you don't take it."

"Oh my goodness, this is way too much. Thanks."

"No, thank you again. One more thing. Be vigilant."

Vigilant. Why? Isabella wonders. She turns the knife over and sees an inscription that she doesn't recognize. "What's this say? Is that 'good knife'?"

T smirks. "Close. It says 'good knight.' "

"I didn't know you Trefars have a sense of humor."

"There is a lot you don't know. Goodbye."

In a blink, the entire herd of elephants carrying the Trefars lumbers off.

Isabella can't keep from staring at this marvelous knife. *How in the world do you grind down a diamond into a blade? The size of that diamond must have been massive. Where are the rest of the pieces?*

Chloe asks, "What's that, Mom?"

"A present from T. Let's get everyone and go home, baby."

"Okay, I'll get Alex. She's probably kissy-face with that Gus guy." Chloe grimaces.

Alex says, "Thank you for everything, Gus."

"It was my pleasure, Alessandra."

"I am truly happy that we ran into each other again."

"Me too. I really thought it was just my imagination," Gus says, beaming.

I am watching and smiling. If Gus falls for Alex, Tabitha will need consoling. And who's a better consoler than I!

"Dylan, you come inside with us." Mom grabs my shoulder.

"Yes, Mom. But I'm the prince."

"Not out here, you're not. No one can hear us."

Gus grabs Alex's hand. Tabitha and Pup are nearby, watching. Gus realizes Tabitha is watching and decides to bow instead of kissing Alex's hand.

Chloe yells out, "Alex, it's time to go. Mom's ready."

And Alex does the unthinkable, and kisses Gus on the cheek and yells back, "Coming."

That sets off Tabitha, as Gus knew it would. Before Gus takes another step, Tabitha confronts him.

"What in the world was that?" Tabitha inquires, frowning.

"She kissed me goodbye, that's all. She's leaving, probably never to be seen again."

"Any more kisses like that, and your little friend will be missing her sweet little head."

"Come on, sweetie, she means nothing to me. You're the only girl for me, I swear," Gus pleads.

"Don't sweetie me. Go wash your face. That tramp is lucky I saved her life. I won't be that kind next time," Tabitha states. "I don't like others kissing you. Do you understand?"

Tabitha has never been the jealous type. Maybe being back in Rockland and all the memories of Gaylok have set her off.

"Okay, never again. Understood. Geez, calm down," Gus pleads.

"Calm down? You calm it down."

Pup intercedes and tries to calm Tabitha, but she doesn't succeed.

"I'm taking the subway back with the prince," Tabitha says. "Gus, you can ride back on your own. Pup, I'll see you at the palace."

Pup, not wanting to get in the middle of this lovers' quarrel, says, "Yes, will do."

At that moment, Pup feels a little sorry for Gus. Tabitha leaves in a huff.

"Where is the prince?" Tabitha asks a royal guard.

"We are awaiting his return."

"Okay, I shall wait with you."

Grock must see us, and a hole in the rock hut opens. Inside, I hardly recognize Tara. She is wrapped up in a blanket, speaking with Grock.

Isabella says, "Hello, Tara. Are you ready to travel?"

"Yes, dear, I'm ready. I brought you a gift."

"I already got your gift from T."

"That was nothing. This is your real gift." She points to what looks like replicas of Lil Magik and Big Magik. "I know you must have lost them in battle, so I wanted you to have replacements."

"How did you … never mind. Thanks. You are too kind."

Then, in a booming voice, Grock bellows, "*Hello*, how is everyone? So glad to see you all. This is the largest group I have had in a while and I cannot wait for a nice long chat."

"Yes, Grock. We are in a big hurry and next time we will have a nice long chat." Isabella sighs.

"I understand, and next time we shall have a nice long chat."

"Yes, indeed. Dylan will be staying behind. You can let him out in a minute," Isabella reluctantly tells Grock.

The kisses and hugging and crying start up again.

"Mom, no more tears, please. Everything will be fine."

"Okay, Dylan. We have a deal, right? I hope you know what you're doing."

"I also hope I know what I'm doing. Yes, Mother, we have a deal."

Chloe and Alex grab me for one last hug. I grab Grandmother and pull her in for a group hug.

"Don't forget to tell Grandpa hello."

"I will, dear. We will miss you terribly. Are you sure you want to stay?"

"Mom, explain to Grandmother our deal again."

I see the blue pillowcase and think about the blue pillowcase in the kingdom. It should be a case for the FBI, named "The Blue Pillow Case." That pillowcase is cursed, for sure. I blow some kisses. A crack opens in the rock hut, and I slip outside.

"Mom, where are we going?" Chloe asks.

"Home, sweetie. This will take us directly to our house. Hold on to my hand and don't let go."

"Don't have to worry about that, I'm holding it forever."

"How about you, Mom," Isabella says, "you ready to see Dad?"

"I'm ready to see that old goat. I miss him more than *air* itself."

"Okay, everyone, hold hands and let's go home."

Chloe, Alex, Grandmother Elizabeth, Tara, and Isabella each grasp a hand tightly. Isabella lays her head upon the blue pillowcase, and they all disappear.

**

I get back to the subway and see Tabitha standing outside.

"This is a nice surprise. What can I do for you?"

"May I get a ride back to the palace with you?" Tabitha asks.

Before I step on my tongue, I think and, in my sophisticated voice, say, "Yes, surely. Of course, please do." I need to calm down—my blood pressure may be up.

"Where is your friend Pus?" I ask.

"You mean Gus?"

"Yes, Gus."

"He is riding a horse back. He needs some fresh air to compose himself. He's acting like a complete fool. I—you know, I'd rather not talk about him." Tabitha smiles.

Works for me, I'm thinking. *This may be the greatest ride ever.*

She says, "Maybe this ride will be better than the last time, when we almost drowned."

"I hope so," I reply. "I didn't bring any swim trunks."

We both laugh. Out of the corner of my eye, I see Gus watching us walk back to the subway. I'd better watch him. He's a big dude. Ah, I forgot, I'm the prince. I could probably have his head cut off. *Wow, I need to stop thinking like that.*

"Where are my manners? Are you hungry? Watch this. Food, please."

"Yes, Your Highness, at once."

Shortly after we sit, food tray after food tray is being brought in.

"Isn't this a waste of good food? Who will eat all this?" Tabitha remarks.

"I thought you were hungry," I reply.

"Not this hungry."

"What did I do? I can see that you are extremely upset."

"I'm sorry. It's nothing you did. I hate all men right now."

"All men?"

"Not really. Just one. I'll be fine. He doesn't have to be nice to everyone, does he?"

"Who is too nice, me?"

"No, not you," Tabitha replies. At that moment Tabitha finally breaks down and starts crying hysterically.

I ask everyone to leave us.

Tabitha's words burst out. "I miss him so much—I'm lost without him!"

"It's okay. He'll be back at the palace soon enough. I'll have him—"

"Not Gus, you moron, it's Gaylok I miss."

"Oh yes, Gaylok." I should have seen that coming. So much for my being a mind reader.

I let her cry until she calms down. "Maybe I can have a monument placed in his honor," I remark.

"Really? The royals who killed Gaylok and all their friends are going to honor him with a statue. Have you thought this through? Or do you always say stupid things?"

Oh boy. I'd better stop talking. Is it me, or is it true the angrier Tabitha gets, the prettier she looks? Maybe there is something wrong with me.

"By the way, what happens when the real prince returns?" Tabitha asks.

"I have been thinking about that."

"What are you going to do?"

"I was hoping the transporter will be ready, and I will get out of here."

"Really? I was beginning to like you."

What's going on? Two minutes ago she hated all men, now she's flirting with me. I need someone to give me some advice on women. Who shall I ask? I could have asked Alex. What does she know. "I really like you, too." *Did I say that out loud?*

"You do, I knew that. What are you going to do about it?"

"What, do, what, what?" I think I turned purple.

Then the subway ducks underwater, and I change the subject on a dime.

"Hey, look, we're underwater and still moving." What would dare attack while Megan is on watch?

"Yes, we are. It's so romantic, isn't it?"

"I guess so."

"Why don't you come sit next to me?" Tabitha taps the couch cushion.

"I'm okay over here."

"Aah, you're shy. That is so cute. Come on over, I won't bite."

Tabitha takes her cap off and shakes her head. Consequently, her hair is cascading from the top of her head. This is the first time I have ever seen her hair and it reminds me of a raging waterfall. She is always wearing a cap or hat. Her hair is bright red and very long. It's flowing past her shoulders and it looks luminous.

I think, *That must be her natural color and it's kind of cool looking.*

"Oh, okay. Your view isn't as nice on that side of the room," I reply, blushing.

I move over to Tabitha's couch, and someone raps at the door. "Your Highness."

"*What?* I'm busy." I slide back to my side and notice the subway has stopped. We have left the water and are now back on land. "What is it? I do not want to be disturbed."

"Yes, Your Highness, so sorry. Someone is blocking the subway."

"Can't you move them so we can proceed? I'm kind of busy here."

"No, Your Highness. It's Tragoon."

"Trago. What's that?"

"Tragoon, Your Highness."

Tabitha, instantly at my side, whispers in my ear, "It's a dragon. His name is Tragoon and you know him well."

"Yes, of course, Tragoon. I couldn't hear you the first time. What does he want?"

"He has asked for you."

"Now is not a good time for me. Set up a meeting at the palace."

"Yes, Your Highness."

Just my luck! Tabitha was starting to warm up to my advances, and now this Tragoon thing.

I say to her, "Where were we?"

"Are you kidding me? Tragoon will kill Pup. I'm out of here." Tabitha departs in a flash.

"But, but what about us?" That went sideways quick. I hate that Tragoon thing, messing up my day. I had her right where I wanted. I'm thinking of my first edict: Tragoon dies.

Pup is watching Tragoon and sees Tabitha exit the subway. Since Grull is riding on the back of Tragoon, he is not prepared for a fight at this time. Tragoon takes off with Grull. What a battle that would be!

The subway starts to move again.

Back at the palace, I storm in. I get to my chamber as Jelab arrives with a plate of my favorite foods.

"Welcome home, my prince. How was your journey?"

"It was lousy, and I'm not hungry."

"Sorry, Your Highness. Where is Tabitha?"

"Hence the problem. She dumped me at the subway. She's nuts, just like the rest of them."

"Yes, Your Highness. How about a soak? That should cheer you up."

"Yes, that would cheer me up. I would like a soak. A full soak, Jelab."

That would cheer up anyone, I'm thinking. *I hope he understands that when I say a full soak, that means water nymphs.*

"Yes, at once, Your Highness."

Chapter 19

HOME

It is something more than a miracle when Isabella returns safely home to Key West, Florida, with Elizabeth, Chloe, Alex, and Tara. The first call Isabella makes is to her brother Tony.

"Oh my goodness!" Tony exclaims. "That is the best news I have ever heard in my entire life! Let me put you on speakerphone."

"Hello, everyone. Guess what? I'm so excited I can hardly talk," Isabella says. "I'm sitting in the den with Alessandra, Chloe, and Mom. Hey, Dad, Mom is here and she can't wait to see you. She's so excited, I'm not sure she can talk."

Isabella leaves out the part that Tara came back with her. Tony may not understand, so she will explain it to him later.

"Hello, my love. Hurry home, I need a bear hug." Grandma begins to tremble.

He starts crying and can't speak.

"Sensational—excellent news. We are packing up and leaving right away. See you soon, sis. Great job." Tony takes her off speakerphone and walks into another room to finish their conversation in private.

"Sorry I wasn't much help. Where's Dylan?" Tony asks.

"That's another story. He stayed behind. He is now the prince. It's a long, long story, and I would rather tell you when you get here. I'm not happy about it."

"Okay then, it's my turn, and I hope you're sitting down. I will be bringing your other son, Michael. He's here with me."

After a long pause, Isabella cautiously asks, "Are you serious? He's with you? How did you pull that off? Now, that is excellent news. How's he doing?"

"Another long story. I want you to tell him what's going on and what's been happening in the kingdom. He's been to your house and saw all your pictures, and is very confused," Tony replies.

"I bet he is. Do you think he'll ever forgive me?" Isabella asks.

"Sis, he will love you. You're his mother. Don't worry, he's a nice kid. Just been brought up a little differently than most. He's a sixteen-year-old that's been raised to act much older than his actual age. I've got to go pack. I want to leave at once."

"You'd better. See you soon. When you're on the plane, give me your estimated arrival time."

"Will do. Love you. See you this evening."

Tony walks back into the den. "Dad, how are you feeling? I bet you're on cloud ninety-nine."

"Son, if I could explain my feelings, I wouldn't know where to start. I love your mother beyond anything else, and I'm not sure how to act. Do you think she still loves me?" Vincenzo asks.

"Dad, you must be joking. You two make Romeo and Juliet seem dull."

"Okay, everyone, let's all get packed and ready to roll in five," Tony announces. "Michael, remember the first house you were transported to by mistake? We are heading to the airport now and flying there."

"The place that has all the unexplained pictures?"

"Yes, one and the same. Plus, my mother will also be there. You know her as Socreen."

"Socreen? Really. This is going to be bizarre! I have so many questions."

"Save them for my sister Isabella, your real mother. She should be able to answer most of your questions."

"Bye, Matt," Vincenzo says, turning to him and Jake. "You two be careful with my machine. She's a beauty, and I would like to see her again."

"Are you talking about your car or your wife?" Matt smiles.

"You two enjoy. Jake, keep an eye on him. He needs constant care." Tony hugs Matt and Jake goodbye.

Then Tony and Vincenzo start packing for their flight to Key West. Michael doesn't have anything to pack.

**

"Hey, Torch, you remember my father, Vincenzo?" Tony says when they enter the plane's cabin. "We are ready when you are."

"Sure do. Welcome aboard. Key West is our next stop," Torch broadcasts.

"Could you show me how to fly this machine?" Michael asks.

"Sure. We can start with this flight." Tony smiles.

Torch announces, "Waiting for the tower for departure. Should be a smooth flight, no storms brewing as of now."

**

Isabella is excited about the entire situation, though she is a nervous wreck about meeting Michael for the first time. The last time she saw Michael was when she gave birth to him. Alex can sense Isabella's anxiety and embraces her mother.

"Mom, I finally took a thirty-minute shower, and may never leave this place again. I'm sorry, that kingdom place is horrible. Why did you go back so often?" Alex asks.

"It was a much different place years ago," Isabella replies.

"Whatever. It sure is dreadful now. I hope Dylan knows what he's doing. The only reason I would go back is to see Gus again. He's the only thing in that place worth visiting. They are so out of touch with reality."

"I think that's on purpose, Alex. I've got to make sure Tara is all set up and comfortable. I'll be right back," Isabella says.

Tara is staying in Isabella's guest quarters. It's detached from the main house, but not far from it. Basically, another great view overlooking the water.

"Hello, Tara. Is there anything I can get for you?" Isabella asks.

"No, thank you, my dear. You have a lovely home and a magnificent view, one that I never would have imagined. Thank you again. I wish T could see this." Tara smiles.

"Maybe one day he will visit."

"I doubt it, dear. He would never leave his beloved land. I needed to see this with my own eyes before they expire on me."

"My brother Tony is coming to visit, and he is bringing Michael with him."

"Michael, your firstborn. That should be exhilarating for you!" Tara exclaims.

"Exhilarating is probably right. I'm a nervous wreck and worried I'll do or say something wrong."

"Listen, dear. Women have been in charge for as long as my memory has served me, and whatever you say or do will be fine. These children have no idea what we go through every minute of every day. I still worry about T, which is senseless. It's what we mothers do. It makes you tougher than the next person."

"Thanks, Tara, I needed that. Good night."

Isabella thinks, *Getting advice from a four-hundred-year-old woman is somewhat comforting.*

**

Now that Dylan is alone, reality is starting to set in. *Am I really ready to run the entire kingdom? Now that the king and queen are gone, what am I supposed to do? A soak is exactly what I need to calm my nerves.* I slink into the warm water one more time.

Later, Jelab asks me, "How was your soak, Your Highness?"

"It was fine, thank you, Jelab. I was wondering what happened to my helpers."

"You need help, my prince?"

"No, no, the bathers, girl helpers." I am embarrassed to ask.

"You mean the water nymphs, Your Highness?"

"Yes, them."

"Oh! You have to request them. They thought you no longer needed or liked their services since you haven't requested them recently."

Oh, I can't be that stupid. "Yes, Jelab. I do like their services and would like to request them in advance for my next soak."

"They will be pleased, Your Highness."

That's all I had to do. I should have known it would be that easy. I am so stupid.

"I would like to take a walk around the palace."

"Of course. I will call your guards to escort you, Your Highness."

"Thank you, Jelab."

Jelab returns to my chambers with two giant guards. "Dank and Skame are here."

"Great, let's go."

"Yes, Your Highness. We are at your disposal."

"How's your day going, guys?"

Never having been directly addressed by royalty before, both guards stare at each other, not knowing how to respond.

Dank finally answers, "Good, Your Highness."

Skame is still speechless.

"Good," I respond.

I'm opening doors, going through hallways. I have no idea how big this place is, but it's the largest building I've ever seen. When people notice me, they stop whatever they're doing and bow. It's as if they have never seen royals walking the halls. I'm talking to people and asking questions. You'd think I have the plague.

"Dank, take me to the school."

"Yes, Your Highness. Follow us."

I have discovered that the schools here are very different from the States. Schools are mainly for teaching skills to keep the palace running smoothly. My first stop looks like a classroom full of eight- to ten-year-olds. I sense that these kids have never been this close to royalty.

"Good day, everyone. What are we studying today?" I ask.

A few hands shoot up. A young girl stands and says, "Are you Prince Mako?"

"Yes, I am. What is your question?"

"I would prefer to be with the animals," the little girl announces.

"Excuse me?"

"Don't worry about her, Your Highness, she's confused." The teacher grins. "She will be reprimanded. Sit down, Andi."

"No. Please continue. I would like to hear what Andi has to say."

"Yes, Your Highness."

"I like animals and don't like learning about generators."

"You see, Your Highness, her father works on the generators team, and we felt it best to keep it in the family. So—"

My hand has gone up to stop teacher Mimik. "Quiet. Continue, Andi."

"I want to work with the royal animals. I don't like generators. I would like animal care classes."

She sounds like Chloe, and I want to help the poor girl. "Then maybe you should be moved to the animal care class."

"Your Highness, that would—"

My hand is up again. "Tomorrow she gets transferred to animal care class."

"Yes, Your Highness, as you wish."

Before the guard can stop her, Andi runs up and hugs my leg. She can't be more than two and a half feet tall.

"Thank you, Prince Mako. I will study hard and be the best animal care person there."

"I'm sure you will."

I can tell Mimik is not happy with my decision, so I lean in and whisper to the teacher, "If any harm comes to Andi, I will hold you responsible."

"Yes, Your Highness." Mimik bows, with an unusual look on her face.

"Thank you all. I must be leaving now."

Dank and Skame follow me out of the classroom.

"I wish I could have asked to change professions. I wanted to be a beekeeper," Dank tells Skame.

"I know. You remind me daily," Skame replies.

Chapter 20

REUNION

The anxiety builds as Tony, Vincenzo, and Michael are on their way to Key West, Florida. They will meet up with Isabella, and hopefully a pleasant reunion will commence.

After the plane reaches cruising altitude, Michael suddenly realizes something. He points to Vincenzo. "This means you are my grandfather and Socreen is actually my grandmother."

"Yes, I believe it does." Tony smiles.

"This is so peculiar for me," Michael says.

Vincenzo replies, "It's scary for me too. I'm not sure what to say to his mother, or to you, for that matter. It's been so long." Vincenzo stares at Tony.

"I know, Dad. It's going to be alright. You know how much she loves you," Tony replies.

"Maybe I'll get her some flowers. She loves flowers."

"Yeah, Dad, that would be perfect."

"She also likes gelato. Maybe I'll get her some gelato. I can't remember her favorite flavor."

"Sounds perfect. She'll love whatever flavor you give her."

"You know, I've gotten older. She may not like the way I look."

"I bet you she will."

"Maybe she wants to break up with me. You know, it has been sixteen years."

"Dad, stop! All she wants is you. Don't worry. I doubt she waited sixteen years to come back, and then break up with you. You guys have never stopped being in love, so don't worry. Hold her tight and never let her go."

"That sounds about right, son. I just remembered the house is a mess. Oh my, that will upset her."

"Isabella has your house cleaned regularly, so don't worry." Tony smiles.

"Hey, Doc, I have a blip on the radar and it seems to be following our flight plan."

"Are you sure it's not another plane, Torch?"

"Could be, but I doubt it. It's not acting like another plane," Torch responds.

"Okay, keep on course." Tony imagines it could be Grull.

Tony's cell phone starts blaring "On a magic carpet ride / Well, you don't know."

"Hey, sis, we're in the air. You beat me to the phone," Tony says.

"Did you have anything to do with what happened in San Francisco?" Isabella asks.

"Let me say yes and no. It was the king's men who blew up the San Andreas fault line, which caused the entire city to collapse into the ocean. Absolutely horrific, and another long story. Matt and I barely escaped the catastrophic event. And that's where we snatched Michael."

"Tony, do you have any idea of the casualties? It's in the millions."

"I do realize the magnitude of the event. You could ask Michael when we arrive."

"What are you saying? Michael did this? I created a monster." Isabella starts to cry.

"Calm down, sis. He can explain it better than I. The kingdom needs water."

"Well, that explains a lot. I almost drowned while in the kingdom."

"Listen, sis, be watchful. I'm afraid part of the kingdom is here in America, and I don't know what they are up to. I'm fairly certain my flight is being followed."

"That's not good."

"We will catch up. I'll be there soon enough. Call that captain friend of yours."

"That's a good idea. Everyone here is worn out and sleeping. See you soon."

**

Captain Rogers's cell phone starts blaring "L is for the way you look at me."

"Hello, Isabella."

"Hey, Bill. I'm home, and I'm sure you have lots of questions."

"Not really. I'm just glad you're back home, safe and sound."

"Why don't you come by?"

"Are you kidding? I'm heading your way—the siren might be on."

"You're so silly. See you soon."

Captain Rogers arrives and clutches Isabella to plant a big kiss on her lips.

"If you promise not to ask any questions tonight, I'll give you some news," Isabella says, hugging the captain.

"Okay, it's a deal," the captain replies.

"Here goes. Tony, Dad, and Dylan are on their way back here to Key West, on Tony's jet. Dad and Dylan have been staying at Tony's house in Santa Fe."

"Why didn't you tell me that earlier? How did Dylan get—?"

"No questions. You agreed," Isabella states. She does not want to get into the fact that it isn't Dylan, but Michael.

"I'm sorry. You're right. Great news."

"I'm not finished. And no questions. I'm not really ready to answer any." Isabella starts to cry uncontrollably, and Captain Bill Rogers pulls her close and hugs her firmly.

"I'll cancel the APB and—"

"That's not it," she says, wiping her tears away. "Mom is back home."

"What are you saying? Your mother!"

"Yes, my mother is home, sleeping in her bed."

"Where was she, abducted by aliens?" the captain asks.

"Possibly. No questions, please. Not now. I'll explain later. Now hold me."

**

"Hey, Doc, whatever it was, it followed us the entire trip. Never landed, though."

"Thanks, Torch. I'll be here a while, so enjoy the town."

"Yellow Submarine" starts blaring on Isabella's phone. Having fallen asleep, Isabella jumps up to answer her phone, scaring the captain half to death.

"Hello!"

"It's me, we're here."

"What time is it?"

"One oh three a.m."

"Oh boy, I fell asleep. See you soon."

"Hey, babe, do you mind taking off?" Isabella asks the captain. "I want to see everyone on my own."

"You going to be okay?"

"Sure. Thanks for watching over me. I know I'm a wreck."

A car pulls into the driveway, and Chloe wakes up. She walks into the kitchen to find her mom pacing.

"Is that them, Mom?" Chloe asks.

"Yes, dear, I'm sure it is. Why don't you go back to bed."

"Oh, Mom, I want to meet Michael."

"Listen, sweetie. I'm sure this a lot for him to take in, and it's very late. First thing in the morning, I'll come get you. Okay?"

"Okay, I think I understand. Good night."

"Thank you. Good night, sweetie."

"I'm going to love him as much as I love Dylan." Chloe smiles.

"That's nice. He'll like that."

Isabella's heart jumps a beat when the front door opens. Even Brandi is awake and wagging her tail.

"Hey, babe!" Tony exclaims, and gives Isabella a big hug.

Isabella grabs her father and hugs him.

Michael is staring at everyone, and gives Isabella a little smile. He puts out his hand as if she is going to shake it. Isabella does shake it, not knowing what to do. He looks just like Dylan.

After a few minutes, Isabella suggests everyone goes to bed, saying, "It's late, and everybody can talk in the morning."

They nod in agreement.

"Dad, Mom is at your house, so you go on home."

"I'm a little scared. What do I say?"

"Come on, Dad, you'll figure it out. Go home. Take a golf cart."

"Okay, honey. Here goes nothing."

"Tony, you know where your room is, and I'll take Michael to Dylan's room," Isabella excitedly says.

While Isabella is walking with Michael, he stops and says, "I'm not comfortable calling you Mom. May I call you Isabella?"

"Yes, that would be fine."

"Good night, Isabella."

"Good night, Michael."

Vincenzo heads to his house, which is essentially next door to Isabella's. Vincenzo slowly opens his front door. He can see the light in the bedroom is on. He gently tiptoes through the house, towards his bedroom, and then he hears: "Take a shower and put on your pj's."

After his shower, he puts on his pj's and opens the bathroom door.

"Assume the position," is all Vincenzo hears.

He gets into the bed and lies on his back. Then his loving wife lays her head on his chest, and he starts to cry like a baby.

"Shoosh, quiet. No words need to be said."

Vincenzo mumbles, "I'm never letting you out of my sight, ever again."

"Deal," Grandma replies.

**

Isabella can't sleep and is sitting on the dock, waiting for the sunrise.

"May I join you?" Michael asks, with Brandi in tow.

"Yes, please do. You couldn't sleep either?"

"Not really. It's all so peculiar to me." Michael grins.

"I bet it is. It's a lot to take in."

"Did you recently return from my kingdom?"

"Yes," Isabella answers.

"Could you update me as to what is happening in my kingdom?"

"I shall try. I guess my brother filled you in on our family—your family?"

"Yes. He said you would inform me in much more detail."

"Did he also tell you that my other son, Dylan, and you, are identical twins?"

"Yes, again he said you would elaborate. Why don't you start by filling me in on current events in my kingdom?"

"Okay, I'll get right to it. The king is no longer living and the queen is in exile."

"By no longer living, you mean dead. How did the king die? Who killed my father? What do you mean, exile? I haven't been gone that long. How did all this happen so quickly?"

"I am fairly certain that the queen had the king killed, and is also trying to kill you, which is really your twin brother Dylan. She departed the palace soon after the king's death."

"I have an idea why she would want to kill the king. Why would she want to kill my twin brother? How did she know I have a twin?"

"The queen knew. Dylan replaced you when you departed."

"You're confusing me," Michael remarks.

"I'm so sorry. I'm nervous."

"Are you saying that Dylan is now the prince? And everyone is okay with this result? How did he get away with it? He should have been caught as a fraud."

"He should have, but the Trefars transformed him into you. The way you walk, talk, mannerisms, hairstyle, birthmarks, and it worked."

"You're really confusing me."

"Maybe I should start at the beginning," Isabella replies.

"Yes, please do. I want to hear everything."

"Sixteen years ago, I was visiting the kingdom with my mother, whom you refer to as Socreen. By the way, she doesn't like that name anymore, so when you speak with her, and only if you remember, she would prefer to be called Elizabeth. This whole ordeal has been tough on her. Sorry, I digress. My mother and I went to visit your kingdom, as we have done many times, and this time I was pregnant and wasn't aware that I would go into labor. I went into early labor, which then caused a premature birth at the most inopportune moment. You were ready to come into this world and came out you did. You were an easy birth, at the wrong time and in the wrong place.

"The queen's guardsmen located us. My mother and I tried to get back to the trans-portal and she couldn't keep up. The queen's men overtook you both. I, fortunately, escaped and got back to the trans-portal. I returned home and gave birth to Dylan. My mother and you were captured and brought back to the palace. I planned on returning as quickly as possible. It turned out that was impossible. You were so small, I wasn't sure you would survive. By the way, the queen had every one of those guardsmen killed. The secret could not be found out. It has taken me sixteen years to return to your kingdom. I never knew if you or my mother were alive. I would have never imagined that you would become the prince. I had no idea you guys were identical twins. I am so sorry."

"So, you went back home and forgot about me?" Michael comments.

"Oh, sweetie, I never forgot about you. I think of you every minute of every day. I made a decision and I had to live with it. You have no idea the toll it has taken. I think of you every day. I named you Michael Dylan, and Dylan is Dylan Michael. It was the only way I could maintain any sanity, naming you guys with the same names."

"The name stuck. I'm still called Michael. Most refer to me as Prince Mako. Socr—I mean, Elizabeth, made sure of that. Please continue."

"Elizabeth filled in a lot of the blanks. The queen had a miscarriage and replaced you as her baby. The king never knew that you were not his flesh and blood. The only persons who knew the truth were the queen and Elizabeth-Socreen. Anyone else who knew the truth was killed. You lived, and became the prince. If I would have had both babies back in your kingdom, you both would surely have been killed. At least one of you would have."

Michael reluctantly asks, "Do you think the queen is evil enough to kill a newborn infant?"

"You tell me. She raised you," Isabella replies.

"She's not the kindest woman in my kingdom. How did Socre—sorry—Elizabeth keep the secret so long?"

"The queen warned her that if she told anyone, she would kill you."

"I guess that answers the question of whether or not she would kill an infant. Why not kill Socreen?"

"Not sure about that. I think the queen relished the idea of torturing my poor mother all this time."

"How did my father, the king, die?"

"He was shot by an arrow."

"That is impossible. Detections have been positioned in the palace for that type of attack."

"True, but crazy events happened prior to his attack. During your birthday celebration is when the attack took place. Oh my, I just remembered—I have no gifts for you. I am a horrible mother."

"That's okay."

"No, it's not. I will remedy that."

"Please continue."

"Someone attempted to stab the king with a knife, and Dylan tackled the assailant and saved the king. So when Dylan tackled the assailant, they both fell off the side of the rooftop. Chaos ensued, and at that time an arrow came and struck the king," Isabella explains.

"Why would Dylan save the king? Better yet, why was Dylan there?"

"Your twin brother took your place as Prince Mako. It was his—your birthday party."

"When did all this happen?"

"When you were transported to the States, the Trefars transformed Dylan into you, Prince Mako. The hard part was already taken care of. You look exactly alike."

"You mentioned the transformation. And no one questioned this?"

"Guess not. It seemed to have worked. Dylan is now the prince."

"Are you telling me that my twin brother has replaced me in the kingdom, and no one has realized it?"

"Yes, Michael. It seems to have worked out that way."

"We will get back to Dylan. What about the queen?" Michael asks.

"When the king was on his deathbed, the queen made her escape. She went into exile. That pretty much confirmed that she had hired someone to kill the king. And at the end of his life, I told him the truth about you and Dylan."

"How did he respond?"

"The king looked me directly in the eyes and thanked me for telling him the truth. And said if I saw you again, to tell you that he loves you very much. His last words were to pronounce that Prince Mako is the new ruler of the kingdom."

"Who is my real father, then?"

"He's .... We're no longer married. We're divorced."

"Can I meet him?"

"Sure, if you would like. I'll call him later this morning."

"Does he know about me?"

"No, he doesn't. Sorry."

"Okay, hold off on contacting him for now. So why did Dylan stay behind?"

"That's a tough one to explain. I wasn't happy about his decision, but I allowed it on a temporary basis. He was concerned that the kingdom would collapse if the queen took over the palace."

"He may be correct on that point. She would be the next in line if something were to happen to me. And then the kingdom would be in complete chaos. If I understand you correctly, you're telling me Dylan is now in charge of my kingdom. Someone who has no idea how things work, especially our day-to-day operations. What chance does my kingdom have? He doesn't know anything about it."

"Yes, my concern also. He wanted to stay and make sure everything went as smoothly as possible. Times are very turbulent after the king's death."

"I bet they are. I should go home."

"I think that would really cause an issue. Can you stay for a few days and see if you like it here?"

"Sure, let's see how it goes."

"What do you like to do?" Isabella asks.

"I like to go fast."

"You mean run fast?"

"No, automobile or airplane fast."

"Oh, okay. I do owe you a birthday present. Have you ever been on a jet ski?"

"What's that?"

"Later today, I'll have Tony show you. It's a small boat that goes really fast on the water."

"On water!"

"Indeed, on water." Isabella smiles.

"That does sound enticing."

"Great. I have a few Sea-Doo RXPs at the dock. I'll have Tony take you out later today. Come see, I'll show you what they look like."

She leads Michael to where they are moored.

"Wow, those do look explosive. I can't wait to take it for a ride."

"Perfect."

Tears are swelling up and dripping off Isabella's face. Michael comes over and hugs her tightly.

"It's okay, Mom, it's okay," Michael says as he hugs her.

Isabella is shaking uncontrollably and all she can say is, "I am so sorry."

They don't let go of each other for a long time.

Chapter 21

PUPPIES

After the long hug, Isabella says, "Michael, come with me. I would like to show you something that you may appreciate. Chloe will be upset—I didn't wake her, but I think she'll understand."

They hop into a golf cart and drive the short distance to Isabella's office.

"Now, this is awesome! What do you call this thing?" Michael asks.

"It's a golf cart. You can drive it back home when we are done."

"I will be pleased to. Thank you."

"Hey, Teri, let me introduce Michael, Prince Michael, my oldest boy. It's a long story."

"Hello, Michael. He looks like Dylan," Teri remarks.

"He should. They are identical twins."

"Oh my. So this is Michael from the kingdom."

"Yes, it is."

"And Hari?" Teri asks.

Isabella starts to tear up.

"I figured something went wrong when Hari didn't come back with you. My heart sank a few days back and I had a bad feeling about my true love. Can we finish that story later? I'm ready to give birth." Teri grins.

"Of course. After you give birth, I will explain to you how brave your Hari was. He literally saved my life." Isabella smiles.

"That's okay. You've had a few things on your mind." Teri grimaces as the first puppy comes out. "He would have been a great da—"

Michael's eyes are wide as he watches Teri give birth.

Four puppies later—two male and two female—Teri is excited and starts licking her puppies.

Teri is admiring her puppies. She smiles, and yells out loud, "This is for you, Hari!"

Isabella says, "Teri, I can't tell you enough how heroic Hari was. He saved many lives, including mine. He will be missed and is having a proper burial in the kingdom."

"That's great. My memories of Hari will last me a lifetime. Now I have his puppies to remind me. I wish he could have seen them."

"Did he know?" Isabella asks.

"No, I didn't want to tell him. It would have given him a bigger head than he already had."

They both laugh.

Michael has been observing. "This is pleasing. Thank you for letting me witness this beautiful occasion."

"Anytime, Michael. I need to sleep now." Teri lies down to rest.

"Yes, you need rest. I will be back to check on you. I'm sure Chloe will be at your side soon."

Isabella and Michael depart. Isabella slides into the passenger seat. "Okay, she's all yours." She shows him how to start the golf cart and points to the way home.

"I have driven an automobile. Yours, I presume," Michael says.

"Oh yes, I am missing a car."

"Sorry, I left it at the Miami airport. It was my first time driving in your land."

"And you had no mishaps. That is an accomplishment in itself. Miami is a tough place to drive around, experienced or not."

Michael is thinking, *That's a pretty stable person, not to be upset about his stealing her automobile.*

After a smooth ride home, Isabella tells Michael, "Good job. You may become a race car driver one day."

"I can race cars. Is that like an automobile?"

"Sure is, if that's what you want. I can see people are stirring inside. Are you ready?"

"Yes, I am prepared."

"It's my two girls you haven't met. You have already met my brother and my father. I think you'll be pleased."

Sitting at the kitchen table is Tony.

"What kind of place you running around here? I had to make my own coffee," Tony says, and smiles. "How did you sleep, Michael?"

"Got a little rest. I was very pleased to see Teri giving birth."

As Michael is finishing his sentence, Chloe comes walking in, just in time to hear "Teri giving birth."

"Mom, is it true? Teri gave birth, and you didn't wake me."

"Yes, sweetie. I wanted Michael to see it with me. Teri is waiting for you to check up on her."

Chloe stops and stares at Michael in a strange way. Then she runs up and gives him a giant hug and says, "Welcome home, Michael."

Michael, smiling, says, "Thanks, Chloe. It's good to see you."

"Can I see the puppies now, Mom?"

"After breakfast. She just gave birth and is resting."

Tony clears his throat. "What am I, invisible?"

"Oh, sorry, Uncle Tony." Chloe turns and gives Tony a big hug.

After a nice hearty breakfast, everyone is relaxing.

"No reason to wait for my oldest daughter, Alessandra. She may not get up until noon. Tony, can you go get Mom and Dad? I'm sure they're up and ready to come by."

"Hey, Chloe, you want to come?" Tony asks.

"No, I want to wait here with Michael. Mom, when can I see the puppies? How many?"

"You may visit soon. She needs rest after having four pups."

Tony sees the lights on in his parents' house and before he can knock, the front door opens.

"What took you so long?" Elizabeth remarks. They hug forever.

"I had to make my own coffee, that's what took so long." Wiping his tears, Tony smiles. "How did it go, Mom?"

"Magnificent, enchanting, charming, and delightful."

"Okay then, sounds like it went well. Hey, Dad, how's it going?"

"Great, son. Not sure why you are so worried. Everything is fine here."

"You all ready? Let's go. Isabella is chomping at the bit to see you. So is Michael." Tony grins.

"Oh my, Michael. Is he okay?" Elizabeth asks.

"He's fine. It will be a long road, but he seems like a good kid."

"He's a great kid. Remember where he comes from and how he was protected from everything. You be nice to him. Both of you. You hear me?" Elizabeth points from her husband to Tony.

"Yes, ma'am," they say in unison.

"See, son, she's just as ornery as the day she left. Nothing's changed. She's still in charge."

"You're right about that," Elizabeth replies.

The greeting between Elizabeth-Socreen and Michael is epic. They hold each other for at least two minutes.

"I can't believe it. You're here, safe. I know you must have a million questions. And they will all be answered. Isabella is the greatest mom ever, so you'll be fine here."

"Socreen, it must have been difficult for you to keep that secret."

"It was agony. Please call me Elizabeth. I have buried Socreen."

"Oh yes, I forgot."

"Not a problem."

"Does Siena know you're here?"

"Oh my. Michael, Siena has passed."

"When? Why? She was so young. How did it happen? Did everyone die when I departed?"

"The queen killed her."

"Why would she do that? Are you sure?"

"Yes, positive. She died in my arms. She was poisoned."

"I am beginning to dislike the queen more and more, every time I hear a new story about her. Why poison such a pleasant girl?" Michael asks.

"It was meant for me, but Siena drank it. I'll never forget her. She saved my life."

Michael says, "I see no reason to rush home at this point. The king is dead. My only friend, Siena, is dead, and the person closest to me, you, Elizabeth, are here by my side. Plus, my alleged mother, the queen, is trying to kill me and is in exile. Did I leave anything out?"

"I think you should stay here and see how it goes. I live right next door," Elizabeth replies.

"I shall contemplate on it. Sounds like a suitable plan. I want to tell you about my driving experience."

"Yes, I want to hear everything," Elizabeth proclaims.

Finally, Alex awakens and comes into the kitchen.

"Hey, Uncle Tony. Morning, everyone. Dylan, is that you?"

Before Mom can answer, Michael says, "I'm Michael, your other brother."

"I heard I had two brothers, but I was hoping it was a dream. I hope you're smarter than your brother." Alex snickers.

"Alex, be nice," Mom interjects.

"Okay, okay. I'm sorry. If I remember correctly, we have briefly met. I found you tied up and brought you here."

"Yes, and when I awoke, no one was here," Michael replies.

"Welcome home, Michael. Hope you like it here. It sure is better than that place you call the kingdom," Alex mumbles.

"Alex, enough. It's going to be a difficult transition, and I expect both my girls to make his transition as easy and as welcome as possible. Understand?"

"Yes, Mother. It's been an unusual adventure for me, since I was caged for most of my visit and I am still a bit confused. Again, welcome home, Michael."

"Thank you."

Chloe excitedly says, "Alex, Teri had puppies. You want to go see them with me?"

"Can I get a cup of coffee first?"

"I guess so. Hurry. I'm so excited, I'm about to burst. Is it okay if we go soon, please?"

"Yes, you and Alex may go visit Teri. She would like to see you both. She just gave birth, so be careful with the puppies. Why don't you take Michael with you? He can drive the cart."

"Do you want to come with us?" Chloe asks him.

"Certainly. Why not?"

When the younger kids leave, the adults go to the back porch and sit on the loungers.

"Who's that?" Vincenzo asks.

"That is Tara," Isabella replies.

"Who's she?"

"It's a unique story. She's a friend, staying in the guest quarters for a while."

"Why would you bring Tara back here?" Tony asks.

"Not now. We can discuss that later," Isabella replies.

"Do you think Michael will be okay? Has he seen Tara?" Tony asks Isabella.

"He hasn't mentioned her. There is a lot going on right now. It's going to be very unusual for him. He's very young and, who knows, he may like it here. He did inform me he likes to go fast, so you're going to take him out on the jet skis."

"He did enjoy the plane ride. He wanted to know how to fly my plane. He's an extremely bright kid, and is curious about speed and any fast-moving objects."

"You know, his being the prince, no one ever talked back to him," Elizabeth reminds everyone. "He has lived a sheltered life."

"I am aware. Maybe this freedom to roam on his own will have a positive effect on him."

"I hope so. He's a nice boy, and I hope he stays here for a while. I'm so used to seeing him every day in the palace. All I want is for him to enjoy his life. If anyone harms that boy, they will have to deal with me." Elizabeth points all around.

"Yes, Mother, we understand."

Chloe sprints onto the back porch and can barely speak, since she ran home.

"Oh, Mom, can I have one? Alex and I would like the large male and we want to name him Grando." Chloe gasps for air.

"Sure, dear. I don't think Teri would mind."

"Alex and I already picked him out. He is so cute and cuddly. Well, they all are, actually, but he is the cutest of them all," Chloe states.

"I bet he is. And he can keep Brandi company."

"Oh, they are all so cute," Chloe says.

"What are we going to do with the other three, Mom?"

"I'll think of something."

"Oh my goodness, this is so exciting! I'm going to make a name tag for Grando." Chloe takes off running and yelling.

**

Jonny hears that Dylan is back home, and stops by for a visit.

"Hello, Isabella. Is—"

"Jonny, I told you my name is Miss Cabrella."

"Oh yeah, sorry. Is D'man here?"

"Yes. He is very tired."

"Sure, Mrs. C. We're only going down to the beach."

"Could you do me a big favor, Jonny?"

"Will do. What can I do for you?"

"Can you refer to Dylan as Michael? That's his middle name and he would prefer to be called Michael."

"Cool. I'd change my first name too, after his past exploits." Jonny is thinking about a school pool party where Dylan made a complete fool of himself.

"Thank you. See, you can be responsible if you put your mind to it."

"Anytime, Miss C. I was hoping it was some other kind of favor."

"Jonny, you should have stopped while you were ahead. I'll go ask him."

"I can ask him."

"Not this time, you can't."

"Okay then, I'll just wait here."

Isabella sees Alex and Michael talking together, and it puts a smile on her face since Dylan and Alex would only argue with each other.

"Michael, may I see you for a minute?"

"Certainly."

"Do you remember my telling you about your good friend Jonny? He is here and wants to take you to the beach. Probably to meet some girls."

"That will be acceptable to me. I've seen pictures of the girls around here." Then Michael stops. "Hold on. Who's going to be my chaperone?"

"No one. You're on your own." Isabella smiles.

"I've never been allowed to go anywhere by myself. Are you sure?"

"Positive. Enjoy yourself."

Jonny doesn't notice any physical difference, other than the hair color has changed.

"Hey, Michael, you ready to go?"

"Yes, sir. I am prepared."

"Bye, Miss C, I'll have him back for dinner."

"Don't be late. After dinner, Tony is going to take Michael out on the jet skis."

"Where are we going, Jonny?"

"To the beach. Violet and her girlfriends are there."

"Who's Violet?"

"Good one. Play hard to get. Good plan."

"I haven't planned anything."

"Well, you've been planning something. Look at your blond hair. Violet will probably like it. Good move, my man."

"Who's Violet again?" Michael says.

"Ah, playing it real cool this summer. That may work in your favor. Let's see how long that lasts."

"It is kind of you to refer to me as Michael."

"No problem. How about you call me J'cool? No, J'man. No, J'stud. No. I don't know. I'll think of something."

"Why not J? That is a good solid name."

"Really? You think that will stick?"

"Certainly should."

"Okay then, you can call me J from now on."

"Okay, J, where are we going?"

"To the beach, dude, that's where the chicks are."

"Chicks. What kind of chicks?"

"Dude, you are playing it big time. Girls, here we come."

"I am prepared. I've seen pictures of these young ladies." Michael smiles.

**

Isabella returns to her office to check up on Teri.

"Hey, Teri. How're you feeling?"

"Not bad. How's Michael taking to his new surroundings? I assume he knows that you're his mother."

"Yes, so far so good. It's going to be a long process, but he's young, and I'm hoping he begins to feel at home sooner rather than later. Time will tell. I'm walking on eggshells."

"Be yourself and everything will be fine. You ready to name your pups? Chloe and Alex already claimed theirs," Teri comments.

"I'm sure Chloe has been by here at least ten times already. Chloe and Alex have named one Grando. He is a perfect Grando. Huge." Isabella smiles.

"Who's Grando again?"

"I told you about him. He is the thirty-foot saber-toothed tiger who saved Alex and Chloe."

"Oh my, that is a big boy." Teri recollects Hari for a minute.

"Yes, that's why your largest pup is being named Grando. I want Mom and Dad to have one. How about we name her Siena?" Isabella asks.

"That will work. Isn't Siena the poor child who died in your mother's arms?"

"Yes, that is the one. She loved her very much. I really think Siena is a perfect fit for her. I wanted your permission to name the next male and give him to Michael," Isabella inquires.

"Sure. What do you have in mind?"

"Hari. If that doesn't cause you too much pain."

"I love it. He looks like Hari," Teri replies.

"The last female will be for Dylan. Only if you agree, since this one will have to go to the kingdom."

"Of course I don't mind. It seems Dylan will need a companion. Have you named her?"

"Not yet. I do have one name in mind," Isabella says, and smirks.

Chapter 22

KING D

Isabella and Elizabeth cooked up a good ol' homemade Italian spread.

"That was the best pasta I've ever had," Vincenzo comments while rubbing his stomach.

"Thanks, Dad, even though you say that after every pasta dish." Isabella grins.

Vincenzo asks, "Michael, what did you think of your mom's cooking?"

"It was pleasant. What do you call this again?" Michael points at the serving dish.

"Pasta primavera. It's not the traditional primavera. I make my own pasta and add my own ingredients from our homegrown garden," Isabella says.

"It tasted fine, and I didn't regurgitate. I mean that in a nice way," Michael adds.

"That's a good start," Isabella says.

Everyone laughs.

"Can I give some pasta to Grando?" Chloe asks.

"No, sweetie. He's too young. Maybe when he grows up," Isabella answers.

"Okay, I'm done. I'm going to see the puppies. Anyone want to join me?" Chloe grins.

Everyone shakes their head in the negative. No one can move, they're so full. Tony needs a few minutes before he goes to crank up the jet skis.

"Isabella, honey, we're both tired. Your father and I are going home. See you tomorrow." Elizabeth kisses her daughter.

"Okay, Mother, I understand. Good night."

"Michael, would you mind taking them back home on the golf cart?"

"Certainly. All by myself! I enjoy driving that golf cart machine." Michael jumps up.

"When you get back, we will get the skis in the water. I should be able to move by then." Tony rubs his stomach.

"You doing okay, Michael?" Elizabeth asks.

"Yes, I'm tremendously confused, Soc—Elizabeth. It's something I would have never imagined. It's very bizarre."

"I'm sure it is. If you ever need to talk, you know where I am. I can sense your being here has made Isabella extremely happy. I hope one day you also will be as happy." Elizabeth kisses Michael good night.

"It's a unique place. Good night."

Michael wants to ask Elizabeth about the Trefars he has seen nearby. He has not mentioned that he has seen a few Trefars around the guesthouse, and remains curious as to why Trefars would be in the concrete country.

When Michael returns, he and Isabella walk down to the dock and see Tony.

"Well, Michael, are you ready for your first jet ski lesson?"

"Yes, sir, I'm ready."

"Okay, let's see what these machines can do. You going to be okay, sis?"

"I'll be fine. I have plenty to do. You boys go have fun. Be careful, Tony. Michael has never ridden on one of those before."

"I'll be satisfactory," Michael adds, and soon he and Tony are roaring out to sea.

Tara is sitting on her porch, watching the sunset.

"Mom," Alex says when Isabella enters the house, "she's like a statue. She sits on that porch and stares off into the ocean. Does she ever eat or sleep?"

"Yes, dear. She's taking it all in. You know, she's never been in our world, and her time is limited. Why don't you see if she needs anything?"

Chloe joins Isabella on the porch. "Mom, when are we leaving to see Dylan?"

"In a few days, when the transporter is ready. The Trefars are working on it now."

"I can't wait. Does he know we're coming?" Chloe asks.

"I'm fairly certain he does. Don't forget to bring his present."

"I won't forget. I'm making name tags for every puppy. Where is Alex going?" Chloe asks.

"She is going to visit with Tara."

"Can I go with her?"

"Not this time. Let those two be alone for a while."

**

"Good evening, Tara. How are you? May I get you anything?" Alex inquires.

"Nothing, young one. Please sit next to me."

Soon she has Alex's hand in hers, and she closes her eyes and starts some kind of chant. After a few minutes she opens her eyes and smiles.

"Can you tell me what you saw? Did you read my palm and future?" Alex asks.

"I'd prefer not to tell you. It's not wise for someone so young to know their future," Tara responds.

"Is it a good future?"

"Yes, it's a grand adventure." Tara smiles.

"An adventure. Hmm, that sounds interesting. Can you give me a hint?"

"I have already. It's an adventure."

"Will I live a long life? And is there a man in my life?"

"You will outlive me, young one."

Alex thinks, *Outlive you. That's comforting. Your life expectancy is another day or two or three.*

"How about a man?"

"There is a man," Tara answers.

"Is he cute, tall, and handsome?"

"I didn't get all those minor details, young one."

"What type of adventure?"

"Life."

"Life. I know that much. What about my mate?"

"It's an adventure you will enjoy."

"My mate. More details, please," Alex snaps.

"Nice mate."

Alex is getting frustrated. She would like additional information about her future mate. *Minor details. That is the most important part of this discussion. What is wrong with this woman?* She can sense that Tara will not be giving her any further information.

Alex gets up to depart. "I must be leaving now. Bye."

"Thanks for the visit, young one. Will you ask your mother to stop by when she is free?"

"Sure, will do," Alex mumbles.

**

"I hear you wanted to see me," Isabella says, greeting Tara.

"Yes, dear. I wanted to say goodbye. And to let you know that Anna has completed her mission. The transporter is ready." Tara smiles. "Anna is the supervisor in charge of the two Trefars who are building the transporter in the guesthouse. This is the transporter that sends you directly into the palace."

"Goodbye! I'll see you when I get back," Isabella answers.

"I won't be here," Tara replies.

"Oh my, is it time? Should I stay behind? What can I do? Should I check your vitals?" Isabella replies.

"No, dear. There is nothing you can do. It's my destiny."

"Are you sure? I'll have Tony check up on you while I'm gone."

"Do not worry yourself, dear. Thanks again for everything. This has been so wonderful. You have a very special place here. Guard it with your life."

"Yes, Tara, I shall."

What Tara is trying to tell Isabella is that she isn't dying yet. Some other events will occur that are out of her control.

**

"We're finishing up here. We will test it to make sure it conforms to your needs," Anna informs Isabella.

"Great, Anna. Thanks for all your hard work. Did you and your team ever sleep?"

"We will rest when we get back to the kingdom."

"How does it work? The cushioning you chose is the same color as my blue pillowcase," Isabella remarks.

"That's why I used the same color blue, to make you feel more comfortable."

"Excellent. That is a nice touch. Thank you again."

Anna explains to Isabella all the nuances of the new transporter. "Since these transporters are linked together, all you have to say is 'Take me to the main palace.' On your return, say 'Key West, Florida.' Once you are comfortably seated, announce your destination, then close your eyes, and you will arrive at your intended location. Do not carry any electronic devices or gadgets, and wear no jewelry. That includes your watch display. It's really not necessary to announce your destination because these two are linked as one, but it will be more efficient if you do."

"How many will it transport at one time?" Isabella asks.

"Maximum of four at a time," Anna replies. "Thanks again for allowing us to use your blue pillowcase to transport back and forth. After our conversation, the new transporter will be operational."

**

Teri is outside wandering around the house, with her puppies in tow. Teri is concerned about something; she doesn't recognize the unfamiliar scent in the air.

"You keep an eye out. I'm taking the girls to Dylan's coronation," Isabella tells Teri.

"I'm going to take one more lap around the house. This unusual scent disturbs me."

Four devoted pups trail after their mommy. The scent Teri smells is Tragoon.

**

Dylan is getting worried about the welfare of Tabitha. He has not seen her since their subway ride. "Jelab, have you seen Tabitha?"

"I was informed that she has just arrived in the palace, Your Highness."

"Great. Good news, thanks."

I've been going to so many memorial events, it's bringing me down. Thank goodness the king's funeral memorial and processions are almost over. It was a spectacular send-off, but enough already. Grando also had a magnificent send-off, but Hari's was private. I bet the Trefars did him right. I am so depressed, and hope that Tabitha's appearance will cheer me up. I need to get out of this sad frame of mind. Now, where is Grande? He could become a problem if he resurfaces.

"Jelab, is today the last day of mourning? I am very excited about my upcoming coronation. All these memorial services are getting me depressed."

"Today is the last day. Would you like a soak, my prince?"

"No, not now. Please depart and check on Tabitha."

If Tabitha sees me soaking with all those girls, it could be big trouble. She seems to be the jealous type. Like it matters. We don't even date; however, I would like to. Maybe after my coronation she will be more attentive.

Jelab later returns to tell me, "Tabitha is resting comfortably in her chambers."

"Excellent, thank you." *My next move is to get Gus out of the picture, without Tabitha accusing me of sabotage.*

I figure it would be best to keep Gus nearby. That way I know he is not with Tabitha. Even though she is in the palace, he will not venture into her chambers. I know Tabitha likes him and he likes her, but with my sister coming, I may be able to stir up some trouble. I need Alex to convince Gus to visit her back in the concrete country, otherwise known as Florida. I'm starting to talk like these people. That's probably not a bad thing.

If Gus does visit Alex, that would alleviate any threat to my Tabitha. He is curious by nature and would probably jump at the chance to visit the concrete country. I can tamper with the transporter and make it inoperable after he departs. With him out of the picture I can have Tabitha to myself. If he disappears, I will have to take my chances that Tabitha doesn't blame me. I know my sister likes him, so it should be an easy scheme. I plan on asking Tabitha to teach yoga from the palace balcony. This may help with the harmony and, better yet, keep her close to me.

**

Isabella, Alex, and Chloe are ready to get transported back to the kingdom for Dylan's coronation. Alex is mainly going back to visit with Gus.

"Okay, girls, are you ready to go?" Isabella asks.

"Yes, Mom," Chloe screams.

"Yep, I'm ready," Alex replies.

"Chloe, do you have Dylan's present?"

"Yes, Mom. See?"

"It's only us girls. No cell phones, no jewelry, which includes watches."

"I guess Michael's not coming?" Alex asks.

"No, Alex, that would be a disaster. He's with Uncle Tony. I can't get him off the jet skis, which is fine with me."

The new transporter is a luxury, compared to the blue pillowcase. Plus, it transports everyone directly into the palace.

Alex remarks, "Wow, that was much smoother than my last experience, even though I do miss Grock."

Chloe is nodding her head.

"Hello, Igagbee. How is everything going?" Isabella asks.

"Everything is fine. How was the journey, Princess?"

"It was perfect. Thank you again for getting the transporter repaired. It really makes it easier to come and go."

"I told you I would have it repaired. Remember, if others find out, it may be used for misfortune," Igagbee comments.

"Do you have someone watching it at all times, day and night?" Isabella says.

"We do on this end. Do you?"

That is a good point. Isabella never thought anyone would find out about the transporter in Key West. She is hopeful it will remain a secret.

"I'll take you to His Highness. It is a great day." Igagbee sighs audibly.

The hugs, kisses, and crying all start. Mom grabs me and gives me a giant hug with as many kisses as she can, before I pull away. Then Chloe steps in with my gift.

"Hello, Dylan—I mean, Mr. Prince Mako. We brought you a present."

She hands me the little puppy. "Oh my goodness. He is the cutest," I remark. "Is he a German shepherd and Rottweiler mix?"

"Yes, and excuse me, he's a she." Isabella smiles.

I notice the name tag around her neck: VIOLET. As I put her down, she takes off running.

"Funny, Mom. That's hilarious, in an odd kind of way."

"Teri, Hari's mate, had a litter of four pups. We kept three and gave you the fourth." Isabella grins.

"Cute. Thanks for bringing Violet. She will love it here. Igagbee wants me to inform you that Hari had a splendid send-off."

"He was a great friend and protector. Teri hasn't said much, but I know she misses him. The puppies are keeping her very busy."

"Alex and I have one!" Chloe exclaims. "We named him Grando. He is so smart. I just love him to death. And Michael named his Hari, and Grandma named hers Siena."

"That sounds perfect. You guys follow me."

"Have you seen Gus?" Alex joyfully asks.

I play it nonchalant. "Yes, he comes by from time to time. He should be around today for my coronation." *Knowing good and well that Gus is always nearby.*

"Is Pup around?" Chloe asks.

"Probably. Why don't you ask Jelab? He's right outside my door. Show him my new friend."

Both girls are gone, so it's Mom and me.

"You know I miss you every minute of every day," Mom says.

"I miss all of you guys. Haven't thought of Violet until today. Thanks again for that, by the way."

"You look like you've grown up just in the past three weeks."

"I feel like I have matured. Every day is a new day. It's quite amazing."

"I bet it is. Have you picked a day to return home?"

"Let's see what today brings."

"Have your advisers not chosen a replacement?"

"Not yet, they haven't."

"Son, I can't let you stay here. So once summer is over, it's time to come home and meet your brother, Michael."

"Michael. You mean the real prince is living with you?"

"Yes. Why is that so unbelievable? He is my son."

"I know, I know, it's strange for everyone."

"No, strange is you staying here in the kingdom!" Mom's voice is agitated and loud.

"Calm down, calm down. It's all good. What's he like?"

"He is your identical twin. You look so similar. He has some of your mannerisms."

"What does he do all day?"

"Same as you. He hangs out with Jonny and the gang. I think he has a thing for Violet."

"He what? You're kidding me. That's a trick. You're tricking me. I don't want him near Violet." I begin fuming inside.

"Calm down, son, calm down. He hangs out with Jonny and your friends."

"Are you saying Jonny can't tell it's not me?"

"I'm telling you it's hard to distinguish the differences by appearance. You guys are so similar, it's almost spooky."

Jelab knocks and enters. "Your Highness, we are ready."

"Thank you, Jelab. I will be there in a moment."

"Okay, Mom. Can we finish this discussion later?"

"Yes. Remember, you promised me."

**

I enter a huge grand ballroom full of dignitaries. Everyone in the room is dressed up in their best attire. I am not prepared for all this pomp and circumstance.

Mom, Alex, and Chloe are sitting in the front row with Igagbee. Tabitha is in the second row, staring at Alex. There is a giant chair in the middle of the room, and I sit in it.

Then all I can hear is a loud echoing gong.

"Everyone, please *stand* for this jubilant occasion."

A rather smallish man walks up to me, holding a crown, and places it on my head.

He turns to the crowd and calls out, *"All hail the king.* I now pronounce you *King D."*

Isabella falls out of her chair, but Igagbee catches her before she can hit the floor. She can't comprehend what she is seeing and hearing. Her son is now King D, in charge of the kingdom. She'll never get him home. Isabella begins to cry.

The entire place explodes into cheers and clapping.

In unison the crowd yells, *"Long live the king, King D! Long live the king, King D!"*

My discussion with Jelab, before Mom arrived, was simple.

"Crowning a new king is very special, Your Highness. Have you chosen a name that you would like to be referred as?"

"I think so. King D."

"That should do nicely."

EPILOGUE

Matt and Jake pull into Isabella's driveway. They are greeted by Teri.

Jake's never seen a Rottweiler, and if he had, it would not have been this large.

"Hey, boss. What's that? I'm not getting out of this car!" Jake exclaims.

"It's merely one of her pets. I'm surprised only one came out to greet us. Come on, she won't hurt you. She's a sweetheart," Matt responds.

"No way. I'm staying in the car. It looks like she's going to eat me. She looks hungry and is big as a *horsey*."

"Well, then, ride the darn thing. Come on and man up," Matt says.

Matt gets out and pets Teri. She wags her tail and stares at Jake.

Matt looks over and says, "Oh, that's my new acquaintance, Jake. It's a long story." Matt talks to her as if she understands. Matt knows most of Isabella's pets are extremely smart. And after talking with Tony, who knows if her pets can understand or not? Matt tries the front door, and no one answers. Jake's still in the car, watching Teri.

"Doesn't seem like anyone's home. Let's try Vincenzo's place."

When they pull up to Vincenzo's house, Teri is sitting on the front porch, playing with some puppies. Matt gets out and starts petting the pups as they climb all over him. "Must be yours, huh?"

Vincenzo opens the front door. "Hello, boys. I see my car finally has made it home. How are you, Matt? Why doesn't Jake get out of the car?"

"He's scared of Teri. Who are these cute pups?" Matt asks.

"This one is ours, Siena. The other two belong to the grandkids. His name is Grando and that one is Hari."

"Teri has been a busy girl." Matt smiles.

"Come on in, and get that goofball inside, please. Lizzy would love to see you."

Vincenzo waves for Jake to come inside and leaves the front door open. Jake slowly opens the car door, and Teri looks his way.

"Good *horsey*. Me not hurt you." Jake shakes his head.

Teri asks herself who he's calling a horse. She might bite him just to prove she's not a horse. Then Grando jumps on Teri's head, and they both fall down.

**

Chloe has gone to see Pup. Alex is with Gus and could care less about Pup.

Pup is pregnant. That was the real reason she didn't attack Trigon.

Isabella is still in shock and can barely move.

**

Tragoon and Grull follow Tony's plane to Key West.

"I can smell a Trefars nearby," Tragoon observes.

"It seems everyone has departed, my friend," Grull remarks. "Yet you think someone was left behind."

"That would be Tara."

"Tara. Are you sure? What is she doing here?"

"Not sure, but she is here," Tragoon replies.

"That is a bonus. Maybe we should take her to the queen. We will be richly rewarded for this prize gift! We take her tonight." Grull laughs out loud.

**

The queen was not prepared to leave in such haste. She did not have time to plan on a destination, and elected to hide within the carousel palace. The carousel palace is far, far removed from the main palace. The carousel palace is full of cutthroats and criminals. Her plan is to recruit as many of these cutthroat prisoners as possible for her evil deeds.

The generator power to the carousel palace is cut off, so it is extremely cold inside and the queen is freezing.

"Someone put more *wood on the fire, now!*" the queen bellows.

**

Being king has its many pluses and a few minuses. One of the king's jobs is to hear complaints and disputes. This dispute in front of the court happens to be between two loved ones.

The advisor court consists of fourteen people, a mix of seven men and seven women. If a vote comes to a tie, the king casts the deciding vote. Better yet, even if the court has decided fourteen to zero, the king can override the fourteen votes with his one vote.

This dispute is between a dragonfly, Gilda, and her husband Justin, a butterfly.

"Please begin."

"He is always flirting with other butterflies, and I want a divorce," Gilda says.

"I am just talking with others, nothing else. She is so jealous," Justin replies.

One of the court advisers speaks. "Haven't you been in a few times, with the same complaint? If I'm not mistaken, you come every sixty days."

"Yes, we have, but I am fairly certain this time he really has done it."

"What have I done this time?" Justin asks.

**

Kati the Kondo and Greg the Graeter are flirting during a yoga session. She passes gas and knocks down ten students. The both of them laugh, and since he can't pass gas he belches, and twelve people fall over.

**

CNN has reported that millions have died and millions are considered missing in the San Francisco earthquake.

**

Transporting Gus back to Key West is going to cause some unique circumstances that Dylan may be overlooking.

**

I could get used to this King D thing. I may rule the world one day. How hard can it be?

CAST OF CHARACTERS

Alessandra Cabrella (Alex, 21-year-old daughter of Isabella)
Angelina (Tony Rome's housekeeper)
Anchor (beetle)
Andi (palace student)
Anna (Trefars)
Blinky (airplane pilot)
Brad (attorney)
Brandi (Labrador retriever)
Brian (giant grouper)
Buddy (T's friend)
Buffalo (dungeon guard)
Caitlin (T's elephant)
Captain Bill Rogers (Key West police chief)
Carolyn (88 butterfly)
Cato (snow leopard, king's guard apprentice)
Chloe Cabrella (10-year-old daughter of Isabella; younger sister of Alessandra and Dylan)
Cranky (Trefars, guardian of the west gate)
Crate (king's assistant)
Dank (palace guard)
David (palace hound)
Dylan Michael Cabrella (15-year-old son of Isabella)
Elizabeth Cabrella (Socreen, Liz, Lizzy; Vincenzo's wife; mother of Isabella; grandmother of Alex, Dylan, and Chloe)
Erica (hippopotamus)
Fang (Calypsos leader)
Flobak (Prince Mako's American chaperone)
Gaylok (rebel leader)
Gilda (dragonfly)
Gloria (veterinarian assistant)
Graeters ("Excavators"; a species that chews and eats gum)
Grande (30-foot saber-toothed tiger, father of Grando)
Grando (20-foot saber-toothed tiger, son of Grande; king's guard apprentice)
Greg (Graeter)

Grock (rock hut)
Grull (bright white hairless albino)
Gus (Asparagus, palace guard)
Hari (German shepherd)
Harkin (assistant principal)
Hayley (zebra)
Igagbee (Trefars, Dylan's handler)
Isabella Cabrella (Bell, Bella, Princess Xandra; veterinarian; mother of Dylan, Chloe, and Alessandra; Vincenzo and Elizabeth's daughter; sister of Tony Rome)
Ivy (spy)
Jacob (zebra)
Jake (pirate)
Jelab (prince's valet)
Jena (palace maid)
Jim (Matt's father)
Jonny Everette (Dylan's best friend)
Justin (butterfly)
Kaci (palace maid, pastpathic)
Kaptuk (200-year-old cheetah, king's guard master instructor)
Kayda (loves dragons)
Kati (60-foot Kondo)
king, the (of the Kingdom of Bonita)
King Primis (first king of the Kingdom of Bonita)
Koper (king's assistant)
Korey (palace headmaster)
Lantern (creature in the kingdom)
Lightner (moon)
Matt Robertson (Mathew; ex-Navy SEAL; Tony Rome's associate)
Mayo twins (tiger sharks)
Megan (megalodon shark)
Mimik (palace teacher)
Moonbeam (3rd moon)
Moonie (4th moon)
Moore, Dr. (Boston hospital MD)
Mrs. Roberston (Matt's mother, Lucy)
Prince Mako (Michael)
Puddin (20-foot Kondo; Kati's daughter)

Pup (young female dragon; Tabitha's companion)
Py (elephant)
queen, the (of the Kingdom of Bonita)
Queen Tafnut (first queen of the Kingdom of Bonita)
Queenie (2nd moon)
Razor (giant eagle)
Regina (prince's dance partner)
Sam (Samantha; friend of Alessandra and Tami)
Samantha Stoner (Violet's mom)
Shai (female teaching assistant of the king's guard apprentices)
Siena (queen's handmaiden)
Skame (palace guard)
Skulleater (dragon in dream)
Socreen (*see* Elizabeth Cabrella)
Sophiabee (Trefars; mother of Igagbee)
T (Trefars leader)
Tabitha (Pup's companion)
Tagot (a king's guard)
Tami (friend of Alessandra and Sam)
Tank (Trefars)
Tara (T's mother, 400-year-old Trefars)
Tazer (commander of king's guards)
Teri (Rottweiler)
Tic (Trefars)
Tony Rome, Dr. (Anthony; archaeologist; Isabella's older brother; Vincenzo and Elizabeth's son)
Torch (airplane pilot)
Tragoon (adult male dragon, Trigon's brother)
Trigon (adult female dragon, Tragoon's sister)
Trefars (masterful elf-like warriors who ride elephants)
Venus (hostess)
Vincenzo Cabrella (Elizabeth's husband; Grandpa; father of Isabella and Tony; grandfather of Alex, Dylan, and Chloe)
Violet (Dylan's love interest and schoolmate)
Zetha (king's guard apprentice)
Zhann (Jelab's father)

About the Author

The mystical and enchanting Tennessee mountains of his childhood home inspired Roger Lawrence Quay to write fantasy novels. The author delights in sharing his storytelling with young adult and adult readers alike. Roger enjoys life with his wife and best friend, Carol, at their oak-arbored retreat in Mandarin, Florida. Learn more at OneIronPress.com. The author invites you to email comments and questions to RLQ@OneIronPress.com.

The Blue Pillow Case in the Kingdom is the second novel in a trilogy series, preceded by *The Blue Pillow Case* and followed by *The Blue Pillow Case Is Closed.* Available from your favorite retailer and through OneIronPress.com.

www.ingramcontent.com/pod-product-compliance
Lightning Source LLC
Chambersburg PA
CBHW030926210726
48290CB00007B/2085